Ales Adamovich

Khatyn

Glagoslav Publications

Khatyn
By Ales Adamovich

First published in Belarusian as "Хатынская аповесць"

Translated by Glenys Kozlov,
Franes Longman and Sharon McKee
Edited by Camilla Stein

Ales Adamovich's Russian texts copyright © 2012
by Natalia Adamovich, Vera Adamovich

Translation rights into the English language are
acquired via FTM Agency, Ltd., Russia, 2012

English translation rights,
© Glagoslav Publications Ltd, 2012

© 2012, Glagoslav Publications, United Kingdom

Glagoslav Publications Ltd
88-90 Hatton Garden
EC1N 8PN London
United Kingdom

www.glagoslav.com

ISBN: 978-1-909156-07-4

"According to documents of the Second World War, more than 9,200 villages were destroyed in Belarus, and in more than 600 of them almost all the inhabitants were killed or burned alive; only a few survived." *WWII Archive.*

"I jumped out of the car and began elbowing my way through microphones. 'Lieutenant Calley, did you really kill all those women and children?' 'Lieutenant Calley, what does a man who killed all these women and children feel?' 'Lieutenant Calley, do you regret not having killed more of women and children?' 'Lieutenant Calley, if today you could go back to killing women and children...'" Lieutenant William L. Calley (responsible for My Lai massacre in Vietnam) in his book *Lieutenant Calley: His Own Story.*

"It is incomprehensible, unfitting to think that on this planet there could be war that brings grief to millions of people." Soviet cosmonauts Georgiy Dobrovolsky, Vladislav Volkov, Victor Patsaev in their *Public Address to the People of Earth from Space,* June 22, 1971.

"There's already a whole platoon here!" the man in dark glasses, holding a white metal cane in his hand, said loudly. The boy in a light-blue raincoat sprang into the noisy bus in front of him, looking around for an empty seat.

The man in glasses lingered by the door, listening to the silence evoked by his voice; there were deep lines round his mouth, his face, which narrowed towards his chin, was unattractively pointed, while his forehead was wide and bulging like that of a child. His mouth quivered with the guilty smile of a blind man.

"Daddy, there's a seat over there," said the boy in the transparent raincoat and he immediately touched the trembling hand that was held out to him.

Once again the bus buzzed with noise and shouts, but that recent, sudden silence also remained like something beneath it all. The voices, the cheerful shout were too hasty.

"Gaishun, come over here, old man!"

"Flyora, come and sit with us!"

"Come on, over here!"

The man with the fixed quiet smile of a blind man was waiting for someone. The metal cane tinkled dryly and hollowly as the blind man brushed against the seat support.

A man in a sweat, wearing a crumpled cloth suit, had put a sack down on the bus steps.

"Where's this bus going to?"

"To Khatyn."

"Where?"

"Khatyn."

"Ah!" the wearer of the cloth suit drawled in an uncertain voice, picking up the sack.

A woman appeared in the doorway, wearing a flowery summer dress and carrying a bag and a raincoat on her sunburnt arm. She climbed onto the step, her dark-complexioned face smiling at the side of the absolutely white cropped hair of the blind man.

"Glasha, come over and sit with us!"

"Come and sit here with the third platoon!"

"She's got fed up with your lot in the forest, haven't you, Glasha?"

Softly saying "hello", the woman touched the blind man's elbow, and he walked down the bus. There immediately became noticeable the leisurely manner forming a bond between them and the strained smoothness that one finds when two people are carrying a full bucket.

"Come over here, Daddy, there's a seat here," the little boy shouted to the man; he had already settled down with his back to the driver's cab, pressing his palms down on the seat on both sides of him as children often do.

A very young-looking and noisy passenger got up from his seat and grabbed the blind man by the shoulder.

"Flyora, you sit with my missus, and I'll sit with Glasha."

"Kostya," said the wife of the noisy passenger, reproachfully. She gave the blind man a friendly smile. "Don't get in the man's way. Look what you're doing!"

The man in dark glasses held his hand out in front of him as he usually did; people greeted him, touching those thin fingers, which slightly trembled in response.

"Things all right, Flyora?"

"Who's that? Is that you, Stomma?"

"You recognised me? Yes, old man, it's me."

"Whose head is that?"

"It's Rusty's. Do you remember who he is? Say something, Rusty."

"Make yourself known," the blind man pulled his hand back. "Make yourself known. Is it really you, Rusty?"

"Hello, Gaishun." The passenger got up a little and shook the hand of the blind man awkwardly as if it were a child's hand.

While the process of recognition was going on, the woman stood behind her husband. She was smiling, too, but she was not looking at anybody, while the dark glasses of the blind man focused on each voice attentively.

A thick-set passenger with a squint in both eyes caught hold of the blind man's hand.

A camera strap was cutting his soft shoulder in two, and be seemed somehow to be all oval in shape, bulging out of his new dark-blue costume.

"Do you recognise me? It's Staletaw."

"And you're here as well," the blind man was surprised.

"Where else should I be?" Staletaw sounded offended.

But the woman had already led Gaishun further down the bus. He brushed against the knee of a stout man, who was tall even when seated. Like a pupil who was too big for his desk, he was sitting sideways, blocking the gangway.

"Hello," said the stout passenger softly and very calmly. "Hello, Flyora," he said again.

For a moment his voice caused everything to fall silent again, as if the silence had shown through the noise like the bottom of a shallow lake.

The expression on the woman's face changed immediately and she quickly caught hold of Gaishun and whisked him forwards. She sat him down and she herself took a seat facing the driver's cab and with her back to everyone.

The little boy called out, "It's better over here, Daddy."

"Well, you sit there then!" his mother snapped at him.

The stout passenger, too, would have been more comfortable sitting by the driver's cab, facing everyone. But he did not sit there either.

...Kasach! That was his voice. The confidently quiet voice, of a man who knows and is accustomed to people always listening to him. That was a voice that I would discern among thousands.

Look what Glasha's hand was like now—it was as if she had stopped me being run over by a car!

What is Kasach like now? Well, whatever he is like, he, at least, is not blind like her husband.

The noise of the motor and the tinkling sound of the bucket under the seat drowned any general conversation. Only the most piercing or the most cheerful voices reached them, clinging to one another and overlapping:

"Last year...", "You've already got grandchildren...", "A bomb will explode, a cloud will rise...", "Well, Kostya, who do you think you are! Don't keep interrupting...", "There are Kasach's men everywhere, I tell you...", "No, I'll tell him, our Chronicler, that...", "Heh, Staletaw...", "He's doing exams for the Institute of Foreign Languages..."

Unreally, impossibly familiar voices from way, way back in the distant past flooded the bus. The accidental words of the present day floated on the surface like pieces of rubbish, and the familiar voices are pouring into me apart from the words, brackish and scorching....

There were about twenty of our partisans. I had already heard some of them, had picked them out: Kasach, Kostya, our chief of staff, Stomma, Rusty, Staletaw....

Kostya still had that same little boyish voice that would break into any conversation: he would guffaw, shout out surnames, nick-names, intentionally meaningless words ("You haven't forgotten Grandpa?... Staletaw, take a photo of us for history. You do that really well... Grandpa, where did you get that hat from?... Mensch!... Don't interfere, old girl...").

Yes, that is what he was like, our chief of staff, Kostya; with him around, it's crowded even in the middle of an open field; he will bump into everyone, embrace them and immediately make fun of them. He was not very respectable for his post. Twenty-two or twenty-three, he must have been. They liked him then as now for he knew his job and he knew how to fight. Just as well as Kasach.

Kasach was here, close by, behind me. "Hello!" That "hello" was meant for Glasha as well, but he detected something in Glasha's look, and excluded her from his greeting saying, "Hello, Flyora." Now what had happened to Glasha's hand. It shook with fear and became hard as it tensed up. She was sitting next to me, bolt upright and tense. I may not be able to see but I knew.

Was he still as huge and strong? His voice sounded the same anyway.

I have always wanted to know whether he himself noticed his constant irony which sometimes appeared to be involuntary.

"I can tell him straight!" a voice came from somewhere behind him. "We pulled him out from behind the stove where he was hiding, made him a partisan by force, and now..."

Who were they talking about? Whose voice was that? It was nervous, and irascible. The lads were already egging him on, our lot always knew how to do that.

"His secretary won't let you in."

"But you'll ring him up, won't you, Zuyonak? Or you'll send a telegram." Of course, it was Zuyonak. He had been the guardian of our partisan heraldry. Zuyonak always remembered exactly when, in what year and even what month people came to the partisans. And who deserved to be respected and how. The whole of Zuyenok's family had been wiped out by the Germans when in 1941 he went away into the forest. Many of our monuments have been erected thanks to his long and persistent letters. And the one we were going to unveil, too. It is the first time that I was going; when I could still see, such things were not yet common practice. Zuyonak even used to get into trouble for trying to get us together. "What kind of meetings are these? Who needs them?" they would ask.

"We'll be crawling along till nightfall at this speed!"

"Oh, Grandpa here is used to aeroplanes!"

It was Zuyonak's idea as well that we should call at Khatyn at the same time although it was not exactly on the way to our partisan country. For me it was especially important to visit Khatyn. Although what would I see there? I would not see what there is there now, but what was there before. I know our Khatyns... I know that..."

Grandpa who had been in charge of supplies in our partisan detachment kept on worrying whether we would manage to get there and back in time, and whether that would make us late. How old was he? He had seemed an old man to us even at that time. When he spoke it was like someone eating a hot potato, making hoarse sounds, blowing and wheezing after every word. And there was the uncertain chuckling of a bustling, good-natured peasant. Somehow Zuyonak had managed to get us all together in this coach, those from the town and those from the surrounding area.

"Never mind," someone responded (it appeared to be Rusty), "they have waited longer for us."

You could even detect certain irony in Rusty's voice. This is probably something he had acquired after the war. Formerly they had all played tricks on him and he had just snuffled through his peeling nose and promised:

"Next time you try it I'll punch your nose!"

"What kind of monument is that, Zuyonak?" someone asked from the back seat.

"A burial mound built up by schoolchildren."

"And what kind would you have liked?" shouted Kostya Chief of Staff.

"For some reason I did not think about it when we were walking—do you remember—through the burning marshes. We walked round in a circle as if on a string.

The faces flash in my memory as if they are being shuffled like cards but none of them fits the voice with the quiet cough.

"It's all the same for the lads now." (Grandpa.)

"All the same, no, not quite!" (Stomma.)

"I would not like to lie under one like the one we saw last year."

"Zuyonak, take people's wishes into account!" (Kostya Chief of Staff).

"No, but do you remember Chertovo Koleno, how we walked around through the smoky marshes? When you tell people, they don't believe you!"

Who is recalling that burnt-out swamp at Chertovo Kolyeno? That voice has such a familiar, gently subtle cough. Can it be Vedmed?

Well, of course, it is! What is he like now, I wonder, without his cartridge belt across his chest and round his waist? It was very uncomfortable and impractical to carry cartridges like that for they used to go rusty and in battle you had to pull them out one at a time and push them into the magazine, into the cartridge-chamber. By the First World War a convenient cartridge clip had already been invented; you put it in the slot, pressed it with your thumb, and immediately the rifle was loaded with five cartridges. But Vedmed stubbornly dragged his belt around with him as if he were dressed for some film, and he himself was thin and stooping and wore glasses. His thoughts were not about impressing the girls like those of the scouts and aids-de-camp who sported weapons and belts for the purpose, but on being fed. Any peasant woman immediately saw that he was a fighting man and gave him something to eat or was it perhaps a passion for the cinema already burning in Vedmed's sickly chest? We went to the cinema once and when the film started Glasha exclaimed softly, "Oh, Flyora, our Lev Vedmed must be the producer of this film!"

I usually go to the cinema with Syarozha. We would go in right at the beginning of the performance, so that the audience was not bewildered by the fact that someone who cannot see has come to the cinema.

To begin with Syarozha whispers to me what is happening on the screen until I catch what the authors are trying to say and then I help him to watch it, listening to the film as if it were on the radio. Some films seem to be made for me for everything is explained out loud and is obvious. But when the audience suddenly fell silent in front of a screen that had become dumb—and all that could be heard was hundreds of people breathing, just as happens before yon cry out in a dream— then my own screen would switch itself on and light up, I would perceive my own picture against the background of the sudden shouts and shots coming from their screen. I could see what no one else could see.

"Are you a partisan as well. Uncle?" Syarozha pestered Staletaw who had moved over to the driver's cab, and now I could hear that he was sitting opposite me.

"We're all partisans here, laddie." Staletaw had not appreciated the question. "And are you a Pioneer?"

"Of course, I am." Syarozha was indignant as well.

"Don't get your shoes on the gentleman," Glasha warned Syarozha. From the moment she had seen Kasach, everything in her seemed to have hardened; I could hear it in her voice.

"Were you one of Kasach's men, too?" Syarozha tried to find out. If he starts bothering you, then you've had it.

"Oh, no," Staletaw was gladdened by the question. "I belonged to the Stalin Detachment."

Staletaw was now sitting facing Kasach; and they could see one another. He had a peculiar sort of squint, towards the sky and towards the ceiling.

"Nor is your Dad any kind of Kasach man, he's from the Stalin Detachment."

It is one and the same: according to our papers we belonged to the Stalin Detachment, but in the villages they probably remember Kasach's men now."

That Staletaw was a fairly exotic specimen, even among such a variety of people as the partisans were.

At first, when the mischievous instructor from Germanised schools who had travelled around the area giving lectures on "Hitler the Liberator", was

15

brought into our camp at Zamoshievo, he was a podgy fellow with eyes that appeared at that time to be squinting with fear. But they did not shoot him; they left him in the brigade (he proved that he had supplied those in the landing force with a typewriter and some kind of stationery to boot), and then we found out that his eyes were naturally like that. Naturally like that and, as it turned out, very much in keeping with Staletaw's nature.

In the wake of that fear-filled squint Staletaw was overtaken by a rush of enthusiasm that swamped us all to such an extent that the lads did not know how to get away from him. He would steal up to Rusty, Zuyonak or Vedmed and would stand in front of them, looking adoringly at them and squinting at the sky. Their heads definitely, it seemed, were up there somewhere in the tree-tops of the forest. He made you feel like an idol basking in worship.

"What do you want?" the partisan would ask, surprised by this attitude towards him.

"Me?... Nothing. Perhaps you'd like some lunch as well? I'm going over to the cook-house."

"Why not, get me some. Yes, get me some, old chap."

Once we returned from an operation and Staletaw was nowhere to be seen, either in our dug-out or anywhere close by. He was at the camp but he no longer seemed to be taking any notice of us. It turned out that Staletaw was already working as a clerk at headquarters, or to be more exact, as a chronicler. He had managed to persuade someone who had come to us from the brigade

HQ that it was absolutely vital to write down the histories of our detachments. The front was already rolling forward, other brigades will suddenly start thinking about it and there we are, ours will be all ready.

Staletaw no longer toadied to Vedmed, his squinting eyes moved to others; somehow they did not seem to pick us out any more.

That man did indeed have strange eyes. He seemed to be measuring you, setting you up against something invisible, pulling you upwards slightly like a tailor straightening out your collar or the back of your coat; but his eyes seemed to sentence you, even exhibiting disappointment, as if saying, oh dear, you're just not up to it! Not good enough for history, is that it? He would pull you up straight yet again with his glittering black eyes, which seemed at times like those of a madman, but there was a smile in those eyes, so subtle and derisive. You cannot deceive me, you know. He would cast his eyes upwards to the sky one last time, leaving you standing there as if in front of a swiftly departing lift. Any phrase would make him prance with excitement as he enthusiastically incriminated people: "Oh, no-o!" If you were to tell him that it was 12 o'clock, he would immediately incriminate you by saying, "Oh, no-o! It's two minutes to twelve!"

No one knows how the chronicle of the brigade turned out. He was suddenly thrown out of Kasach's headquarters just as rapidly as he arrived there. Kasach made no bones about doing things like that, and his protector in the brigade HQ did not help Staletaw either.

It came to Kasach's ears (they had been grumbling in the villages) that "one of your lot with a squint" had beaten up some old fellow, had threatened the womenfolk with a rifle, and had tried to put someone up against the wall.

"We are fighting here," Staletaw tried to justify himself, "and some chap is sitting over there, hiding behind his beard, and you're supposed to go and liberate him. I wouldn't let them all go back."

"Fighting, are we?" Kasach inquired again. "Well then, go and fight. You can compile your history later on. To begin with, put him in the guardhouse!" So Staletaw did "make history", only not the kind of history he was so anxious about.

We joined up with the army. Some went to the front, others started to get the economy going, and suddenly there was a hitch with those who had stayed in the area to work. Staletaw's file came to the surface and it turned out to contain such things (especially about Kasach and about the others, too) that when they summoned the lads, they did not even begin to read it out loud, but just ran their fingers along the lines. They could not bring themselves to utter the phrases that Staletaw claimed to have heard in our detachment. It is hard to say what he actually heard there and what he made up. The partisans really did discuss all sorts of things, sometimes very heatedly and openly. He possibly heard something at headquarters as well. But, it appears, he put too much arsenic in it: one deadly dose of arsenic is fatal, but ten doses may just cause vomiting and clean out your stomach straightaway. You couldn't bring half a detachment back from the front anyway. The matter was dealt with by someone who was no fool. Staletaw had to try to vindicate himself, for the "Hitler the Liberator" lectures as well. For a long time, nothing was heard of our Chronicler but suddenly he turned up reading essays on the radio and writing articles. He had come to life! He even published a brochure on the heroic deeds of the members of the landing force (those to whom he had handed over the typewriter). Soon Staletaw began to appear at meetings. I did not go to the early meetings but I heard that Staletaw had appeared, that the eyes of the Chronicler, squinting towards the sky, were again filled with rapture and adoration. At first, I don't think they stood on ceremony when it came to reminding him of the brigade's "history", but it looks as if they have got used to him again. Our hot-heads do not bear grudges.

"Oh, no-o," Staletaw drawled, as if testing the reaction of those in the bus, "No-o, your Dad and I are partisans, and not some kind of" (Kasach's men, but he did not say it).

They were already singing songs, two or three at the same time.

It was a while before it dawned upon Syarozha that his father was different from the others. And when his child's heart finally perceived it—he once looked up and suddenly understood—he screamed and cried; it was as if from that moment on that everything happened to me: "Who did it to you, Daddy? Don't be afraid to tell me. It was the Germans, wasn't it, the Nazis? Tell me, please tell me!" He ran over to his corner, grabbed his German-made red clockwork windmill and began to break it, crying loudly, and threw it on the floor. Glasha and I tried to assure him that his toy was made by other Germans quite different ones....

From that time on, not a day passed that Syarozha did not begin to talk about my "little old eyes". He and I discussed a plan as to how I would be cured and see him with his freckles and his black eyes. Syarozha laughed uncertainly when I told him how he would appear before me and I would fail to recognise him.

The first operation three years before was a failure. I decided to have another one for Syarozha's sake. He and Glasha came to see me at the clinic and talked a lot. Syarozha laughed excitedly, lie was quite sure that, when they took off my bandages, I would be able to see him and to see everything again. Then they took me home still in that same darkness. Glasha wept softly and stroked my hand. Syarozha sat in front, next to the taxi-driver, and I could not hear a sound from him.

Syarozha never spoke about "my little old eyes" any more. Sometimes I could discern from the way he breathed, from his sudden sigh, that he was looking at my face, studying it sorrowfully. My eyeballs began to hurt me and they definitely became rounder. It was even suggested to me that I should have them removed to stop the pain, but I did not consent, for Syarozha's sake, as well.

Today Syarozha was cheerful and full of beans; he was going to the former haunts of the partisans and he was, moreover, among people who needed no explanation as to who his Daddy was. On the contrary, he could listen to what they had to say and ask them questions.

The noise of the engine drowned the voices in the bus. We were going into the forest, and, when the trees parted, a field opened out. I could clearly discern the voices, even on the back seats. All the time, I was trying to imagine what each of the people looked like. I compelled myself to make allowances for time, for it was twenty-five years since I had seen them.

I imagined myself just a decade ago as well, what I was like when such a thing as a mirror still existed in the world, and reflected in the mirror was a pale, narrow-faced man with swollen eyelids, with the hair on his temples turned white and with deep, arched lines round his mouth which sustained a guilty smile.

Glasha married a man like that but she probably saw me in some other mirror, not such a pitiless one. In her memory I was connected with her girlhood. And with many other things as well, with Kasach, too. But how she hates him! Or she is afraid of him? She is afraid of herself. No, it is I who is scared. A cowardly and envious blind man! And an ungrateful one.

While I was still like everyone else (my eyes only began to become red and hurt suddenly from time to time). Glasha and I did not get on very well together: what brought us together, divided us and tormented us, was our time in the partisans together, it was Kasach. We did not talk about it, we did not recall it aloud, but it was ever present. When the most awful thing happened to me (over a period of six months), it was as if Glasha had become someone else, her voice, her hands, the way she touched me had all changed. And she herself wanted to give birth to Syarozha.

Once again Kasach was next to us. He was behind us, he had sat behind us all the way. I could feel that Glasha had not forgotten that even for a moment. How silent she kept, all tensed up. I myself had insisted that we should go to this meeting when Zuyonak wrote to us. Glasha did not want to, but Syarozha and I insisted. I was doing it in revenge for all that had happened before, to spite myself. That is a blind man's gratitude for you....

The bus buzzed with loud, cheerful conversation. It is always easier for me when people are distracted like that, then I could observe them instead of them observing me.

"Under him even that one sat in the waiting-room as good as gold." (Zuyonak.)

"That's how it was, one in front of the other! In our village there was one..." (Grandpa.)

"Suvorov talked about China... Do you know what Suvorov used to say?..."

He was here, too, Ilya Ilich, our company commander. Gypsy-like with that small beard of his, he always had a little book in his pocket or in his bag... God alone knows where he used to get those books. In the villages they had smoked the last bibles already in their hand-made cigarettes.

"Let's have a singsong!" Kostya, our chief of staff, shouted now and immediately began singing "Oh, what a welcome there will be at the station when we come back with flying colours!..."

Kasach remained silent. He alone was not drawn into the loud conversation. It was interesting what he would have said and how, what he had been thinking all those vociferous years. Immediately after the war he worked at the local Soviet's executive committee, then he was made manager of the peat factory and later chairman of a state farm. What he was doing now I did not know, nor did Glasha. For all that, they had incriminated him for being taken prisoner by the Germans and possibly for something else contained in Staletaw's notorious file. He himself was a sufficiently complicated person with surprising traits of character. It was the first time that I was attending a partisan meeting, but I could already see (from the conversations, the rejoinders, and from his deep silence) that they were not making much of an effort to converse with him, nor he with them, for that matter. He had never been sociable and companionable, he was not like Kostya, our chief of staff. It was probably because in our minds Kasach was linked with much that did not dispose one to cheerful gossip, things that were buried deep down in our memories. War is war, but in the company of Kostya, it was a completely partisan war, with noise, anecdotes and recollections of all kinds of adventures; with Kasach you recalled something quite different, more drastic and poignant. Kasach was not inclined to pride himself upon and boast about his exploits as a partisan like the rest of his men did, nor did he tend to see those partisan days in an increasingly romantic light as others did, as the years went by. He was going to this meeting like a stranger. Anyone regarding him from outside would decide that he was the only one who was not one of Kasach's men.

I have heard or read somewhere that people who have known each other in especially agonizing and degrading circumstances are not very keen to meet afterwards. It happens now and then, but not more often. It is difficult, even impossible to live with your secrets constantly, bared as if they are concealed in an open basket. The families of such people are seldom friends. I myself was acquainted with two men who had survived Auschwitz in the same barrack. They would bump into each other in the corridor or the smoking room at the teacher-training institute and would sometimes check the camp numbers stamped on their arms with a definite lack of concern ("I'm 120 thousand people younger than you..."), but you could tell from their conversations that they knew nothing about each other, not even on which street each one lived.

What's the use talking about it, I would not tell Syarozha everything either (even when he becomes a student), although we do not apparently have anything to hide or be ashamed of. I know for certain from my own students that there are some things that you cannot communicate to those who have not experienced anything like it.

My third-year students heard about an incident when the commander of a partisan detachment, ambushed by the Germans and trying to avoid an encirclement which meant sure destruction, allegedly ordered a child to be killed that kept on crying in its mother's arms and betraying the detachment's movements. They told me the story indignantly. But it was an interrogation as well to find out how I would be able to answer with my "universal science of psychology". They were convinced that after this incident the detachment would most certainly break up, for people who have betrayed and lost sight of the purpose of their struggle would come to hate each other and themselves and their very lives bought at such a price. Just as indignant as they were that such a thing could happen, I could not agree for all that

that it would have ended like that. I reminded them of the defensive mechanism of the psyche without which war would be unthinkable in general, unendurable for man.

I did not see the faces of my students, but for the first time I sensed—from the tone of some of their voices, and from the reticence of others—not simply disagreement, but antagonism. It seemed as if my blindness itself, my dark glasses were unpleasant, repulsive. No, they would not have given way to any "defensive reaction" if they had been in the place of that detachment.

And thank God for that. Although too many things recur in life, they were right in not wanting to believe that such a thing had happened for all that. Spring that does not wish to know that autumn and winter recur is right. Youth is right which does not want to believe that life began in just the same way for others. Blessed is the river that takes its source from a pure, clear spring; even if the spring were to know that the lower reaches of the river are befouled, this would not make its waters turbid. The river can be cleansed. That would be quite pointless, however, if it were not for the initial purity of the spring and the underground sources that fed it.

The first person I was in love with in the partisans was not Glasha at all. My love for Glasha which came later seemed to take source in my adoration of Kasach. Yes, Kasach! Boyish and funny as it was, with its reveries, fantasies, grievances and joys, you could not call it by any other name but love.

Even before I joined the detachment, I had heard a lot of things like: "Kasach's men, oho, they don't take just anyone!", "Armed like commandos", "All Kasach's men are experienced soldiers, they know how to fight!", "Kasach's men are waging battle", "Kasach's men, Kasach's lads..."

I did not simply dream of becoming a partisan, for quite a few of them passed through our village, but one of Kasach's men for sure.

I managed to get hold of a weapon without which you could not even ask to join him. Fedka Sparrows' Death told me how to do it. He, the son of the collective farm's book-keeper, had freckles all over his face like the speckles on a sparrow's egg. He was only fourteen years old, two years younger than me and, in order to make my constant advantage in that appear less, Fedka kept on trying to find things to boast about. This time he pulled two small hand grenades, out of a hollow in a tree trunk and showed them to me as I stood under the tree.

"Well, what do you say?" he asked with a proud ring in his voice.

My amazement must have been so delightfully gratifying to him that he decided to finish me off. He took me into the marshes. From beneath an uprooted tree stump he pulled out, wrapped in a piece of tarpaulin, what I had long dreamed of, a rusty rifle, its butt rotting slightly, but the genuine article nevertheless. Now even a fool could have seen that the advantage I gained from being two years older was sheer presumption and effrontery on my part.

"All right," said Fedka, becoming kinder, "they've got plenty where this came from."

I was perplexed.

"The little old dead men," Fedka explained. "So what?"

Involuntarily I glanced at my fingers which immediately opened out and which had suddenly become sticky. This was why the wooden parts of the rifle were so black, as if they had been scorched.

The next day we set out for the graves. There were many of them in the pine forest on the sand dunes. This is where they buried them in 1941. They were interred where they were killed, each in his own trench. The battle thundered on for a long time here in Polesye, among the forests. The Germans had already taken Smolensk, but here in the forests and swamps they were checked by armoured trains and the cavalry of Oka Gorodovikov with his big moustache.

The yellow sandy mounds of the trench graves had settled, grown over with heather like a camouflage net disguising them. Fedka sat down under a bush and had a smoke.

I stood in front of him with the spades, ready to beg "Better not do it!"

"Well?" he inquired sullenly,

I did not know what he meant.

"Have you hired me? Arbeiten!"

I, most likely, blushed.

"Give it to me!" he tore the spade out of my hand. "Dead men don't get tooth-ache!"

The damp yellow sand, bright like fresh blood, gradually built up around us and we kept going deeper and deeper down into the ground. I sprang out of the trench suddenly for the earth seemed to be moving away, sliding slipperily under my bare heels.

"You running off for some water?" Fedka shouted scornfully.

"It's cramped with both of us in there," I explained, choking on my sticky saliva.

Fedka threw something black like a piece of burnt paper out onto the yellow sand.

"This is a German the buttons are German there's not a thing here!"

"Why?" I forced myself to take an interest, although if I had been alone now I would have liked to have left, to have run away. I had the feeling that I had lost something for ever.

Fedka banged about in the pit with his spade, trying to detect the sound of metal.

"I've already told you! They don't have them in their graves. It's a proven fact. They buried their dead without weapons."

A sound like the thud from wood thundered in my cranium. Fedka looked me in the eyes.

"Little helper, eh! Well, get on and fill it up. Am I your slave?"

He walked away to one side and lay down with his eyes shut, and I began to fill the pit up with the already dry sand.

It was not until we dug the third pit that the spade (his, not mine) rang out as it struck something. At this, point, I forgot about everything else.

The rifle was lying in fresh sand and we were standing over it. The metal, was so rusty that it was yellow like a buttercup in spring, and the wooden parts of it which were as black as coal were impregnated with the odour and dampness of death.

"We've got it," I cried out.

It was with this very rifle that I asked to join Kasach's men. (I had to put a new canvas strap on it).

I did not begin by telling Mum, knowing how difficult it was for her to make such decisions, but got straight down to business. Twice we went (and we took Fedka with us) to saw down telegraph posts. The lads we knew who were with Kasach were rewarded with cartridges for taking us with them. Fedka hid them away somewhere. But Fedka was again racked with envy,

"It's all right for you. You haven't got a father."

But I did have a mother. I summed up my courage, summoned all my ingrained fearlessness of a rather unsatisfactory pupil and told Mum that her son was a partisan.

My little sisters, twins of seven, examined the partisan who had suddenly announced himself in their family with enthusiastic and pitying expectation, for they thought that he was going to cry now. Our Mum was quick to go for the belt und even for the stick. Then she herself wept, but you would be likely to howl before she did.

This time she was the first to cry. She wept softly and helplessly, looking at her twins' little mugs, flat like saucers, casting a glance round at the walls, and the corners of the house, as if the family needed to run away immediately, to leave everything.

She went into the kitchen without uttering a word. She busied herself there around the stove and wept, and we talked in whispers.

"Will they give you a horse?"

"I'll get one myself. Kasach's men get everything themselves."

"Will you let us have a ride on it? Will you sow the seeds in our kitchen garden? Otherwise it will be hard for Mummy."

"I shall come and do it. You're a partisan's family now."

"Mummy's crying."

"She always does... When Daddy went away to fight the Finns she did as well... You were too little to remember that."

Our twins were not regarded as beauties, even Mum would speak of them with a pitying smile (when they were next to one another it was hard not to smile): "Good heavens, little old ladies are growing; its bad enough having one, let alone two."

I loved their flat faces with their thick lips although I often used to shout at them, like a bad-tempered lout when they would not leave our band of kids alone. But in our own home we were friends. Anyone would have been touched by that pair of submissive smiles on those kindly little mugs, a double portion of respect for an older brother.

Now, when Mum cried and looked at them in that way and at the walls, I felt guilty. For the first time it struck me well and truly how everything might end. These were times when no family could feel safe, let alone partisan families, who needed a great deal of luck and good fortune if they were to survive, for the Germans hunted them down all the year round."Come on, let me sew your father's collar on for you. Get up in the loft and bring it here," said Mum, turning towards us from the stove; we had immediately stopped talking. "Some devil will find it and take it anyway. Or they'll burn it."

I rushed out into the inner porch and flew up the ladder. Among some rags near a deck-chair I unearthed the sleeve of an old jersey reeking of tobacco. The sleeve contained the only valuable our family possessed, an astrakhan collar rolled up in tobacco leaves to protect it from the moths.

Mum sewed the collar with its gleaming black curls onto my faded red-brown school coat, while we sat by there in a communion of silence and expectation. Mum's straight, thin shoulders shuddered with the cold, and I ran and brought a warm old shawl from the cupboard. When the shawl was round her shoulders, Mum's figure did not seem so angular and she seemed to become kinder through and through, more sorrowful and pensive. It was when she was like this, with the shawl round her in the chilly dusk, that she would tell us about life in the town, about her youth, and about father. (I came from the town, but my little sisters were born in the country. My father himself had requested the job at the tractor pool and he was manager there right up until the war with Finland started. Then something incomprehensible and stunning happened—he was taken prisoner. Two letters had arrived from somewhere in the north before the new war started.)

Mum's shawl and the astrakhan collar that Father had bought for his coat were all that was left of our "manager's" life style. We had begun to sell our things from the town even before the war started.

Mum finished sewing, and she looked at my coal with the luxurious collar and even smiled, "It came in useful at last."

Gladdened by her smile, we hastened to try on the coat: the twins held it like a fur coat for a rich gentleman to don, and I was ordering them about like valets. The astrakhan smelt of tobacco as if it has already been worn. It probably seemed like it to Mum as well.

"You'll smell of Dad's tobacco."

I breathed in deliberately cheerfully and loudly and smelt it, afraid that she would start crying again. My little sisters poked their noses, in as well, but I ordered them to wipe their noses first, and they wiped them obediently.

The first days and weeks at the partisans' camp were for me a veritable feast of things to learn. Discipline in the detachment was almost like that in the army, Kasach's men prided themselves on this for all their neighbours to see. But they were partisans all the same; everything they did was with inventiveness, cheerful swearing and with a small portable gramophone with one record for all moods "Stop being angry, Masha". This "Masha" sounded different when things were going well and when the dead were brought back and the partisans wandered round the camp gloomily and without saying a word.

We, Kasach's men, loved to see ourselves as others saw us. Once a captured polizei man, told us how he had hidden in the cellar and how he had heard us attacking from there, what we had shouted, our very words. We used to make a special effort to go and listen to the man and, being aware that he had hit the nail on the head, he did his utmost to make up the most complicated swear-words that we were supposed to have said.

It was considered obligatory to fight in a cheerful manner. It was only the beginners who described the fighting seriously and in detail; Kasach's experienced men talked of it as amusing, almost ridiculous adventures. Someone would come tearing along, having barely hooked it from the Germans, his eyes each as big as an apple, but he was already thinking up a story, trying to find something funny in what had happened just as if he had been playing some kind of cruel, but cheerful game with the Germans. If it had not turned out all right and the Germans had made our tails hot, that was made out to be funny too. And only when the dead were brought back, it was best not to go near if for some reason you had not been involved in the fight, for they would bite your head off as if you had been a stranger. In the evening they would sing songs softly and listen pensively as a prewar baritone assured Masha that "our life is splendid on sunny days".

Kasach was respected in the detachment, perhaps even feared, but feared very much in a partisan way, too: they would say that that was just the kind of handling they deserved, that you should look sharp and be able to slip away even from Kasach, otherwise you were not Kasach's man!

All the same, there was something about him they did not understand, even I noticed that. Yes, he was tough, perhaps even too tough, but then he was brave, and Kasach's men knew that he would never leave them lying there wounded as others sometimes did; even when we were ambushed no one would have dreamed of breaking loose and running unless commanded. The courageous man would not run because he was courageous, nor would the coward run because he was a coward and he knew that Kasach would decide his fate for him.

But that mystifying smile of his, the ironical attitude it revealed towards everything, whether good or bad! That smile annoyingly made everyone and everything level. It was as if Kasach only saw and remembered you when you were in front of him. Each time he appeared to be noticing you for the first time.

But perhaps this did not disconcert others. But I, I was in love, you see!

There I was, standing at my post near the headquarters' dug-out. The camp was slowly falling asleep, and the unsaddled horses under the awning were sonorously sorting through the dried clover. Someone was walking towards the headquarters, making the last year's leaves, which were slightly stiff with frost by evening, rustle loudly. In the chilly twilight I recognised the big figure of Kasach in his short sheepskin jacket and cap with ear-flaps.

"Who goes there?" I called menacingly, glad that he would hear me, my partisan's cry, but I was a little shy. For I had recognised him, and he knew that I had recognised him; it was as if I was suggesting we played a game."Password!" I demand, more softly this time.

He kept walking towards me out of the darkness, without saying a word or slowing his pace. I pulled back the trigger, but said immediately, "Is that you, comrade commander?"

I might as well shout out, "Ah, I recognised you, aha!"

Kasach walked quickly up to me and pushed my rifle to one side as if it had been a stick.

"Why didn't you shoot?"

A game is a game, but what a game he was proposing to me!

"I recognised you straightaway."

"If a person does not give the password, then shoot him!"

"But I..."

"It makes no odds." Kasach looked into my perplexed and aggrieved face closely and attentively and grinned: "Two days in the guardroom." This was probably to make it clear to me that war was a game in earnest and a fierce one.

But this was where Kasach's men took notice of their commander's character. It was really nasty, chilly and uncomfortable in the guardroom in the daytime: the bunks made of alder poles were cleared away and, standing or squatting in the freezing cold dug-out, you would breathe into your collar permeated with the smell of father's tobacco... But then a nights! At nights you enjoyed all the privileges, the extra special care of the guards.

I wonder if they told Kasach, even after the war, how they fed those under arrest out of headquarters' rations.

I had a hand in that too, when I had to stand on guard near the cook-house. You used to stand there, knowing that they would soon come out. (The rattling of saucepans instead of a password).

"Watch out when you're on watch!" someone like Rusty or Zuyonak would sob with a chuckle, their sleeves rolled up to the elbow. He would pick pieces of meat out of the smaller "headquarters" kettle, blow on his fingers, and you, the sentry, would have to hold the mess-tin as well. One mess-tin for all those under arrest.

Kasach was sitting behind me, just as he was, but quitel different as well. I do not know what he is like now, though.

At that time, we gave the man something of our own, something good and something bad, so that he took something from us with him.

And now we had taken back what was ours, retrieved it, and although he seemed the man he used to be, he was different for that matter.

People live this change in different ways. Some would be terribly surprised and take umbrage: "Only yesterday their life and death were in my hands, and here they are, each having the right to live, as he pleases, as if he and his fate had not been completely in my power just a short time ago". Some would live and keep pondering what they could have done yesterday, how they could have dealt with you!

I do not think Kasach is like that. He knew how to command. But I do not believe that was all there was to it. His ironical, at times even incongruous smile seemed as if he was somehow looking on from the side at what he was doing so skilfully and firmly. Most likely he was not getting his own back on the Germans, on the Nazis alone, but on something else as well. May be it was on the war itself? Perhaps this was the reason why he was less of a Kasach man than all of us and this was why the things he did so exactly and firmly did not bring him closer to people. Yes, we had given up to him something of our own and he bore within him something of ours. But it was not a cheerful sense of desperation like Kostya, our chief of staff, but something quite different. Perhaps it was a human need to wreak vengeance on the war by waging another war, to avenge himself on the war for it falling to his lot to come face to face with it.

Perhaps I am making Kasach a more complicated person than he really is. But he is not to be oversimplified either.

And I ought to say that I hardly know Kasach as he is today.

All the way there he did not say a word. Both he and Glasha were silent. When she saw him, possibly her face did not betray anything of what she felt. People learn to keep their face straight, but their hands will give everything away, and her hand had been resting on my shoulder.

I had always thought myself an ugly person, even when I could see. As if a person who can see can be an ugly person. But before I met Glasha, I did not pay much attention to that. When I became a member of the detachment, I even thought very highly of myself. I had a rifle and grenade, I was a partisan, what other beauty could a person wish for!

And then a girl looked at this partisan. She burst out laughing for the whole street to hear, and all at once became different.

As if on purpose, that day came along damp, cold and muddy. The hay under me which I had taken from a meadow flooded with water from melted snow was also damp and heavy. Lying on top of a high cartload of loose hay, I was going down the village street, looking for a house to have lunch in... Suddenly I saw Kasach riding a strong, fiery stallion, followed by the adjutant wearing straps and with hussar's whiskers. While my thoughts were wandering in admiration of us, Kasach's men, Zhenka the adjutant and I changed places (all in the mind, of course); he was now sitting on my cart and I was bounding along on his steed; I was so lost in my fantasy that I completely forgot about my own horse, old fat-haunched Goering, and it, the fascist critter, played a right trick on me, too. I was suddenly aware that the cart was tilting, that I was slipping and sliding together with the hay, slowly and inevitably into one of those puddles you get in spring.

'"Go on, fall in, it will be drier there!" shouted Zhenka, absolutely letting me down in the eyes of Kasach, who looked round at us angrily. But we all looked round when we heard the girl laughing loudly. I was ready to do away with myself and Goering as well and that laughing creature, too, who just had to choose this moment to appear. With the long legs of a baby stork stuck in huge worn out boots like pink candles in candlesticks, she held a dirty bucket on her graceful outstretched arm and in the other hand a big, thick sheepskin mitten. She was gathering up for the pigs the manure that the horses had been kind enough to leave behind, and she was getting a real laugh out of it too!

Glasha likes to recall that incident; she finds especially funny my indignation at the time at the way she held her bucket in a ballet-like pose. But it turned out that it was Zhenka with his sideboards, pulling faces that made her laugh, and not me and my cart at all.

Kasach and Zhenka turned into her yard. They had also decided to take a short rest. I was in no fit state for that.

Glasha lived with her mother who was still a young, shapely woman. She had only ever seen photographs of her father, smiling from ear to ear. Maintenance from him used to arrive from somewhere in the Urals. One day another photograph arrived showing a whole bunch of smiles like her father's. These were Vera, Nadezhda, and Lyubov, Glasha's little sisters on her father's side who lived far, far away.

In the village Glasha and her beauty of a mother were referred to as Glasha-Win-Ten-Grand and Ulyana-Win-Ten-Grand. It so happened that they had been lucky enough to win this sum on bonds; it had even been reported in a local newspaper. It was at that time that the owner of the house got his head turned, and embarked on a series of heady adventures that carried him as far as the Urals where he finally settled down.

At first it was not Kasach that Glasha was attracted to, but Zhenka "if only he hadn't been so free with his hands". She and Zhenka used to argue, throwing water over each other; they would almost come to blows and try to justify themselves loudly and angrily, she to her mother and he to the commander with the words "Let him (her) not start it!"

In the summer of 1943 the Germans started to bomb the villages where the partisans lived. Glasha suddenly came to be in our detachment. It was her mother, Ulyana, who begged Kasach to accept her, although even in the cook-house and the medical unit we had men working almost exclusively. Glasha's mother justly thought that it was safer at the partisans' camp anyway than in the camp for families where she herself moved with the rest of the villagers.

In the beginning a short-haired girl as skinny as a bean pole, lanky, shy and swift began to be seen around the cook-house and the medical unit. She was fairly tall for her seventeen years, but she had such narrow shoulders, drawn up tightly together as if in embarrassment. She had such joyful blue eyes that at times she seemed just like a little girl.

What happened did not do so immediately, but after another blockade, that is, the Germans' attempt to encircle and destroy the detachment. The blockade ended, and we began to notice many things around us again. People usually came out of a blockade as if they had just been through a wasting illness, exhausted but longing incredibly for quiet, sleep, laughter, voices, and the light of day. Day would become day again and the night night; the moon was no longer like a Hare, and human shadows like graves.

It was at that time that we discovered a "commander's woman" living around us.

The Germans had destroyed our previous camp, burned it down. Now we were living in a different tract of forest. We were no longer sleeping in dug-outs but in cabins built of branches and fir tree bar, or just under the trees.

Towards morning you would keep watch in this temporary camp surrounded by the fir trees, bashfully naked and shivering from cold now they had been stripped of their bark. Suddenly, in the cabin farthest from the road you notice a pair of bare feet slip out from under a sheepskin coat and be drawn back again under the coat startled. Kasach's voice could be heard in the cabin, implausibly good-natured, as well as Glasha's laughter, all of a sudden the resonant laughter of a woman.

If Kasach were to leave at that time, he would be followed by looks full of love and jealousy as Glasha and I watched him go. Once our glances met. Kasach rode past me thoughtfully, his horse going at a trot. I watched him go and then looked round at the cabin. Glasha sat there, pulling the sheepskin coat round her knees as she felt the cold. When she lost sight of Kasach in the trees, her eyes accidentally came upon the sentry. I do not know what she read in my glance, but it would seem that it grudgingly allowed her to love the commander. Fear flickered across her face, and she withdrew into the cabin.

Now the "commander's woman" used to get up later than everyone else. But I understood that this was because she was afraid of us, of our little smiles, and our looks. Everything that Kasach possibly did not notice depressed her doubly as soon as morning came and day broke.

So, our camp would wake up, its occupants coughing, laughing, having a smoke and washing in the yellow water of the swamp looking like cold tea. Some would be gnawing on rusks, some were rubbing flints together or were bringing lighted wood from the kitchen to make a little camp fire to protect themselves from the mosquitoes and some were examining their weapons. Night had come to an end, but day had not yet started. It was the very time to shout to one another loudly across the camp, to have a discussion or a laugh about something or someone.

It seemed as if there was no one at all in the commander's cabin. The "commander's woman" used to appear before us already dressed and with her hair done. She would walk round the side to the barrel of water, and would wash without making a sound as if she were afraid of waking someone up. More often than not, she would be wearing neat boots and a grey German sweater, which did not cover up her skinny neck, but on occasions she would appear in a ridiculous black silk loose-fitting dress on her narrow shoulders. She wanted to look as much an adult as she possibly could in front of us, but she appeared even more unprotected in that long dress. Especially with that flat and unpleasant, somehow alien female whiteness showing through the black silk.

That was our "commander's woman" for you, her eyes cast down, her lips pressed together, her face sleepy and unfriendly. But if someone, someone older and kinder, were to call to her or say hello to her, she would shudder, blush from head to foot startled and joyous, and the hunched up narrow shoulders would move around, struggling with a feeling of awkwardness and embarrassment.

But when Kasach was in camp, she would forget about us and herself as well. She only had eyes for him. Just as a shadow quivers as a ray of the sun catches and overtakes it (gradually becoming lighter and growing in it), so would she blush and brighten up when Kasach was around.

We were getting ready to go on a mission. The general formation of the detachment was in a clearing overgrown with stunted bushes. Everyone else was standing, only we, the drivers, were sitting on the carts. We could see everything as we were so high up. Shardyko, as the detachment commissar, addressed a few words to the men. As long as I can remember, he always walked around with his hand or arm bandaged or a dressing round his head. The bullets seemed to make a special effort to hit that agile little body. Kostya, our chief of staff, once explained why this happened. "You're a smart one, you are, commissar. You want to keep pace with everyone everywhere at once. If you're running through the rain, you will catch all the drops, yours and other people's as well. You're used to making home-to-home rounds on a collective farm, telling people what to do. No, let each person find out what he has to do for himself!"

Kasach listened to the commissar's words, his head hung, buried in thought or simply waiting to give the general order.

Glasha was waiting among the supplies platoon boys and the wounded. I could see how she was waiting for him to look at her. (I even became angry with him at times that she should have had to wait like that, and he, cross about something, did not notice). At last, he raised his head and looked her way. He looked for an indiscreetly long time, his mind on some problem of his own. His eyes shifted to the commissar. But it was already too late. As if summoned, Glasha moved towards the middle of the clearing. And, as if on purpose, she was wearing that same dress, that awkwardly long silk dress.

The whole detachment observed her strange, sleep-walking movement. The commissar stopped speaking and looked at Kasach disapprovingly, Kostya, our chief of staff, gave a laugh after saying something.

My heart stood still as I watched Glasha going towards the centre of the glade without remarking either the sudden silence or Kasach's sullen face behind the grin. But suddenly she noticed it as if she had pricked herself. She stopped, looked round horror-stricken, like someone who has found himself on an ice-floe that has drifted away from the shore. Kasach turned away, and she ran off into the woods.

If there was something about her that I loved at that time, it was precisely the fact that she was so in love with Kasach. It was a reflection of my own feeling for Kasach cast on her.

In my childhood I was in love with the brother of a gin in my class, in a reflection in just the same way. For me he was a living model, a copy of his sister. The eyes were the same, the mouth was the same, you need not be afraid to look, you could look to your heart's content. The little boys tormented the weak-willed, whining son of the teacher who had come from other parts, but I watched over him and protected him. Sensing my incomprehensible dependence on him he, in his turn, tyrannized me and acted capriciously. But this made him even more like his sister and made me even more attached to him. When I was with him, I could mention the name of that girl, unintentionally as it were; I could say it aloud in front of everyone, out loud—this is what it really meant to me, this was the special sweetness of it.

This is apparently how I perceived Glasha at first. It was almost like that. But she did not heed my secret, conspiratorial kindness, my guardianship, she did not notice our triple union. This was the case right up to that very meeting in the glade where the red grasshoppers flew away and sprayed out from under your feet.

Sometimes it seems to me that these sparks, these swiftly moving points on the black screen of my blindness are not little shivers of pain, that they issue from there, from our drilling. I had been to the glade before that, often seeking my Goering there, but I did not notice the red grasshoppers although they were, of course, there the whole summer through.

But summer was already drawing to a close. The damp, warm forest smelt of mushrooms, blueberries, and oily rotten stuff like an old cellar. The woodpecker could be heard tapping on the trees. At first it seems like the firing of a machine-gun far away. You listen hard—no, it is close at hand, the woodpecker is making a real effort. There will not be any fighting today, it will be tomorrow, towards morning. My immediate boss,

Sashka, was sitting in camp, greasing his machine-gun. I was in charge of the horses and the cart. Something serious must be going to happen if they were taking the machine-gun carts. I could see the grey back of our trace-horse in the bushes on the other side of the glade. This meant that Goering was somewhere around. I was busy, lathering nuts. There were so many nuts that you could pick them with your eyes closed. You would catch hold of the brunch, crumple up the dryish leaves that pricked your palm until you found the solid, heavy cluster of nuts. The green flesh of the nut left a sour taste and a coolness in your mouth....

At first the hazel-nut grove dragged me into the dark thicket of the forest and then led me out and pushed me out unto the other side of the clearing.

There I heard the weeping of a woman and then a child.

I espied Glasha lying under an oak tree, her narrow back quivering under the black silk, I myself was at a loss, unable to understand where the crying child was. Then the muffled sobbing of a woman turned into the sobs of a child. The woman was lying there on the hard rib-like roots sticking out of the ground under the oak-tree in her long silk dress and choking on infantile tears. Her little boots stood by her head with the puttees hung neatly on them to dry. Her bare legs and feet shuddered angrily in response to mosquito or ant bites.

Greedily and frightened, my eyes scrutinised the whiteness of her woman's skin sharply set off by the black silk. Glasha suddenly sat up, tucked her legs under her, and grabbed her boots.

"Oh, it's you...," she said in such a tone as if it was only Goering breaking out of the bushes.

"I'm looking for my horse," I explained why I was there at all.

How neatly the little boots stood at the side of her, the weeper.

When the war was over, Glasha recalled: "I used to walk right through the camp, talking to people if anyone spoke to me, laughing and guffawing, but I would be going to have a cry. The camp would be behind me, no one could see me, but I would still not have burst into tears; I would be hastening towards my glade, to the oak-tree. I would run to it, pull off my boots, make myself comfortable, hang my puttees up to dry—now everything was comfortable and nice—and at last, I would give way to my tears, such sweet tears because they had been held back for so long."

I found the fact that frightened, tearful Glasha looked almost ugly with her swollen lips, lack-lustre, furious eyes, very touching. She must surely have become plainer and lacking in vitality specially for me so that it was simpler and easier for me to be with her. Grateful that she was so generous and kind, although she was unattractive (she even sniffed like a boy), I stood there and did not go away, amusing her with my notions regarding the lighting the near day. It must be a big garrison if we were taking the machine gun carts. It was good that we were going to have a shot of strength. There had long been talk of another blockade (they would come in the autumn, to grab the harvest) and our detachment was right in the very salient of the zone controlled by the partisans. We needed to widen that salient and in general we had not seen much action for a while.

"I don't go on the operations," said Glasha, without hearing my discourse out, "I'm the lady commander, you see!"

She looked at me as if I had called her that, as much as to say, "All the more fool you are!"

I readily agreed. That went without saying, it was obvious.

"Well, now you can do what you like with your commander. I'm going to have a baby. Even if you all fall apart with malice!"

I looked askance in fright, just as if this were going; to happen right now. There was something about me, something about my lanky, flabby figure that meant that Glasha was not shy of me at all.

"That's the very thing to do," I said gladly, "You've got the right idea. When the war ends, you'll have..."

I could have said "we'll have": I eagerly thought of her as one of us in that imaginary world of mine where Kasach and I were close friends, and Glasha did not interfere with that.

"You've got the right idea!" Glasha said, mocking at my enthusiasm. "You're a right little fool, aren't you!"

She looked at me in such a way, however, as if begging me to repeat that stupid remark. And I was quick to do so.

"So, you're going to be a Mum, then!"

It was as if I had dealt a blow at her with that word: she suddenly blushed agonisingly, turned away and got to grips with putting on her boots.

"Yes, of course our commander's..." I dragged on and tried to help Glasha to continue our conversation. "When the war's over..."

"Do you think I don't know that you have a 'mother-in-law' in every village?"

And again it was as if someone was rubbing salt into the wound, she even groaned. She stood up and walked across the glade. Somehow I could not put an end to the conversation, I kept dragging it out idiotically in her wake, I just went on talking. Glasha remained silent, almost hostile, and at last I stopped talking.

She was ahead of me, I was about ten paces behind her. We were walking among piles of logs that had collapsed. The warm, sour odour of the rotten stuff tickled the nostrils. Before the war firewood used to be cut and sawn here. Blocks of birch, aspen and hornbeam wood were rotting away, caked and stuck together, covered with a frothy, foam-like fungus.

A thick carpet of dense, young, spreading bushes stretched between the piles of logs. If you were to throw a stone into them, it would bounce back as if it had fallen on rubber. Glasha was taking steps slowly, pensively. The bushes were so dense that you had to balance on one foot while searching for somewhere to put the other foot down, and this pose probably cheered her up. It was just like the ballet posture she had taken up that time with the bucket.

"Look, it's pink!" she said, referring to the jagged-leafed, spreading bushes. And it was true, they were completely bespattered with red. It was the woodland grasshoppers hiding in the warmed, dry shade of this green carpet tinged with red. They would shoot out from under our feet like flames from a camp fire, fly through the air and fall on the jagged leaves where they would immediately stay as if lifeless. A grasshopper sat on my palm like a little piece of charcoal smouldering away and coated with grey ashes. Glasha took it from me and put it down on her funny narrow hand. She let it shoot up into the air, and, like a flying spark, it went out amongst the green and pink leaves.

I began to say what I was thinking out loud, that perhaps they were adapting. The war, the conflagrations, look how long that had been going on for, and there was not even any hope that it was going to come to an end.

"Perhaps they only live for a day," Glasha objected. "What will they remember!"

Then I began to feel sorry for them. What if they were born on a rainy day, then they would only see clouds! They would never know that the sky is sometimes clear and blue as blue can be....

Glasha caught my furtive glance and looked at me mockingly and encouragingly as if I had not thought it but had said something aloud about her eyes. She turned away and began to laugh.

"What a funny boy you are! Especially when you're on your cart. You'll make the Germans laugh themselves to death."

(This is what struck me most about Glasha at that time. She would sometimes be surrounded by lads laughing at one another softly and at her, and she would be like a thin stalk in the wind. Her long arms and the whole of her upright figure would be tearing themselves away from our glances just as girls do, and her huddled shoulders would move as if performing some kind of embarrassment dance. But her blue eyes were surprisingly daring, laughing eyes. They betrayed a joyful awareness of the strength that gathered and held us around her, the power that a woman has over us.

In Glasha there was, nor did she lose it later, the awkwardness of a girl, a feeling of embarrassment when she moved and the audacity in those blue eyes that knew what effect they had).

Almost thirty years have passed since we were in that green and pink glade. But how many times I have returned there in my dreams. The ground suddenly begins to smoulder with the red raindrops of the grasshoppers. Glasha and I look round at a loss as to where to put our feet. Then we run back. Above us, thundering like a train rumbling across a bridge, the wave of fire rolls across the tree tops of the forest, showering us with hot sparks. When you wake up and for a long time you cannot understand where you are and where you have come from as you make efforts to open your eyes....

When you lose your sight, the first terrible thing that happens to you is that you cannot open your eyes. You keen on trying but you cannot. This happens over and over again in your dreams. But at the same time you are tormented by the fact that you cannot close them either. They are forever open to the world! And to your inner self, to your memory.

I followed Glasha step by step, watching the flying, dying sparks shooting out from under her little boot and my stiff boot. I could hear the hard cracking of the leaves underfoot while my own footfall sounded like the light cheerful beat of a sonorous drum. And I knew that the fighting (and perhaps injuries or death) would not catch up with me until the following morning—a whole eternity away.

"Flyora, where did that name come from?" Glasha asked, turning round in such a way that she herself was standing still while her adult's dress continued to swirl round her legs. She had long, straight legs and she did fine that trick of swirling her dress round them.

I told her what "Flyora" meant (I had read it in a calendar).

"A flower?" Glasha laughed. I laughed as well. Some flower I was with my monkey-like smile stretching from ear to ear, in that baggy German full-dress uniform and baggy trousers which I had exchanged with the scouts for my coat from home. "Let me have a shot." Glasha was already eyeing my rifle.

"We're not allowed to here," I warned cheerfully, taking the rifle off my shoulder, "Kasach's orders."

That name suddenly sounded unfamiliar, even somewhat taunting, and, just as if I were arguing, I said in a dull voice, "It's only right, too. They'll soon be shooting up the limp."

Glasha was not listening, she left me on my own to face any possible trouble. She was aiming at the bottom of a tree. I swiftly lifted the barrel of the rifle.

"Press it against your shoulder." I took hold of her by the shoulder and elbow to show her how to do it. The silk was so slippery that I seemed to burn myself.

"I'll do it myself."

She moved the rifle like an anti-aircraft gun and at last she fired. She handed me back my rifle and burst out laughing.

"You poor thing, you'll be in the guardroom again."

"They've got to prove it first."

I sat down on a tree stump, pulled out my cleaning rod and fished around for a little bottle of oil in my gas mask bag.

"How did you come to find this glade?" Glasha was walking about in front of me, kicking over the fly-agarics which flared in such bright splashes of colour amidst the grey-green aspen.

"What do you mean? Surely that's not difficult?"

She had probably fled here so many times to have a good cry that she regarded it as her own secret glade.

That evening we left the camp so as to have the garrison surrounded by morning. What garrison we would find out when we got there. Because it was like this, the feeling with which you usually prepared for and went on a mission was doubly intense. A link has already been forged between you and someone there (you do not know where or whom) for you have to kill each other. Because you are aware of this, but he does not yet know it, you imagine what it will be like for him, how he will hear the first shots striking home, how will jump up in fright. For you yourself those first deafening shots are so familiar that they sound like a knock at the door, and you are filled with relief that you are at last coming face to face with the danger. "There it is!" you say to yourself.

When the detachment which had formed up was listening to the commissar, I was perched high on my cart once again at the back of my platoon, watching and waiting for Glasha to go over to Kasach. But he himself rode up on horseback to those who were crowding round the edge of the clearing....

It had gone quiet in our bus. Drowsiness was even overcoming Kostya, our chief of staff. Only my Syarozha kept chattering away, painstakingly telling me what he could see through the window at this moment and what had just gone by. Suddenly he burst out laughing and exclaimed, "Oh, Daddy everything's moving across your dark glasses... Oh, there's hare, a hare! Look, it's in the clover!"

"No-o, it isn't, it's in the buckwheat," the words resound in the sleepy calm.

I was shell-shocked during the fighting at that time. The detachment was launching an offensive on a railway static from the direction of a stream and a meadow overgrown with birch and alder bushes. We had a long time to wait for the sun to rise, hiding in the bed of the stream, to which we had brought our cart down as well. At exactly five o'clock, without firing, we rushed towards the allotments above which the brick water-tower showed up darkly like the tower of a fortress.

Our company commander, Ilya Ilyich, warned us just before the attack, "Keep your sights on the water-tower. I wouldn't mind betting there's someone up there with a machine-gun! You can look after this for me."

He threw up to us on the cart a little book by Nekrasov "Who Can Be Happy In Russia".

We placed the horses so that they were shielded by the low bank, at least leaving them concealed and we remained face to face with the tower.

Shots had already rung out—the fighting had begun. Floating in the mist that precedes the dawn, the tower suddenly began to spatter flashes, teasing us unmercifully with a little red tongue of fire. Yes, that was a machine-gun, all right! Sashka immediately entered the duel with it. At first the German ignored us, firing on the attackers. Somehow Sashka just could not get the machine-gun in the right position and kept ordering me to move the horses from one side to the other. Our "Lewis", tall as a bicycle, was fixed on the mounting from a "Maxim", which was not a very comfortable hybrid as you could neither lie down behind it nor sit behind it unless you crossed your legs. And we did not have anything to shield us.

Finally Sashka found the right position and the "Lewis" spoke through its nose in a bas clef, something like a bulldog. It chewed up its ribbon, turning it into a flat wafer. I handed him another one and helped to fit it into the slot. And then our turn came, but it hit the water behind us just as if stones were raining down. Sashka set "the bull-dog" on them again (that is what we called our machine-gun). I was holding another half metre long ribbon of bullets across my palms, rather like a waiter. There was nothing else for me to do except count the little stones dancing on the water around us. Suddenly a red snake appeared in the water, lithe and unhurried, becoming longer and longer. I did not realise straightaway that it was blood. Swiftly (in my mind's eye) I felt myself all over. There did not appear to be anything wrong with Sashka either. The horses were standing there calmly and indifferently, but Goering kept lowering his muzzle to the water as if trying to catch the red snake with his lips. But it continued to grow long, winding with the current, floating away from us yet unable to tear itself away.

"Hurry up!" shouted Sasha. "Get your skates on or he'll nail us."

Now the firing intensified, now it died down, but it was already clear that the nastiest thing had happened: we had not crushed them in a single swoop, and now everything depended on who had more ammunition and time. We had loss of both.

German mortar shells were pounding the allotments. We could see the black peaks of the explosions. You simply wanted to groan at the thought that they were ripping and rending our men apart who were lying low up there. Sashka let loose another stream of bullets into the little black aperture of the tower which was becoming more and more visible with every minute, its dark colour gradually becoming brick red.

Immediately we felt we had got him, we had hit the German.

"Come on, let's get another one!" cried Sashka, rubbing I his sweaty freckled nose and his short-cropped hair with his sleeve from sheer joy. "I'll make him pay."

I put up four fingers. That was how many cartridge belts were left in the boxes.

Clumping through the water, someone was running behind the bushes. It was Kasach's aide.

"What are you doing here?! The commander ordered you to go over there, on the fringe over there... closer to the forest... on the flank! Come on, get a move on!"

But "our" German came to life again. Showered with little stones, Zhenka fell towards the cart at my feet.

"Did you see that?" Sasha bawled at him. He was ever such a kind man and would get worked up at the slightest thing. He had been with the partisans a long time, joining the detachment along with Kasach. There had been time enough for his nerves to become frayed. He pressed the trigger again. With a rumble, "bull-dog" accurately counted off ten cartridges. It chewed up almost half the cartridge belt.

I showed Zhenka how few cartridges we had left.

"Come on! Kasach's orders," he shouted without even looking and ran off. The German released another shower of bullets. We heard them hit the wheel directly below us.

"All right, let's go, it's an order," cried Sashka. We were reloading the machine-gun when Kasach swooped down on us. Yes, it was certainly Kasach.

"What do you think you're doing? Firing at the skies? You bloody..."

Never before had I seen that large and at the same time sharp-featured face so close. It looked sharp because of two scar-like furrows running down his cheeks from his eyes to his chin. And what eyes he had. His eyes were particularly striking. They looked furious and yet seemed to be grinning all the same, not a hint of mercy as he looked at me. But at last it was precisely me that his eyes perceived and recognised.

"Come on, up there!"

Neither hearing nor understanding what Kasach and Sashka were shouting to one another and what they were doing, why they were trying to pull the butt of the machine-gun out of each other's hands, I rushed towards the horses consumed by a burning sensation that what had happened was irretrievable and fully prepared to do some last, terrible thing, which alone could put right what had gone wrong. I dragged the horses on by their muzzles. Goering's ear had been torn by a bullet (that was where the red snake had come from). Blood was trickling down into his distraught eyes and his foaming nostrils and stained my hands and the green sleeves of my German uniform. When I jerked the cart out of the water onto the bank, I tore it and the machine-gun away from Sashka and Kasach, and they immediately came to their senses. (When I went over it afterwards in my mind, I realised that Kasach had furiously and contemptuously pushed Sashka off and seized the machine-gun himself, but Sashka, swearing like a trooper and almost in tears had refused to give way). In the end, Sashka pushed Kasach away, ran up to the bank and tumbled onto the cart. "Get moving!"

And move I did. For the first hundred metres probably because of the fit of temper and the dreadful bone-shaking we got as we raced across the hummocks in the meadow it seemed as if we were speeding along like lightning. I thrashed the horses with the whip-handle, bouncing up and down in agony on my knees, and Sashka, still holding on to the machine-gun for all he was worth, kept shouting, "Get going, move it!"

When we flew out onto the meadow, the tower rose directly above us, drawing closer to us, all aflame with the red rays of the rising sun. But the forest seemed to be miles away now. Mine and Sashka's eyes met for we both got the same feeling at the same time; we already knew that we could go on rushing along like that for only a few more seconds. That feeling was quite distinct, as intense as if someone were counting out those seconds aloud. It was as if we could see ourselves from up there on that tall red tower: there we were, in a cart pitifully and defencelessly creeping across the meadow. We could see the German training his machine-gun on us, he would hit us any moment. Something snapped beneath us, the cart became warped, but we still kept rushing on, trampling down those last seconds. Then, just as if they had stumbled the horses dropped with a crash right in front of us, caught by the explosion, and the cart flew on in a semicircle before overturning and hurling us out. (All the time I was flying through the air I was remembering where the heavy machine-gun was and where my head was...)

There were explosions all around us. I was tossed up into the air, torn away from myself and let down into a state of ringing silence. From there I looked out as if through a thick window glass at Sashka, crawling along so slowly, so terribly slowly. I could see what had happened to his leg, but he did not understand as he hastily pushed himself off the ground with that shuddering red stump, shedding blood on the grass. His boot and what was in it were trailing on a long trouser leg far behind. His huge eyes were full of expectation that he would see something any moment. I awkwardly stripped off my German jacket and crawled along that bloodstained path. I caught hold of what remained of the leg, but could not wrap it up in my jacket. It pulled itself out of my hands as I tried to catch it and kept crawling away like a frightened little wild animal. It seemed to me that I could hear the piercing shriek of that little wild animal, creeping along that red path, shivering hurriedly.

Anyone who has been wounded or shell-shocked even once is not the same person as he was before. He already knows what it will be like. Before that he only knew that he was mortal but now he has actually felt it.

I went round the camp, smiling at everyone. I had discovered that it was cheering to be mortal, that there were masses of advantages to it.

First of all, everyone starts to notice you and becomes fond of you. A wounded person is a highly respected individual among the partisans, noticed by everyone to such an extent that you feel uneasy because you are not used to that and you try to get rid of your bandages and crutches as soon as possible, so as to become like everyone else. (True, sometimes the opposite occurred; someone would enjoy wearing bandages as if they were epaulettes, but here the most awful thing would await him—people would suddenly lose interest in him; he would still like it, but instead he would get distrustful grins and scornful indifference...)

Well, secondly the mortal one was an adult, on a par with everyone else. (Only children were immortal.) Immediately to become closer to them, to the adults—that was worth losing immortality for. You could go there where they all were, where Glasha was....

When they brought me in, deaf, limp owing to the noise in my head and suffering from nausea, Glasha ran over to the cart where I lay. Suddenly I saw her blue eyes against the floating grey sky— she had bent over me. Many carts had already passed, bearing the dead and the wounded, and she appeared, leaning over me and weeping. She had run up to those who had been killed, to the dead and then she spotted the faint, awkward smile of someone who was alive. She was so happy about it that she kissed him, the person who was alive (somewhere near his eyes) and it was not apparently until later that she realised she had kissed me. Such a shocked expression registered on my face which had been inert owing to nausea up till that moment that Glasha started back in her girlish indignation, but she smiled straight away and stroked the spot that she had kissed with her fingers, leaving it to me.

Three days later I was already able to walk about the camp; it was silly to just lie there when you could get so many kind affectionate smiles. I strolled around, gathering them like mushrooms. What I was looking for was Glasha's smile, but she was not there. Glasha was away from the camp for a whole week. I espied Kasach in the distance several times. He did not notice me again. But the shame, ardour and horror at the irretrievable that I had experienced by the stream made me even more attached to this man.

Sashka, who had died from his wounds was buried in the forest by the path. Kasach had stood there, he looked grave and downcast, stooping in an unfamiliar manner. It was not allowed to sound a salute near the camp. Kasach threw down a handful of earth like the others, but he kept his fingers clenched round a lump of soil and I saw him take it right back to the camp with him....

I used to go out into the clearing and sit there for a long time, deaf, lonely, and mortal. I no longer heard the dry patter of the grasshoppers as they rained down and I only watched the noiseless red sparks of them. The scales of things had become imperceptibly intermingled, and here I already seemed to be in the fiery redness of the explosions with a pulsating rumbling recurring in my head. A sense of alarm would come stealing up on me and begin to grow as to what would happen if there was fighting in the camp and I was sitting there deaf and knowing nothing about it. Something may have changed in the world drastically and menacingly and only I knew nothing about it. If anyone had seen how I used to return to the camp, so cautiously with my weapon at the ready, they would have decided that the real war was not enough for the lad, that he wanted to play at it as well.

Once I fell asleep, warmed by the gentle caress of the autumn sunshine, resting comfortably between the high roots, like the arms of an armchair, of a very fat oak-tree. When I opened my eyes, there was Glasha. She was standing there, staring at me. I had already opened my eyes, but those blue eyes did not even waver, her face rigid, almost stern. At last she noticed that I had woken up, said something and sat down by the oak in the next "armchair" formed by the roots. She threw back her head so that the sun fell on her face, and sat stiff, her eyes closed, only the lids and the lashes quivered a tiny bit under the melting tears. Glasha was wearing a German sweater, open at the neck, revealing her neck that had grown even skinnier. She was wearing, as most women partisans did, a skirt on top of blue trousers which were tucked into her boots.

But it was obvious that she was not seeing herself that day, that she was not thinking what she looked like, she could not care less.

She muttered something without opening her eyes. Had she forgotten that I had become deaf and could not hear? Or was it all the same to her whether anyone heard what she was saying? I could not hear, but then I was glad of a chance to talk. About Kasach, of course. How else could I thank her for coming to sit by my side instead of going looking for him and spending time with him?

Naturally, I know more about Kasach than she does. All these stories do not perhaps make such a difference to a woman's love as they do to a boy's. There was the story of how Kasach appeared in the forest along with seven other escaped prisoners of war who were taken to be German spies and sentenced to death. Both Sashka and Kostya were also among those seven. Sashka cursed and wept from anger and resentment. Kostya Chief of Staff kept asking for a smoke (both while they were led to the place of execution and while he was digging his grave), and the rest acted as if they did not believe that what was being done was being done in all seriousness. Suddenly, down in the half dug grave Kasach said loudly, "When I finish you off, don't whimper! All right?"

He had spoken out loudly (everyone had heard him), but no one knew whom he was talking to. (I do not know whether he himself could explain what he had in mind. It was some kind of bitter, suppressed thought altogether and not a reproach or a threat. He could not have known that the fighting was going to start presently, that the Germans would appear two hundred metres away and that he, Kostya and Sashka, would display their mettle to such an extent that a few months later Kasach became commander of the platoon and then the detachment. The only thing that was strange was that they had already been lined up to be shot, but when the Germans fell upon them, they were immediately handed out weapons.)

I kept on talking and talking, and all the time about Kasach and about the fighting with Sashka down by the stream, and in everything I saw Kasach as being right because he showed himself no mercy, he did not spare himself. It seemed to me that Glasha listened to me attentively and approvingly, although she kept her eyes shut. Suddenly she articulated the words, "Be quiet, you little fool!"

I read it on her lips and in the irate look in her eyes.

She stood up and walked across the clearing just as she had the time before. Something must have happened between her and Kasach! I was absolutely stunned by this conjecture. For things had turned out so fortunately, so well balanced. Where was I to go, whom was I to follow if they were no longer together? Without her for me there was something missing from him. And without him this glade and our meetings meant something quite different, something that I was not ready to think about right away. I was so accustomed to being conveniently sure that we used to go there so that Glasha could voice her thoughts about him and I would help her to do it....

The fighting started immediately and was surprisingly close, not even beyond the brook where the embankment of the demolished, unused railway line lay, but on our side, almost in the camp.

We went through the pine woods with their smell of pine needles and summer sand. As Glasha pushed the branches aside, her wrists became pricked all over by the needles, and she licked them eagerly with her funny tongue. Suddenly she stopped and looked at me inquiringly and beseechingly.

"Shots are being fired!" I read on her lips. She waved in the direction of the firing.

"Are there a lot of shots?"

She nodded.

"Submachine-guns?"

"Yes!"

That meant they were very close.

I heard the explosions myself. My whole body somehow seemed to register them. It was probably mortar shells exploding. If they were already throwing grenades, then things must be really bad.

Glasha was listening to the fighting and watching me just as if it depended on me whether what was already going on would be stopped. And precisely at such a time I was deaf as a stone! Being deaf was like being blind, it meant being open to what comes, being clumsy and helpless. It is like being in a cage; you are caught and anyone can come up and look at you. The Germans would not look for long....

Glasha grabbed hold of my elbow with both hands. From her trembling fingers I sensed that they were shooting very close, right next to us in fact. I loaded my rifle and held it at the ready, looking round, but all the while I still remembered and thought about the fact that I was walking *arm in arm* with a girl like in an amusement park and that now they would see it, those same Germans would see it. It would be even worse (and it did seem to me much worse) if our own scoffers were to see us. And what if Kasach were to see us?

Those fingers were tightening on my elbow and trembling at the nearness of the shots and the explosions. In a whisper I ascertained, "Are there machine-guns? There are submachine-guns, aren't there?"

Glasha looked upwards to show me that there were even aircraft as well. This could only mean a blockade and nothing less. Now the main thing was to get back to our own people, not to get cut off and be left alone. Glasha was either leading me or hanging onto me amidst the shooting I did not hear. In my head I had my own noise, an empty, senseless rumbling. We tried to skirt the shooting and the shouts (later Glasha said she heard German voices shouting) in order to get back to camp. We kept moving to the right to avoid the fighting and enter the camp from the other side. But no matter how far we walked, how much we ran, we were not able to leave the fighting behind us. Glasha showed me that it was going on in front of us, to the sides of us and all around us. I was already becoming angry, thinking that she was probably confusing the shots with the echoes. I pulled her fingers off me and indicated that she should walk behind, that she should drop further back. I set out straight for the camp, I looked round. Glasha was shuffling along obediently behind, smiling guiltily and shyly. Involuntarily I smiled back at her, and she immediately approached me like one forgiven. Once again she put her arm round mine. Something had altered between us and had already changed in me. Now I saw myself as someone quite different, and that someone did not stand on ceremony; it was up to him to save Glasha. This was now the main tiling and let others be embarrassed and feel shy!

Suddenly the pine tree that we were approaching spluttered with white splinters, mute and terrifying as if exploding from within. Glasha had already fallen to the ground and was pulling me down by the flap of my jacket. The pine-trees were blowing up. Shreds of white like foam were bursting from under the bark. They were explosive bullets, but we could not see where they were firing them from.

(Sashka had talked about them once, but then the froth was red; it was as if I was recalling it as I has seen it myself—those red squashy bursts. It was in 1941. He and Kasach were plodding along as prisoners in the dusty columns when suddenly a hare jumped out onto the road. The German guards excitedly and merrily shot at it and into the column at the same time. Right before Sashka's and Kasach's very eyes, the back of the head of the man walking in front of them burst open, spluttering red froth.)

They were firing from the birch woods a hundred metres from us which showed up white beyond the trunks of the pine trees. I pushed Glasha, indicating that she should crawl away and she looked at me as if I could really change something in the whole world.

Dark patches of people appeared against the white wall of birch tree trunks as if filtering through them. They were coming away from the white wall of trunks and falling, coming unstuck and tumbling to the ground as if hit by a mute machine-gun. Then they were getting up again and stretching out in a line.

Glasha, her head raised slightly, was watching me from the ground with her big, defenceless blue eyes. Her face might be about to explode in a mass of red, too.

The trees kept on spraying out white splinters in the silent terror. I moved my legs right up to Glasha's face, indicating to her with a fierce grimace that she should creep away as fast as possible behind a dead fir tree lying nearby. And all the time I was afraid that that face turned towards me would blow up in a red froth. Suddenly I imagined that only the face, those huge blue eyes were Glasha, and her body, hastily crawling away, was someone who had seized her and was dragging her along and this was the reason for the horror and the beseeching look in those eyes.

The Germans walked by right next to the withered fir tree bare of its needles, behind which we lay. I even saw how the German closest to us in a helmet and spotted water-proof cloak hesitated for a moment when he saw the fallen fir tree, probably thinking that he ought to take a look behind it or fire a burst from his submachine-gun. That was such a tense moment that it seemed to me that even the cartridge in my rifle moved. The narrow young face remained turned in our direction for a little while longer. He did not fire his gun, however, nor did he walk up to the tree....

When they disappeared from sight, we jumped up and ran. It was pointless and even very dangerous to run for we did not know who or what was fifty or a hundred metres ahead of us. But we were overwhelmed by the feeling that had been building up within us throughout those minutes, by a desire to get as far away as possible from the spot where we were now. The danger had ceased to be so imminent, it was no longer breathing into our necks, but was perhaps lurking ahead....

"If you stand still—disaster will catch you up, if you run, you'll run into it yourself," This is what Rubezh liked to say over and over again. Timokh Rubezh was a strange, funny man we met two days later. No one in the bus would remember him for they did not know him, that Rubezh. His path and mine came together for a short space of time, but only mine stretched further on and his came to an end. Probably someone somewhere other than Glasha and myself remember him, for he had a family, but all the same you got the feeling that of the living only Glasha and I knew that he had existed and while we detained him in our memory it was true that he had existed.

It was strange how I perceived the people in the bus at this moment as intermediaries through whom I could communicate, *as if with the living*, with them, with Kostya, with Zuyonak, with Vedmed whom I had known and seen many years ago. It seemed as if Kostya, that noisy, laughing fellow, and Kasach who remained silent all the way, and Staletaw, had all come straight out of that distant past of twenty-five years ago. It is odd when your memories suddenly acquire flesh and blood and real voices. The sighted would have to exert themselves to picture in the present what Kasach, Zuyonak, Staletaw, and Kostya had been like a quarter of a century ago. But I did not have to make any effort, for I could only see them as they had been before. Those who were here today just confirmed that everything had indeed taken place....

Glasha was squatting, resting against a tree. After that lunatic dash pallid and flushed patches began to spread over her cheeks, and her staring eyes mirrored an expression of dark fright. I stood over her, wiping the stinging sweat from my face and looking in all directions at once. Glasha indicated that shots could be heard everywhere, all around us.

There was certainly no chance of us slipping into camp. And there would not be anyone there anyway, if that was what was going on.

"Kasach will wonder where you are," I said.

Glasha pulled down the grey sweater, removed a birch leaf from the toe of her boot and scrutinised it.

"It's autumn already," her lips and those eyes watching me said. I took the yellowed leaf from her which was still soft and fresh, as if she had said something vital, something that was important to us at the moment.

If a blockade had indeed started, all this—the firing and the aircraft—was already occurring there now where my Mum and my little sisters were. It would be a good thing if they had had the sense to leave immediately for the "islands" in the depths of the swamps. The people from our village had hidden there in 1941 and in 1942....

Glasha looked at me and agreed with what I was thinking. My goodness, I was already thinking out loud! I was speaking at the top of my voice without noticing it. I went on as if nothing had happened, "There in my forest I shall ride over the Germans whenever I feel like it. They won't be able to reach us there. When things quiet down, I'll deliver you to..." I did not utter the word "Kasach". Her look prevented me from pronouncing that name. Previously she had assisted me in uttering it, had demanded of me that I say it and here she was for some reason hindering me.

We were walking through the forest once more, and again Glasha pointed out where the firing was heaviest. We turned towards the little swamp, green with the long grass spreading over it. I filled my forage cap with water and, raising it above my head, I caught with my lips the stream of water, salty with sweat. Glasha drank from the palm of her hand.

"You're hungry," I guessed. She nodded swiftly and looked at me in a childish manner as if I could pick something from the tree at that very moment and hand it to her. Hell, I had even left my bag back in the camp. It was lucky that I did at least have my rifle and a grenade with me. Glasha had absolutely nothing. Kasach could have given her some kind of carbine, if only for appearances sake. Now we were making for my fellow villagers, and there they would decide that I had simply brought my girl along, my fiancée, and they would wish us all the best. Should the Germans kill us, they would come up and look at us lying there on the ground.

I pulled my elbow out of Glasha's grasp. To do that I made out I had to return to the clearing in the forest and take a look.

Everyone in the bus was half asleep. Glasha, who had bent over, was fumbling about in her bag and passed Syarozha a bottle with a drink in it. She said to him sternly, "Don't spill it."

Now she was looking out of the window. I sensed that she was breathing tensely, and it seemed to me that I caught a glimpse of her blue eyes, just as Kasach behind us probably did, too. Kasach was sitting at the back of us. We were going there to meet up. We were going to an encounter with ourselves.

But you are the one, Flariyan Pyatrovich, who is indebted to the partisan Flyora, that self-assured, angry, deaf man in the baggy, old German clothes, you are obliged to him for making it here, for managing to get through with Glasha. At times I see that Flyora from aside, myself at the age of eighteen. There was certainly nothing of that youth left in me, for he had remained there. Sometimes it seemed to me that Glasha and I were following him, heeding his furious signs, and he, raking through the leaves and the pine needles with his heavy boots, would either disappear among the trees or emerge from behind them with his narrow, skinny back. He still had to think about his mother and his little sisters. With his elbow pressing tightly against it, he would carry his pitiful little rifle permanently blackened by the dampness of the grave, as if that rifle could have defended us all.

...And then we caught sight of people. It was immediately noticeable that they were the inhabitants of a village who had fled into the forest, and that their flight had occurred that very day, perhaps just two hours before. There were no huts built of branches or trenches, no trees obviously used for hanging up clothes and other oddments. People had scattered and then gathered together again, huddling together in a throng, standing stock still and looking in one direction, for over there they were burning their village. The peasants' cottages themselves were not visible, just the spirals of smoke, differing in heaviness and colour, swirling upwards into the sky from behind a hill, but not yet joining together to form a single wall of fire. At first, as if one, the people turned in our direction, started, ready to rush off again, to run off, but they were immediately relieved by our appearance. Only a woman in a clean white jacket which stood out among the worn old clothes, raced towards us, bewailed something, shouted something angrily, pointing at my rifle with a cast iron pot which she was holding for some reason.

Glasha and I stood still for a moment as if waiting for people to lose interest in us, and then we quietly slipped away, along the edge of the forest. We did not want to lose the edge of the forest now that we had gained it by conquering our fear, we did not want to go into the forest again and wander about blindly. We still had to cross some three kilometres of open fields if we were to get to "my" forest.

We kept to the edge of the forest until dusk and saw ever new columns of smoke billowing upwards in one direction or another, some closer, some further away. Aircraft were swinging backwards and forwards between them as if on giant trapezes. They appeared first from one side, then from the other. There had never been such a blockade in our parts before, with so many aircraft involved!

By evening the sky was completely overclouded. The clouds of smoke curled upwards and twirled around as if held down by a low, black ceiling. Suddenly it rained heavily and then, as if that had been a mistake, it stopped raining, and dry sand came whipping through the air, caught up somewhere by the wind and now being hurled right down out of the clouds.

At first the glow spread along the horizon, hugging the ground, and the reflections leapt up to the heavy belly of the sky. Then the glowing patches began to grow and grow until they finally seized hold of the clouds and hung on them. The lower layers of the sky seemed to become smoother and more solid as it were, while the very depths of the sky became increasingly black and gloomy. Huge shadows collided with one another, knocking each other downwards. Night did not fall, nor was it day. The world became long and narrow, the whole of the horizon like an embrasure lit up from within.

Stumbling and tearing the leafy tops of the potatoes with our feet, we hastened across the field, hurrying towards the distant coal black trees of the forest outlined against the glow.

Then we espied people running against the background of the glow, along the horizon. The distant black figures that looked as if they were burning, flickering in the luminous embrasure, would disappear, while others would appear, only to be swallowed up by the blackness as well.

Other people would run out of the blackness closer to us, driving their long shadows before them as they fled. The ever lengthening shadows had already raced past us while the people themselves were only just approaching. Others further to the left were shooting away out of the rye which, like a fish-pond from which the water is being drained away, seethes from the thrashing fish. People did not notice us until they got right up to us. Their eyes would regard us hesitantly for a moment as if inquiring "Who's that?" or "Why aren't they running?" and then they would race past. As you watch them drawing away, you see the eyes again, this time children's eyes. Pressing themselves against the shoulders of adults, as they flew past us the children kept their little heads turned and their eyes fixed on the glow behind them.

Suddenly something happened on that side of the field to which everyone was fleeing. The darkness was pierced by tracer-bullets, and it became obvious that people were running away from there, probably from another village. When they caught sight of each other, the people came to a halt for a moment, perplexed, and perhaps they shouted out (maybe they had been shouting all the time, but I could not hear it). They began to rush about and then, all together, they raced towards the forest out of which Glasha and I had just come. In the forest, the habitual partisan abode, that we finally reached, we immediately felt freer. The forest admitted us, drew us into itself and led us into its depths, its quivering mottled light flickering over our faces and hands like a dog licking us. We walked for another kilometre and sat down for a rest. Glasha found a tree to lean against and immediately fell asleep, leaving this war and the whole of this world to me alone, for she was tired of it. I sat there, looking at her sleeping face with its capricious expression, as if it were slumbering as a challenge to the world about it, and softly, like a madman, I laughed probably because I was so weary and because of my idiotic deafness.

Since that was the very thing not to do, I also fell into a deep sleep, sleeping unconcernedly (as if giving way to Glasha's childish inclination), and nothing terrible happened. It was very cheering to wake up and see a world in which everything had remained just as it was.

At the same time as I awoke Glasha raised her head from her own shoulder and opened her eyes, generously adding to the world with their blueness. We looked at each other for a while, open to everything.

Everything in the forest smelt of smoke, the ferns and the pine needles, your sleeves and probably Glasha's short hair chilled by the dew which she was smoothing down with both hands. The smoke made your eyelids sting.

The sun, which had previously been hidden by the trees, suddenly broke through into the forest in a single surge and then the smoke began to twirl as if it was alive in the motionlessly splaying spokes of light.

We walked through a patch of old, wizzened coniferous forest, gathering the blueberries which had already dried up and turned sugary in the summer sunshine. We needed to get away from there as quickly as we could, but Glasha's hunger would not let us. Her hunger displayed itself in just the same, childishly capricious manner as her sleep had. Cheerfully, just as if we were feeding a greedy rabbit carrots from our palms, we gave it the sweet, slightly warm berries. I did get a few for myself, but the rabbit was so joyous in its avidity that it was hard not to give the berries to it.

The forest cast a spell on us, bewitching us, as it somehow vanished into thin air and became quite unreal owing to the bluish orange smoke, transparently stretched across the sunbeams.

At a certain moment we looked up from the blueberry bushes and discovered that we were walking through a cemetery, a woodland burial ground among the age-old pines and as old as the forest itself. Time and the woodland mosses had eaten into the three-to-five-metre-tall crosses to such an extent that in the first instant you think dully, "There are crosses growing here!" At the foot of the giant crosses lie smaller crosses like children and even smaller ones like infants, scattered about, having rotted long ago like little shadows of the giants. In some places the broken iron railings around the graves still remained standing. Time had caused them to grow together with the thick trunks of the pines. The iron had penetrated right into the middle of the trunk, and the moss had crept along the cast iron, making it appear part of the forest.

So, this is how they used to bury their dead, with a wrought iron cross on each grave. The crosses were not like the usual ones; perhaps they belonged to the Old Believers or the Catholics.

...Yes, Flariyan Pyatrovich, you might well have been lying there, mown down by a round of machine-gun fire, spattering another's cross and another's grave railing with your blood. And Glasha would have been cut down in that same instance. But that time, too, Flyora saved her. Confident and awkward in his baggy German uniform, carrying his little black rifle, he led her right before the very eyes of the Germans who were lying in wait to ambush the partisans in that very same cemetery.

Now we had changed roles. I was the one who was leading that partisan with his little old rifle, and that is what I keep doing, so to speak. But exactly from what moment in time, from what spot?

From the moment when the war ended? Perhaps I replaced him later on? Or, maybe, earlier? Once one of our Soviet tourists played a trick at the museum in Belgrade (when I was able to see, I tried to travel about as much as I could, to take a look at things, secretly suspecting that I was doing it for future use, to have something *in reserve*). It happened that this Soviet tourist took his fellow countrywoman over to a glass case and showed her a white skull. He said it was the skull of Alexander the Great at seventeen years of age.

"But where?..." The woman wished to find out where the skull of the adult Macedonian king was, but then she immediately realised what had been said and burst out laughing with everyone else. But where in fact? Where did we exchange roles, change places, Flyora and I, for example. For I stand completely apart from him. I remember him as if he was someone else, someone who had kept me company, whom I had followed, who had led me out of trouble and had saved me just as he had saved Glasha.

Yes, it needed to have been seen to be believed, how Flyora had dodged and used cunning when he suddenly caught sight of a machine-gun poking through the ramshackle railings, its cyclopean eye trained upon us, and on top of the machine-gun there was a motionless black skull-like helmet! Glasha had not noticed anything. She was walking ahead, fingering the moss-grown tips of the crosses and their velvety bodies with their arms thrown wide above her head in a mute cry. To her great amazement, Flyora suddenly began to wave his arm and shout back in the direction from which we had appeared, "Heh, captain, come here all of you! Look what we've found!"

In a strange voice he stopped Glasha and beckoned to her, "Glasha, wait a minute, I've got something to show you."

He seized Glasha by the shoulder (his hand was shaking, the expression on his face appeared to be one of laughing, but somehow turned to stone). He led her to one side, muttering something senseless, Once again he shouted out, "Heh, you over there, where are you? Come over here!"

They crossed the cutting in the forest, leaving the cemetery behind them. Glasha did not understand what had happened. He neither looked at her nor did he let her shoulder go. It was beginning to hurt her, but he just kept walking faster and faster. Suddenly he cried out, "There were Germans there, you fool, run for it!"

Grabbing her by the arm, he raced into a thick hazel grove.

When they had run a long way from that spot and when she realised what the situation had been there, Glasha started to shiver. Flyora threw his jacket with the aluminum German buttons on it round her shoulders.

Observing his military jacket with its high collar on Glasha, Flyora said, "Mum does not know that I have bartered my coat. The last time I called in at home, she asked me why I had not brought it with me. It had a good collar on it. Let's go back to the farmstead, you know. You're hungry, and I'm hungry, too.

...When we had run away after the cemetery incident, we had noticed a burnt down farm-house or forester's homestead in a clearing in the forest. There might well be potatoes there, even baked ones.

But I suddenly felt that in my deafness I was afraid of the forest. I kept on imagining the black skull of the helmet and the eye of the machine-gun trained on us. The main thing was for Glasha to stay with me, to be by my side.

I said in an angry voice (just in case she started begging me) that I would go alone and she would wait for me in the fir grove. Glasha looked at me beseechingly, not daring to object.

I was already enjoying acting in this way with her, making decisions for both of us, getting angry. When a person is cheerful, especially if his cheerfulness is unbidden and importunate, he always looks as if he is trying to justify himself. Nobody tries to justify himself for being gloomy and sullen. On the contrary, others somehow feel that they are to blame for it. You can get used to that and you like it all your life.

I soon found some food, right there on the road. I had to steal quickly across that road freshly ploughed up and erased by tank tracks. I stepped onto it and right before my very eyes lay a cardboard box. This was such an unexpected sight here in the forest, as if it had come from another world. It even made me jump back behind a tree at first, for I was afraid that it might be something dangerous. But immediately I raced out and grabbed it, as if fearing that my vision would disappear. When I seized the box, it occurred to me that it might well be a trap mine and, when I tore open the carton and bit off a piece of the evenly shaped biscuit, the suspicion did cross my mind that it might be poisoned. The biscuits were very dry, but in my hunger my mouth was watering so much that I was able to eat a second and even a third. I chewed as I was walking along, the faint, vague smell of bread going to my head. I was chewing them, and soothing my conscience with the fact that I had to be sure that they had not been poisoned. I even felt giddy in addition to the usual nausea and noise that accompanied me from the moment when I became shell-shocked.

I got lost and suddenly realised that I was wandering about at random, I could not even cry out to Glasha or rather I could not hear her voice. I had completely forgotten that I was deaf.

Frightened and confused, I began to run and then I felt quite sure that I would not find her, and I became even more afraid. There had been no necessity to leave her and go there on my own. There was no need to make out that I feared an ambush. It was simply that, *like other people*, I enjoyed being morose and in command. What a fool I had been! What did it matter to me how others behaved! Perhaps Glasha had not meant the same to others as she did to me.

I almost fell upon her. She espied me from a distance and ran across my path, alarmed by the sight of me, racing along, my eyes all white, carrying some kind of box, just like someone who has stolen something and is being chased!

This someone bawled, "Eat your fill, they're not poisoned!"

The light in the forest began to dwindle and collect above the trees. At nights the ground emitted a pungent coniferous aroma. We had walked all day long and now we were settling down to have a long, tranquil sleep. We ate all of the biscuits, which went down well with the sour wood sorrel. Our hunger was only slightly sated, but the very awareness that we had eaten bread that day made us feel better, for bread always raised your hopes!

Glasha was sitting under a dark tree, downtrodden with exhaustion, my German military jacket thrown round her shoulders. It was drizzling and damp. I broke off prickly fir tree branches and put them down by her legs.

The rain clouds were descending lower and lower over the forest, but instead of becoming darker, it became lighter as the nocturnal reflections of the fires slid across the forest. We were almost in my parts now. It was some thirty kilometres to my village.

I had got a pile of fir tree branches, and all I needed to do was to drag them into a thick fir grove. I stood my rifle up next to Glasha and dragged my heavy, prickly burden along blindly, moving the densely growing firs apart with my back, for we needed to get into the grove as far and as deeply as possible, away from everyone and everything. Glasha sat there strangely unconcerned as if she did not see what I was doing, and it already appeared that this was not from fatigue alone.

Everything was ready. I went up to her and took my rifle. Glasha looked up at me and handed me my jacket.

"The rain won't get at us now," I said. As Glasha stared up at me, her eyes lit up and there was something inquiring in them and completely unfamiliar to me. But what was so special about this? It was just the usual thing, we had to get through the night without encountering the Germans and without getting lost, and altogether we were dog tired people. I told Glasha how we would leave in the morning and reach our destination by evening. Glasha regarded me in silence. What else could she do, if I was deaf? Everything was just as it usually was.

She walked over to the dense little fir grove with its brush-like branches wet and glistening and was interested to see what I had put together there.

"Come over here, I've even made a roof," I said, walking backwards as I pushed my way through the prickly wall of firs. Glasha followed in my wake, brushing the fir branches away from her face with her hands. I could see her face and her eyes. All of a sudden, she seemed to have become uncomprehending, unable to grasp what was happening, very surprised by everything as if it was the first time she had been in a forest. She had apparently been deciding how to act while she had been sitting there under my jacket and I had been gathering the fir branches and now she was behaving like this, waiting for everything to be shown and explained to her as if she herself had never thought what was there and what it was like. She had found precisely the way she should behave with Flyora.

There it was, our dwelling with both a roof and a bed all made of fir branches. Glasha stood there, confused as to what to do next. "Crawl in," I said to her.

The palm of my hand hastily informed me that Glasha's hair was wet and warm. Glasha squatted down and crawled into the darkness under the bushy roof. I crept into the prickly darkness as well. Glasha's cold hand touched my face, indicating where I should put my head. We had enough fir branches to pile them up the sides and cover ourselves as if with a blanket. Lifting the branches and pulling them out from under our backs, we put them onto ourselves and evened them out. Our tingling hands would meet and would show the best way for the fir branches to be placed. We found it even better when I took off my military jacket, covered us with it and then put the wet, prickly branches on top.

In the end, everything was just right. We had a springy shed of fir branches beneath us, a dense, heavy layer of fir branches on top of us, a rifle between us, and our hands pulled the warm jacket up closer to our necks.

Everything in the world seemed mysterious and distinct as if you were looking through binoculars the wrong way round and everything was distanced from you. It seemed as if everything would happen tomorrow, but for the moment there was this alone, only us. The silence was already making me afraid like some sort of incriminating evidence, and I began to talk, to whisper. Naturally, I talked about the detachment, about Kasach. I said that he must be looking for Glasha and wondering where she had disappeared to. So that she could hear me better, Glasha turned over from her back onto her side. Now she was facing me. Now I could feel her breath which was cool for some reason. Or perhaps it was my cheeks that were so flushed? But I did not feel warm at all. I didn't know why, but I was cold. I kept talking faster and faster, as if saying a prayer, whispering that I would hide her on the "island", how we would then find our lot, the detachment. (Glasha checked with her hand to see that my side was covered up and that I was not getting cold). I still kept on mumbling my prayer, talking about Kasach, saying how strict and taciturn he could be, but then when he told you to run off and do something, everyone would gladly run off and do it. And I understood why Glasha was like that, and why I was like that myself. Glasha already had her arm on top of the jacket. I could feel its trusting weight on my neck. Her adult-like simplicity was splendid. She put her arm like that without even thinking about it, but now all I could do was think about the way her arm lay across me and what that meant.

She had wanted to become adult and had done so right before the very eyes of the detachment. I only grew up in dreams, but in dreams I was sure to be frightened by someone at the very last, the most shameful moment, as if someone was amusing himself with me, always deceiving me in the sameway and always managing to do it.

Glasha was quite quiet, her breathing became more shallow, but I kept on whispering, softly uttering my, prayer. I was already telling her how it all started, how Kasach and Kostya had organised the escape from captivity by breaking a hole in the floor of the carriage transporting prisoners and how they had all tumbled out between the wheels of the train as it raced across Poland....

Finally, I realised that Glasha was asleep, slumbering cosily, as if she were at home, just as she did in any situation.

Immediately everything had changed. Next to me I had a trusting little ball of human warmth. I turned towards it, no longer needing to be afraid and silently I inhaled it and rejoiced in it. I did not allow myself to sleep, although the whole body was being caught up and drawn into that snowballing sleepiness, and as drowsiness crept over as if sticking to me, I had to shake it off again and again. If we were to get killed the next day what remained of our lives would have been spent in that night. You just close your eyes and the next thing you know, it is morning. No, let every minute last, be prolonged as much as possible, let it be torn up into seconds, into moments. Glasha's arm lay trustfully and sleepily upon me, her little knees were warming themselves against my legs, her breath tickled my lips and made my eyelids tingle as they stuck together, begging to be allowed to sleep. You could even close your eyes, but you must not permit the moments to join up to become minutes and the minutes to form hours and the whole of your body to roll into the single, sweet, dead ball of sleep. You must not allow yourself to sleep, must not permit yourself. You had to restrain yourself, to pull yourself out of it, to drag yourself away from sleep. Where were Mum and my little sisters now, where were they at this moment, what were they thinking about? I just had to see them and make sure that nothing had happened to them, that they were still alive.

I sank into sleep as if into water. In what seemed just an instant to me I surfaced into the coldness and the dampness, into a dawn ringing with the resonant echo of shooting. It was still dark in our fir grove except for the strings of drops glistening on the needles as if they had their own light, and the trunks of the fir trees, stripped of their bark high up showing up white in the hovering mist like candles that had never been lit or had been blown out. It was even amazing how they had managed to remove the bark almost to the very top.

"Will they find us? Will they catch sight of us?..."

Glasha's voice, her hasty whispering betrayed fear and those knowing, brave, smiling eyes looked up at me. She seemed to be telling me that it was she and that for the first time, in truth, it was not in a dream, but they were indeed shooting close by. We, however, were alone and our hands were begging, mingling, permitting, prohibiting, helping. They were both affectionate and rudely clumsy, and funny and strong but bashful. Her eyes were so close that they seemed about to dissolve into a huge patch of blue.

"Don't look! Can you hear it!... Can you hear shots?"

I closed my eyes and woke up. Once again someone was playing with me, amusing himself with my foolish cowardice. Glasha was wide awake now and had raised herself up slightly, after turning on one side and throwing off the blanket of fir branches heaped on us. She was concentrating on listening. Sleep had left me, but I was still sleepy, and this prevented me from watching her. Now it seemed that I had really woken up. I looked for my rifle which had rolled away under my side and wiped the rain drops from my face, washing it at the same time.

"Shots are being fired," I said. I had read it in those eyes bent on listening.

There it was, my Beliya Pyaski. I had brought Glasha home to my native village. The village seemed huge because of the sudden emptiness that opened up in it. In disbelief, our gaze was fixed on two or three buildings which had escaped destruction at different corners of the enormous tract of open ground on which the last warm patches of embers were blazing up here and there. My shoulder shuddered under Glasha's trembling hand, and I thought that she now felt the way I felt when I caught hold of the stump of Sasha's leg as it crawled away. I walked away from Glasha. It was almost with an aversion for her, for myself, for us who had not come here yesterday or the day before yesterday when we were still needed, when we could have been of service....

I began to descend from the pine-covered hillock to the road which was showing up white across the meadow in the twilight. Taking no notice of my aversion *for us* or choosing to ignore it, Glasha walked by my side.

Often, when I was walking on this hillside until darkness fell, I used to look at the village. Just in the same way the lights would blaze up in the different corners of the village, in the windows. Just like that.

The road accepted us quietly as if it had been waiting for me when we went down to it; it showed us the way and ran on ahead. The grown up son of my neighbour Yustin had drowned (it had happened just before the war), and Yustin returned from somewhere a day later, when the coffin was already in his house. He walked along the street, already knowing the misfortune that had befallen him. People, neighbours approached him quietly and walked at his side in silence, just as Glasha was accompanying me. The white road ran ahead, showing you where to go, where your grief lay. But at the same time it did not forget to wind as it had long done, even unnecessarily, past the dried up marshes, past the collective farm barn which had once burned down after being struck by lightning. Just like that winding road, I kept drifting away from my thoughts of my mother, my little sisters, the neighbours, and the village and I kept thinking about something else, something quite different....

My cottage was at the far end of the village, and that was where we were going. The mounds where the cottages had stood were being whipped into flames by the wind, and now the stoves appeared corpulently white; the reflections fell upon Glasha's face and mine. It was like feeling that someone was looking at you without seeing who was watching you. There seemed to be some sort of age-old womanly quality about these weakened squat stoves looming white. "And whose is that? It's the Gaishun's lad, Flyora, isn't it? Or whose is it?" As if trying to take a look at or show us, the warm patches in the kitchen gardens suddenly flared up, illumining the surroundings with bright flames. The deserted courtyards had withdrawn from the street only leaving the little benches where they had been previously and the charred fences and the birch trees with their tops thrown back like heads. (Something white scuttled across the street like a dog, but I could see quite well that it was not a dog, but a pig, and just like a wild one at that.) At one time we had spent the summer evenings under these birch trees. The older people would sit, stand, have a smoke and a chat, taking it easy after the working day, and we, the boys, would race up and down the street, around the kitchen gardens, enjoying the sensation that the adults were in such a calm mood in the evening and that the whole of the human world appeared to be reassured, protected, kind. Even now, somewhere in my being, in the very depths of my memory is recorded the momentary feeling that I noted and registered when I shot up the steps to the loft, hiding from the "blue ones" (we were playing at war) and looked down to see mother and father on the bench under the birch tree. They were sitting like a youth and a girl together (just made for each other, as happy as can be!). It was funny that they should be sitting like that, so touchingly; thinking that no one could see, he kissed her by her ear, and she brushed him off, running her hand over his face. ("Petya, have you gone mad, what will the neighbours think!") I felt good and at the same time a little strange, for it was as if I did not yet exist and there were just the two of them. I sat quietly there and looked upon a world in which I did not exist. I myself did not know why, but I cried out loudly as if I was continuing to play a war game, and in actual fact to remind them about me so that I could appear in this world again. Mum looked round, but father was angry, "What are you squealing for?!"

He was quick-tempered and I loved him and feared him. In general, I always liked stern, unaffectionate people, people just like my father. Even when he went away to fight in Finland, my father did not kiss me. He only squeezed my shoulder and pointed to my mother who was weeping and the twins, with shawls wrapped round them under their armpits like the coachmen used to do, leaning against her legs, "Look after them!"

Now I was approaching that same spot where that had happened, where our house had stood. Here the little flames were no longer flickering across the kitchen gardens, there was only heat quivering round the stoves which meant they had started at this end.... A birch tree towered above me, throwing back its tattered head into the black sky. The gate and part of the fence had survived destruction. The darkened ground around the stoves was giving off light.

Glasha walked softly towards the stove, but I still did not enter the wide open gate. Whose hand had opened it? And what had happened afterwards? Little tongues of flame shot up around Glasha's feet, and she left behind her glowing red footprints. Smouldering embers clung to the toe of her boot, sending out a shower of sparks. Just as her boots had done that time in the clearing. What was I thinking about? My thoughts kept on slipping away from me to one side, ignoring what was most frightening. Resolutely and convincingly, to make myself believe it as well, I told Glasha that everyone had run away, that they were all in the forest. Glasha bent over and was examining something. I tore myself away from the gate and ran over there, scared that I was running. Oh, I know only too well what white coals mean! For an instant, it seemed to me that they were white like burnt bones. No, it was the reflection from the stove, our stove whitened by my mother's hands! And the smell was that of charred potatoes and apples, only of potatoes and apples! They have fled into the forest, tomorrow I would find them, I would see them the next day....

I walked up to the stove and touched it, and it felt surprisingly cold among the warm still dying embers. Just as my boots pressed moisture out of the marshes, here they squeezed heat and light out of the ground. The footprints did not disappear immediately; they smouldered, bursts of flame whipped up by the wind, tongues of blue and red flames racing across them.

Beyond the apple trees the stove belonging to Yustin, our neighbour showed up as a white patch. Something was hanging on the fence. It began to seem that it was terribly motionless people.

I went back to the gate. Glasha was already there, watching me approach. She sat down on the bench, and I sat next to her. Something womanly and simple seemed to have emerged in Glasha. She laid my head on her knees and pressed hers against my back. Then I lay down properly on the long bench, and it did not seem strange nor did there seem anything shameful about her sitting with my head on her knees, just as a wounded man does not find it strange or embarrassing. From time to time I opened my eyes and saw Glasha with her head thrown back and her face towards the birch tree. I watched the wind fanning the heat across the ashes and driving the blood-red reflections onto the trees, finding and showing up the apples, those reddish-black apples. Inside my head there was a thudding, becoming fainter so that it seemed that the noise was in the kitchen gardens, and then coming back to me. There was a strange hollowness, now filled by me, now drained. That knocking sound, the smell of the burnt apples and baked potatoes enticed me into one and the same dream, which was interrupted and then continued again. I dreamed that it was morning in our cottage and the twins were whispering and letting out muffled yelps on the bed above the stove. In the kitchen I could hear Mum chopping meat on the board, moving the cast iron saucepans, banging about with the frying pan and was very much afraid that she would come in and see me *lying there in the fir grove on the fir tree branches with Glasha.*

I came round with a bright blue colour flooding into my eyes. The cool top of the birch tree was swaying, the yellow half of its crown looking like hair suddenly turned grey. Sparrows in a dark, crowded flock were not flying away, but somehow floating down from the birch tree onto the kitchen garden. I watched them and finally managed to wake up. Below, on the ground, in the kitchen gardens, it was black and frighteningly empty. The stoves were not white as they had been at dusk, but a dirty grey. When I looked at the yellowed boughs and the sparrows I thought I heard the birch rustling and the sparrows twittering. Now everything around me had grown dumb again and there was only my own noise within myself. And that slight feeling of nausea.

I looked around for my rifle. I could not see Glasha. Pushing myself awkwardly upwards from the edge of the bench, I turned over, lifting myself and resting on my arm. Something hot crunched pliantly under my palm, and a terrible blow to my elbow, to the back of my head caused me to jerk up. With my mouth and my tongue I licked off and sucked the acute pain persisting in the palm of my hand, simultaneously swallowing the tasty burnt squashed potato. Startled, Glasha halted by the gate, holding a piece of black tin-plate like a tray on which there were semi-charred potatoes and apples. She put the "tray" down on the grass and guiltily ran over to me, but I pulled my seared palm out of her hands and grabbed hold of the butt of my rifle which was lying on the ground, but it was warm. I pressed my palm against the gun metal, but it did not help, I touched the grass, but it remained warm. I rushed backwards and forwards, looking for something cold but not finding it. With my heel I dug a hole in the ground and thrust my palm into it. The pain was immediately alleviated, drawn away by the soil, but somewhere, deep down, my hand still hurt as if I had been stung by a bee. Glasha fingered the burnt potatoes as if she were to blame. The potatoes that I had not brushed away were still on the bench, and she was telling me something, probably reproaching me and reproaching herself. My hand was beginning to hurt again and, jumping up; I beat out another hole in the ground and pressed my palm into it. The pain went immediately just like water disappearing into sand. What I was doing, acting in a fidgety manner, jumping up and down, kicking the ground, grabbing hold of it, probably looked quite ridiculous, and I was furious that I could not stop myself doing it. Seizing the moment, Glasha took my hand and blew on my reddened, swollen palm.

"What are you doing? Are you a gipsy or something?" I pulled my hand away and dug it into the cold black earth once again. There was nothing Glasha could do but smile at me, and I smiled up at her, and we both got on with what we were doing; I sat confined to the ground, and she laid our breakfast out on the bench. She came over to me and took from my sheath a German bayonet dagger and began to scrape the burnt skin from the potato, blowing on her fingers as she did so. She had gathered the potatoes from the hottest patches, but they were just embers! From time to time as I pulled my hand out of the soil, it did not hurt immediately, but it always started to hurt again, shooting into my elbow, my head, and the back of my neck once more. I transferred my palm to the metal part of my rifle, and that already helped it. Seizing ever new, as yet not warmed parts of the rifle with my scorched palm, I went over to the fire site, to the little stove. The pain was drawn off by the stove with its deep-seated coldness. I held fast to that cold while looking round at all that was left of the cottage: a few large blackened rocks in the corners, an iron bedstead bent in the middle, the frame of a bicycle which had long lacked tires and a bucket that had been flattened. There had been a sewing machine. It was a good thing I could not see it. There had been no need for them to take the bucket or a useless bicycle either, but Mum would have taken the sewing machine, our most valuable asset. Even before the war Mum's sewing had kept and clothed us, and during the war especially.

There were iron pots in the stove. The one closest to us contained the charred remains of food. The one behind it held soup which had almost boiled dry; the pot was still fairly warm, and I carried it in my palms. I was not aware of it hurting me, for I had forgotten about pain. I put Mum's lunch on the bench and pulled a spoon out of my pocket. I tried the bitter soup tasting slightly of smoke and ale a little. I handed the spoon to Glasha and took a peeled potato from her. Glasha tried the soup and gently put down the spoon.

We finished breakfast. Glasha carefully swept the peelings and the cinders off the bench onto the "tray". I carried away the iron pot and put it on the stove. My hand began to hurt again. I walked through our garden, touching the fairly warm trees and searched among the apples for a green one that was not burnt. I bit a piece from it and placed it on my palm. The ground was strewn with black apples. There were so many of them that you had to step on them as if treading on something living. There were the shreds of linen, oddly singed, that had shown up white on the fence at night. The sparks from our cottage and Yustin's had fallen on it. Why had they not taken it with them? Did they not have time? A sense of uneasiness brought me out in a cold sweat.

Glasha was looking at the sky. Yes, they were already flying. A German reconnaissance plane was always overhead when things were going badly for us. The partisans had repeatedly tried to shoot them down, but had not succeeded. They say that they were armoured.

The plane flew away towards the forest where we needed to go as well. When I had to travel by air after the war, all the time I was bothered by the thought that this was how that flying spy had seen the ground, the cottages, us, the people, how that *someone*, that nameless embodiment of evil had seen us. From that height from which everything seems tiny as if in a model, he was precisely the one who could not yet see the ground and the people. It was probably not with malice at all, but with glee that the Messerschmitts chased the refugees as they scuttled away from the road like ants. This is just how they would aim from outer space at the glassy pale blue sphere admired by those first cosmonauts who were happy about being human....

"Listen, Flariyan Pyatrovich, what is happening to you again?"

These were the words with which my former post-graduate, now Candidate of Science and a psychologist, Boris Boky, usually appeared in my flat. I had never seen him. I only know him by his voice, the hand-shake of his slender strong hand, his rapid footsteps and his energetic, noisy movements. For me he was something black, shining, and pointed. He is probably a skinny little black-haired man with a big thin nose. I noticed that people with funny bird-like faces are always given to the use of irony, preferring to mock rather than be mocked.

My Boky's briefcase was always crammed with books and magazines; he would put it down in the hall with such a loud bang as if he had flung it off his shoulder. Immediately he would shout out the news: they had acquitted another camp commandant, they were banging women and children (the families of expelled diplomats) over the heads with portraits of the "great leader", and Lieutenant Calley had been placed under house arrest as a "punishment".

"What's happening to you again, Flariyan Pyatrovich, in your neck of the woods?"

"In my neck of the woods," meant right here on our planet. It was not that Boris was taken up with it, but he was "wearing in" (as he used to call it), like a new pair of shoes, an idea, a hypothesis borrowed quite openly from some kind of science fiction novel. From the heights of this hypothesis, we, earthmen, did not exist just by ourselves, but were under some kind of observation by a sort of super civilisation conducting an experiment to decide whether we should be allowed to join them. Or whether to "shut down the experiment'.

Everything that I had once told him as a student and post-graduate, which he had heeded with respect at that time, he was now repeating to me, comparing it with a new and increasingly surprising reality. He was presenting it to me again wrapped in irony. Boky had forgotten that he himself was a teacher now and might very soon find himself acting my part. This somewhat deliberate note was upheld by the fact that more often than not Boris would call on me because Glasha had rung him to ask him if he could accompany me to the institute (when I had to be at the institute at the same time as Glasha had to be at school). It seemed as if Boris would appear to vent his feelings for my benefit regarding his thoughts on us, the earthmen.

"Listen, Flariyan Pyatrovich. A thousand million people are yelling with one voice. A thousand million, you mark! No, no, I'm going to put a stop to the experiment, it's hopeless."

"Be patient. It will pass."

"To start somewhere else? You're pretending, Flariyan Pyatrovich, that you can be so cold-blooded about it! You saw for yourself how something like that can end. Once man has been under the wheel, for the rest of his life he ceases to believe in steering and brakes. But it turns out that you are a psychological exception? Or do you have something to tell us about the disappearance or at least the lessening of the 'discrepancies' between technical and moral culture?"

"In the former case, an instinct of self-preservation is sufficient."

"That has not helped all species of mammals. And then it has still not been proven that mankind experiences that feeling, that it has retained it."

"Homo sapiens is precisely distinguished by the fact that he can make a rational choice of alternatives. He did not always make use of that ability, but now everything has become so compressed, so accelerated, so bared, that, it has become easier to choose."

"It has been accelerated! What, with rapid firing missiles, rash ideas? Buttons?"

"But then, something else has emerged," I countered. "How many generations previously were born, lived, and died—and all in a single formation. It seemed to people that the Neros and the Louises, the tyrants were here forever, that slavery, absolutism, and someone's despotism would never end. And now within the lifetime of a single person there is enough space for the first, the second and the fourth to come and go. You can grow wiser, both separately and *en masse!* You can have one foot in the crusades and the other in the distant planets. These are not just words, but real feeling—that we have (at least those who had seen the thirties) that we were the living contemporaries not only of those who had lived fifty years ago but of those who will be here in five hundred years' time. Yes, it always seemed to everyone that their generation was at the very turning point of history. But here there really was a right angle. Surely you must have the feeling that on one plane there were the Neros, the Louises, and the Hitlers, and on the other plane, the harmonious world of Yefremov's *Andromeda: A Space Age Tale?* And you and we are at the apex of the right angle. And you have both in your field of vision, your own life story and that of your time..."

"I get a different feeling when I read Schiller's words that when the gods were more humane, man was more divine."

"When was it that they were more humane then?"

"When they were not darting to and fro in armour-plated limousines, but were sitting on Olympus. People always attributed their own qualities to the gods, imbuing them with their own virtues and vices, but never before did they stuff their own gods with such rottenness, vileness, and baseness as in the twentieth century."

"Historical progress always preferred to partake of the nectar from the skulls of those killed. Do you remember what Marx wrote about it? This is why we say that that is all prehistory."

"But what is history? Is it Khatyn or My Lai?"

"Yes, one foot is still there."

"But aren't we becoming absorbed in it? Don't you remember how they frightened Tolstoy by telling him that in this vast country there were a few men who had volunteered to perform the job of an executioner? At first there was one who was taken from Moscow to Kiev and Odessa to put the "hemp ties" round people's necks. Then a few more volunteers announced themselves, Tolstoy was greatly alarmed. Well, who would be surprised at such news in the middle of the twentieth century? In My Lai it was not even a specially selected team that did the killing, but a normal platoon of ordinary nineteen-year-olds, who had just left their mums and dads. What kind of climate is needed for ordinary people to be capable of that! Doesn't such acceleration, such concentration, prompt you to anything, Flariyan Pyatrovich?..."

"Yes, but when was it that they openly rebelled against war? And where? In a warring, in a strong state!"

"When they collapse into fascism, you'd be surprised where your mutineers get to then. No, no, don't beg me, I'm going to stop the experiment."

I had never seen him, my constant opponent. I only remember his voice, slipping away into misplaced buffoonery. It was not easy for me to argue with Boky, because all too often I had to argue with my own memory. What Boky could only guess at, *I could see* because I had seen it yesterday....

The reconnaissance plane hovered over the forest where Glasha and I were going, either climbing or descending, spying out houses where people were still living. Perhaps it was already summoning the bombers. It loomed over everything, armour-plated and unhurried. It was as if the eye of a huge insect was looking at you.

A dream stuck in my memory, not the events of the dream themselves, but an unusual, ambiguous feeling. It was as if I were up there in the aeroplane, but I was also down below as well. I could see myself and was afraid of myself. I was chasing a small and unprotected person down below, about in an open field like a table top. Suddenly that furious, frightened little person who is also me rolls over on his back and begins to shoot, firing at the aeroplane. I felt that he had hit me and that I was falling; I was flying right at the person who was firing, now we would come together and strike each other to death and I begged and prayed that either the one who was falling or the one who was firing from below would survive, would escape destruction....

The forest welcomed me with its familiar shady paths and cuttings. First we walked through pines and oaks, then came the firs and the damp alder thicket, and beyond it the marshes with the "islands" where we always hid, where our people would be hiding now. In spite of all that had happened, all those events, the forest was just the same as it had always been. I even wanted to show my companion the hideouts in the woods that Fedka and I had, but I just recalled all those pastimes of childhood with a grin. Where was Fedka Sparrow's Death now? His father had not let him join the partisans: "Do you want them to come and wipe out the family, have pity on your mother and the little ones!" He had cunningly disarmed Fedka by informing partisans he knew that his son had a whole cache of weapons. They brought pressure to bear on Fedka, and he gave the weapons up. I learned of all this when I called in at home one day before I got shell-shocked. At that time, Mum was very glad to see me, and my little twin sisters were doubly full of enthusiasm and respect as they examined their brother all hung about with weapons. Only the German uniform distracted them as if there was someone else, a stranger, present in the cottage besides us four. Not in front of Mum, but when she went out into the kitchen, the twins breathed out both at once, "Did you kill him?... That one?..." And they pointed to my uniform. From Mother I found out how Fedka paid his father back. In their garden they had a wild boar weighing about 130 kilos. It was kept in a special pit. Fedka whispered about it to some roaming convivial fellows in exchange for a promise that he would be allowed to join their group. They made off with the boar. To Fedka who was waiting for them by the forest they told: "Be off with you, your father's looking for you. And we've no need for traitors!" Fedka hid in the bushes for two days, while his father walked around on the edge of the forest, shouting at the top of his voice: "Go home, you swine. Go on, you vermin, I won't touch you, although murdering you would be too good for you!"

From Mum's I headed, in full partisan attire, straight for Fedka's, carrying the rifle that he had given me.

"Yet another hero!" the master of the house himself, Fedka's long-armed, stooping Father greeted the one who had led his son astray. "It's a pity you did not get your father's belt!"

Fedka came out of the cottage and walked past us without saying anything.

I followed in his tracks.

He was gloomy, my friend was, sort of drained of enthusiasm, reluctant to talk.

"Well, how's things?" he touched my rifle. "Have you fired it? Or do you spend your time drinking home-brew there? I'm going to get myself a submachine-gun."

He glanced at his cottage where his father was awkwardly dragging a sack of straw up onto the eaves asking someone in a woman-like, peevish, shrill voice, "Where are these heroes then? Where has he run off to already?"

...My hand was still hurting. The burn had caused a thick-skinned deadly white blister to form on my palm. I placed on it everything from which coolness could be squeezed out such as the sticky alder leaves, and the damp moss. We could already feel the marshes underfoot. Glasha and I were plodding on and I was trying to find what was coldest, as though I was to measure the temperature of everything that I came across on the way.

We had left behind the smell of fires, soot, and smoke. Only the baked potatoes in my pockets reminded us of it.

Another smell was already ousting the freshness of the forest, a pungent, heavy odour creeping towards us. That was precisely the odour that we dug up when we were looking for weapons. Involuntarily you wiped the corners of your mouth, but they became unpleasantly sticky again.

But the forest was still just as clean. My eyes did not catch sight of anything out of the ordinary. Suddenly they espied several light coloured, fresh little aspens lashed or cut down by bomb fragments. Below them were black bomb craters which looked as if they were filled with tar. The hollows trailed away across the snaggy ground, towards the "islands". I was almost running now so that Glasha could hardly keep up with me. Uppermost in my mind was that ominous, sticky, familiar smell. Here the marshes were already more rust coloured, with little wart-like tussocks sticking out of them, on which small crooked trees had taken root and were clinging. The mire had been shaken up by the bombs, mud had been thrown about, and brown grass and blackened strings of marsh plants looked as if they had been hung up by someone on the boughs and tops of the little pines and stunted birches that had recoiled in fright. An iron-hard snag had trapped a willow-bush against the water; it had probably fallen from a great height. The round willow bushes like green hay-stacks were to be seen everywhere in the swamps. But there were no corpses to be seen. The smell had become so heavy that even the skin on your face seemed to feel it like a spider's web gently brushing it.

We were already by the first "island" overgrown with dense green alder thickets. (Before the war the villagers used to lay in sedge here for their cows.) All we had to do now was to cross the black strip of sludge out of which the tips of fallen trees and tree stumps stuck like palings. Next to them some kind of little brown islands bulged out of the mire. I did not examine them closely at first, nor did I understand what they were, for they had never been here before. They all looked strangely alike. Suddenly I saw a big round eye showing up white in the blackness of the swamp and above it a cow's horn. It was only then that I realised what these identical little brown islands were. This was a whole herd of floated cow carcasses floating in the mire. They looked like huge brown and black bubbles. Glasha could not stand it. She crammed her hand over her mouth and ran back, splashing herself with the mud. Because the stench became even more oppressive when you saw those bubbles.

But this was the only way to get to the "islands", and I was not the only person who had tested it. How we would flounder about in that stinking slush! If I had been on my own it would have been all right, but then there was Glasha as well....

Slinging my rifle across my back, I took a pole out of the willow-bush that someone had thrown there for some reason and felt my way towards the glistening bubble, using it like a spear. I had to push them out the way. The bloated carcasses rocked heavily, opposed to being disturbed, but that was all. Glasha observed me from a distance, her eyes revealing her suffering and distress.

And I (just like Fedka at those old graves) cheerfully yelled and sang some kind of senseless words, "And we're here now, we're here now! The dead do not get tooth-ache, tooth-ache!..."

I was no longer paying any attention to the waist-high mud and the muggy stench. I had managed to climb onto the rocking fallen tree, stood up on it and fooled about, showing Glasha how amusing and simple it was. I touched the islet-like carcass with my staff and jumped onto it, but slipped off immediately, my feet apparently not even touching the carcass. I banged my head and ear painfully against my rifle. My legs slipped into a void, and my fingers grabbed eagerly at the revolting slippery fur and skin.

Finally, I felt something firm underfoot. I was already standing, although the mud was up to my chest. Glasha, was looking at me with horror when indicating that I should make for the bank. But immediately, as if summoned, she set out, moving towards me and stretching out her hand. That sometimes happened to her just as it did in the clearing when she went up to Kasach, as if sleepwalking....

I did not move, afraid that I would lose my foothold, that I might startle her or be overcome by fear at last myself. If I were to crawl out on the bank again, no force would make me go back into that stench once more. Glasha kept on raising her arms above the mud in her disgust and wariness. First her boots, then her skirt she wore on top of her trousers became submerged in the slime. The black mire swallowed up Glasha's knees, her taut stomach, the blackness rising up the grey sweater to her frightened breasts. Glasha was squeezing them between her elbows, holding her hands in front of her face, near her mouth. I raced towards her, and just in time, for I caught hold of her hand as she was falling and dragged her out. Without giving her or myself time to come to our senses, I dragged her past the bloated carcasses, seizing dead trees and branches with my free hand mid yelling loudly and desperately: "Wonder yonder, whale-flounder! Wonder yonder, whale-flounder!..."

Not allowing myself to think about anything or to feel anything I pushed forward with senseless and dangerous haste, dragging Glasha to the "island". Her face was screwed up with a grimace of revulsion and horror and all bespattered with mud. Several times we completely lost our foothold, then we flung ourselves sideways as if avoiding a fire, seeing the fear in each other's eyes. We had already come to the sedge so the bank must be near. Only waist-deep in mud now, we could have walked the rest of the way calmly, but we wallowed despairingly as if saving ourselves from a sinking boat and clambered up the bank almost crawling on all fours.

We got out and stood among the sedge near the bushes and collected ourselves just as if someone had dragged us and pulled us and suddenly left us. We stood there pitiful and battered as if we had been licked and sucked by the unclean mouth of a monster. Glasha had tears in her eyes. I set about breaking off some alder branches and tearing the leaves from them to clean us up with, to squeeze the dripping brown slime from Glasha's sweater and wipe her hands. She stood there, weeping, her arms spread wide so as not to touch herself and looking at herself with disgust. She had always seemed to me to be slender and straight like a ruler with only her high knees breaking the line sharply. But now when her clothing stuck to her shoulders, her bosom, her stomach and her legs, outlining her figure, I could see that her womanly slenderness was not just a straight line after all. Glasha snatched the branches from me angrily, and now I was only breaking them off and bringing fresh ones to her, while wringing the mud out of my own things at the same time.

Suddenly I sensed that there was someone watching us from behind. I was quite right for there was someone standing behind the bush! He had a rifle on his shoulder. There was nothing menacing about his stance, just curiosity in his look. He was waiting to see what the two who had come crawling out of the bog on to the "island" would do next. It is a strange and complicated feeling that you get when you recall the first meeting with a person who later becomes part of your life. You still do not know who or what he will be to you and everything about him still appears to be optional, accidental like the encounter itself, his smile, his gait, his eyes, and his gestures, for instance. Everything in such a person does as it were, live its own life, but that is in the beginning. Why does a person have to have black, Gypsy-like eyes, if the eyebrows and the hair sticking out from under his threadbare winter hat and the thick growth on his unshaven cheeks are all light, flaxen, straw-coloured? Or how out of place that surprisingly long nose seems on which there were two small protuberances (why two?) if that person has such a serene, clever brow, so large and white! What was the reason for such thin, crooked legs, wrapped in puttees, if the whole of the person is well proportioned and strong, and you could see this for yourself in spite of the shapeless grey sweater that he had pitilessly pulled down under a belt with a huge star-shaped buckle on it. At first it all appeared to have come together by chance, did not seem to combine well, and was almost clumsy just like his leather winter hat amongst the succulent greenery.

Yes, at that time when I scrutinised the stranger who was coming towards us from out of the bushes, I did not know what he would come to mean to me, and what awaited us both, what we were to experience. But now when it is all a thing of the past and remains just a memory, I have a jealous feeling that Rubezh could only be like that and that my memory did not need him to be any different. If a person has found a place, *a spot* in your heart for ever, it is not that he just has filled a kind of vacancy that anyone might have occupied instead. He does not take up that gleaming spot of light, but he creates it, and without him it would not exist within you.

My rifle was on my back, so it was like being lied up when the approaching stranger eyed me over calmly. No, I did not think, did not want to believe that he was from the *polizei*, but, all the same, I would have felt better if I had my rifle to hand. For some reason, it seemed awkward to pull it off my back when he was looking at me. It would be cowardly, deliberate, and demonstrative.

The stranger said something, asked Glasha something. She replied and was telling him our story. Both of them were looking at me, the stranger suddenly with concern and what seemed to be embarrassment. Everything was buzzing inside me and I felt weak at the knees. I understood what they were talking about and why the man was looking at me like that.

When you look back on what you have lived through, you only see a single line of events, but when you look ahead into the future there is a cluster of paths splaying out, and you still do not know yet which is the only one of them for you. You live through a month, a day, a minute, and what was a cluster is squeezed up together again, becomes bare like a little branch that has been pulled through a lightly clenched fist. But even after you are left with a single twig stripped of leaves, you will look back again and again, senselessly hoping to return to the moment when everything could still have turned out differently, the moment when that one bare, merciless truth had not yet emerged....

I was already aware of it, had seen the truth—that black tunnel and the entrance into it. But, hoping against hope, I still kept beseeching someone and did not enter it, as if saying "anything but that, please don't make me face the darkness in there!" I had already taken refuge in my deafness, which distances me from the whole of the truth, postponed the moment when there was no longer any hope.

The stranger was already walking ahead, indicating that we should follow him. His crooked legs, and feet shod in rawhide sandals tore the thick sedge growing straight out of the water, as they became entangled in it. Glasha scooped up handfuls of water to wash the mud off herself, broke off a branch and wanted to wipe the mud from my uniform which has become rust coloured, but I moved away, frightened by her sudden guilty solicitude, her reluctance to look me in the face. I kept trying not to accept the thoughts that had already entered my head, that I already knew....

We crossed over to the second "island" which was even more densely overgrown with alders, walking along boards immersed in the sludge. (We found out later, that there was a similar pathway to the first "island". The *polizei* and the Germans had drowned the cows when they tried to drive them off the "island". They did not go to the second island where the inhabitants had taken refuge and where the wounded partisans were in hiding, and this saved people.)

Armed with long staffs which our guide pulled out of the bushes and feeling our way with them, we followed the stranger along the invisible, slippery poles under the mud. There were two of them and in places three. You had to put your foot across them so we were not moving straight forwards, but sideways. All that distracted me and helped me to take refuge from myself, to convince myself that nobody knew anything yet, that we would get to the place and then we would find out and not until then!...

They were already awaiting us on the second "island", a crowd of women and children and some partisans with weapons were standing by the bushes, watching us and asking our guide about something from a distance. We climbed off the pathway onto the bank, and they began to ask me questions as well but then realised (or someone told them) that I was deaf, and they left me alone except for the children who began to look at me and study me with even greater interest. They looked just like children usually did in our parts at that time — with mosquito-bitten faces and a hungry look in their big staring eyes. All the same, they were very curious and wanted to understand whom it was that a world in which something dangerous and terrible was happening had flung up on their shore. Our guide said, and the women began to stare at me again, having sought me out once more. They kept on gazing and gazing, probably in just the same way as I had looked at Sashka when he crawled along that red path with an unnaturally long leg dragging behind him, and Sashka could discern from the frightened look in my eyes that something terrifying was happening to him.

I did not see a single familiar face, these were not people from our village, but they were looking at me as if they knew me, as if they had recognised me. Everything in me hummed metallically like a hollow pipe that had been struck, whined within me, in my legs and in my hands which had immediately become heavy, I sat down in the sedge, right there in the water. Glasha squatted down as if she had long expected this, took the wet forage cap off my head and wiped the cold sweat from my face.

I feared the twitching lines around Glasha's mouth which immediately seemed to have aged, I hated the clinging, eager compassion shown by women, and tried to find something else in my surroundings, but even in the children's eyes there was something mercilessly sentencing me to face the truth. With that feeling of hopelessness of someone who has been caught, I sought salvation all the same, taking refuge in the hasty thought that I really was deaf, could not hear anything, and therefore could not be sure about anything anyway. But I found myself encircled by faces and eyes whose expression betrayed how pitilessly sorry they were for me: there was nothing I could do but face the truth. Suddenly a crazy idea came to me and dissolved in me like a relaxing and tranquilising narcotic: *they would not murder* my mother and my little sisters now, *they would never kill* them because they had taken refuge in death. It had concealed them from the murderers, from fresh killers....

I remained hanging by that thread of deception for just an instant. Recoiling from the person in me who was not pitying those who had been slaughtered, burned to death, but pitied himself instead, I, now at my own will, was anxious to encounter the pain. I opened up completely and immediately experienced it in tears. I jumped up, ran further away and lay down in the wiry sedge pressing my face to the ground from which a cold moisture was issuing. But the ground no longer removed the pain; no longer drew it out of me, nor did I relinquish my pain to it. I was actually seeking out that pain now to punish myself for not knowing for such a long time that they no longer existed, for turning my back on the truth. I had not turned up to save them, to take them away from the cruel torture, from death....

People came up to me again and surrounded me, standing over me. I was hovering between merciful oblivion and implacable reality. When I was ill as a child and was in a semi-delirious state I would still remember all the time that my mother was sitting at my bedside. And now I imagined this. The reality and the delirium were like two mirrors, each reflecting the depth of the other, absorbing it and then returning it again as if it was its own. I imagined that I was at home, lying behind our florid screen; unfairly offended by my mother, angry at her, I was crying and imagining how I would grow up and no longer love her, I would not love her. A guilty, kind, affectionately ironical hand touched the back of my head, and stroked my hair. Immediately I forgot my silly, childish malice and grabbed hold of her hand. At this point reality returned.

No, it was not my Mum! But it was not Glasha either, as I had thought straight away. A strange woman sat by me, rocking from side to side, her face dark and swollen and frightening. She was saying something, mumbling away, and I could even hear her voice, but it was not audible to me, I knew that I only thought I could hear.

"Where did you get to, sonny, I already thought that you were not with us any more, that I would not see you. I cried and grieved, I thought they had killed you..."

But I thought I could hear other voices, too.

"Auntie Malanka, Auntie Malanka, here's a lad from Beliya Pyaski. He's not yours, is he, Auntie Malanka!"

I was lying there with my face to the ground, but I could still see everything, how the people were standing over me, how they helped the woman with the swollen dark face to get up and led her away. But no, I was hearing it. I could hear!

"Flyora, dear little Flyora," that was Glasha's voice. Now she occupied the place where that woman had been, where my Mum had been. And there were other voices, too: "Yustin who is here with us, who got badly burnt, he comes from Beliya Pyaski, too."

No, it was true, I was really hearing it. But what were they saying about Yustin? Shreds of linen, either his or ours, showed up white on the fence, in the devastated kitchen garden his stove stood next to ours. His son had drowned, and old Yustin walked right through the village, already aware that there was a coffin in his cottage and his son had drowned....

The noise was pulsating in my head just as before, but voices were forcing their way through it and rolling forth; a child was crying and being comforted, and they were talking about Yustin. The effect was just the same as when you covered your ears with the palms of the hands and then opened them. But wait a minute! Yustin? Was he here?

"Where is he? Yustin! He was our neighbour. Where is he?"

I jumped up. I noticed in the look that the children and even Glasha gave me that there was already something frightening about me.

I rushed after the crowd of women and children who were heading for the other edge of the "island", as if I could still change something, make an amendment somewhere, turn the clock back two days. They took me right across the "island". It was called an "island", but in actual fact it was just part of the bog that was slightly drier and overgrown with sedge and shrubs. I was up to the ankles in water, in the stirred up slime. On the yellowed branches indicating where the families lived, clothing was scattered about and smaller children were sitting and lying there. Their soft crying could be heard, but it was not an attempt to attract attention; they were just moaning because of the damp and the murderous rust-coloured gadflies clinging to their little bodies. There was not even a wisp of smoke to be seen anywhere; the reconnaissance plane probably loomed over the forest constantly.

Something red and blue, something that looked as if it was in slimy wet scales was lying on birch branches under the only big tree on this "island". Everything went dark before my eyes when the dry wheezing at every sigh and sob came to my ears (or perhaps I imagined it) of the person who was evidently my neighbour Yustin. By him sat an old woman with a branch, moving it as if gently brushing away the air itself, the weight of it, from the burnt man. She did not look up at us.

"Yustin, Yustinko, someone's come to see you, a lad from your village, your neighbour. Yustinko!"

Several of the women called to the man with burns at once, their voices merging into a common lamentation addressed to Yustin, to me, to this swamp and to the gloomy sky: "Can you hear us Yustin? Someone's come to see you. They burned his Mum to death, too. They slaughtered all of you, setting fire to you. They shut them in the cattle-shed and set light to it. Isn't that right, dear Yustin?... You were all their, your grandchildren and your daughter-in-law, and his Mum, all of you. But you crawled out of the fire, you begged them to put an end to you, you ran after them and beseeched them to finish you off because the pain was unbearable. But what did they do, dear Yustin? You ran and begged and prayed that they should kill you. They laughed and laughed, didn't they, dear Yustin? They laughed and said, "You just go on living, bandit!... Go and breed some more..."

Something dazzling flashed before my eyes and all around it became as white as white can be. The birch trees, the scaly groaning man on the ground, the sedge, the marshes, the people standing near me, and the sky blazed suddenly with an intolerable transparent whiteness which turned immediately to blackness, everything disappearing, myself included. I was in some sort of booth made of reeds. Outside people were walking about, crouching down and busy doing something. I could not seem to grasp whether I was in a delirium or whether everything I had been through was a delirium. But no, everything had taken place and remained just as it was. I was the one whose near ones had all been murdered. Mum, the little ones. I closed my eyes in fright when I heard myself groan.

Outside the voices sounded, husky as if people had sore throats, the voices were angry yet cheerful (I had indeed got my hearing back).

"Heh. Styopka the Conjuror, you could conjure up some bread. What good is your stuffed doll— you won't get any milk or meat from that!"

"He just can't get enough playing, now he wants a puppet!"

I was wearing someone else's shirt of undyed canvas. My own laundered high collared jacket was hanging up on a branch in the cabin to dry right in front of me. My rifle and my belt with the cartridge pouches lay under my elbow; someone had taken my belt off.

Glasha came over, holding a kitbag and stood by the wounded partisans (I was already aware who it was talking and laughing over there); for some reason they had cried out with joy on seeing her. The partisan who walked with a limp, got up from the ground and put a large rag dummy next to him, shouting, "Dear little Glasha, stay with us a while. Haven't you heard, cripples, how the nightingales are singing away again? We've got some fine nightingales, haven't we, dear little Glasha?"

"Come over here to us, Glasha, don't listen to that one-legged wretch. He thinks he's heard nightingales!"

"I hear that from someone who's got no arm!" the expert on the nightingale's song replied cheerfully.

As Glasha drew her narrow shoulders together, her laughter rang out just as it used to in our camp.

"Oh, you've come round!" After her recent laughter it seemed to me that Glasha only pretended to be glad when she glanced at my bed of reeds. She sat down, looked at me and called to someone outside. "Katyaryna Alyaxeyawna, he's opened his eyes, he's looking round!"

Someone else came to look at me, someone with a big head wrapped in a warm scarf. The head started to cough, shaking off the coughing fit with difficulty, and asked in the voice of someone with a bad cold, "Do you feel better, little lad?"

"Now we'll give him something to eat," Glasha said fussily untying the kitbag. Otherwise, we've been worried about him."

For Glasha I was already "he" and "him". She seemed to have forgotten how to address me directly. But then she had got to know others, they had been teasing her with nightingales!

"What's this?" I pointed to my clean shirt.

"What of it?" the blue eyes reflected innocent surprise. "It's all right. I washed yours."

"All right, go away, I won't be a minute."

The trousers I was wearing were also laundered and clean. They had taken them off and put them on again, the devil only knows what they've been up to!

In a lying position, I pulled the belt which had become so long round my trousers and tucked my shirt in. My hands and feet felt awkward and limp, my skin felt prickly all over, especially on my back. Something in my hand was getting in my way as if it was struck up; it was the dry scab that had formed over the burn, now dead tissue devoid of any feeling.

"We already thought you had typhus," said Glasha, fiddling with the kitbag and laying out the food on a piece of cloth.

For some reason my eyes hurt me after that white flash as if something had been sprinkled in them. (By evening, incidentally, they had stopped hurting. Later, when I realised that I was going blind, I told the doctors about that dazzling flash by that groaning, seared man, but they heard out my story politely and somewhat awkwardly and were interested as to whether I had received any physical trauma. Yes, there had been a physical one all right.)

Lunch was awaiting me next to the kitbag; it consisted of a cold baked potato and some apples. Glasha dug something else out of the bag, wrapped up in alder leaves, and smelt it.

"Do you remember the pig, when we were in your village. The one that ran across the street. The day before yesterday the lads went to Beliya Pyaski. Only it's got no salt on it. We left you a piece, but it got. But it's not that bad, it's edible."

Having taken an apple, I hastened to move as far away from the meat as I could. It made me reel.

The wounded partisans (about ten men under a tarpaulin awning and three who were stronger, outside) made loud comments on my resurrection,

"The main thing is to get on your feet."

"If there was only something to stand on."

"You're going to guard the 'island' now, old man, we are not much of fighters now, you see."

I belatedly said hello to them, and they answered me. Although I was walking on my own legs, and they were lying there or sitting helplessly, they spoke to me as if I was the sickest person there.

One of the partisans was doing something very strange, was making a dummy the height of a man out of rags and sticks, and now on a piece of plywood meant to be the face he was drawing a familiar physiognomy with a small moustache, a gangster's forelock, and a round bawling mouth.

The partisan in the winter hat, the one who met us on the first "island" and brought us here, stood there leaning his elbow on the barrel of his rifle and chatting both to the clever chap making the dummy and to his creation.

"They just won't know whether to shoot at you, you raggy scum, or to salute you! Good work, Conjuror, you'll give the Germans something to think about. Well, what have you opened your eyes wide for? They've drawn you, and you already want to start yelling. Look, Styapan, he's bawling at you. Make him squint-eyed for that."

Styapan sat there with his crutch under him. He had an amazingly, even unpleasantly handsome thin face. He kept on smiling, and his smile seemed to be reflected in Glasha's face, even when she was not looking at him.

"I've put something like five of these up already," said Styopka the Conjuror, jumping onto his good leg and plucking the "Hitler" on which he had been leaning, off the ground. (Styapan continuously sat down lightly or leapt up although his other leg was in heavy splints).

"They're both one-legged," they shout from under the tarpaulin, "Conjuror and the 'führer' alike!"

"It'll do!" said Styapan, smiling at Glasha. "You should see how the Germans look at them. They are riding along in their vehicles or on their motorcycles and when they see them, they are absolutely flabbergasted. Who could have dared to do such a thing? And they do not know what to do about it. They are afraid to touch it in case it's mined. They cannot knock it down with a hand grenade either because it's the 'führer'. You'll get a good laugh. You'll be shooting them down like quails while they are gaping at it. Have you understood what you've got to do, Rubezh? Then get moving!"

"Yes, I have," replied my guide, "only I'll put some stuffing into him, fill his guts with dynamite. Then he'll yell for me right!"

"Oh, how I'd like to be going with you," Styapan suddenly yearned for action. Glasha immediately looked at him. It was amazing how they always listened to each other. I used to notice everything, even with some kind of extra keen sight. But it was all somehow occurring at a distance from me. There was some kind of strip divorcing me from what had seemed important not so long ago. What I was seeing and noticing, what was happening outside of myself immediately became immersed in an overwhelming feeling of bitterness with which I was completely overcome, and dissolved in that feeling without intensifying it or making it more poignant.

(I particularly recall the eyes of the Conjuror; they were bright and madly cheerful. His face was so beautiful, just like a girl's, that it seemed unreal. He had long black eyelashes. Later on I imagined over and over again how everything happened here in seven to ten days time: how he hopped away on his crutch from where the German machine-guns were rattling away, hurled an unloaded rifle down on the ground, tore a hand grenade off his belt and sat under the tarpaulin, having pulled towards him the kitbag holding the tolite; how the wounded crawled over to him from all sides, as if to a saviour; he laid them down with their heads towards him, urging them to hurry. All of them pressed their faces to the ground and he looked at the world for them for the last time with those crazily cheerful light-coloured eyes of his. The last person to see those eyes was Glasha.)

Thrusting the dummy into the marshy ground and grabbing his crutch off the ground, Styopka the Conjuror proclaimed, "This will be 'Führer' No. 6!"

"In our lot in forty-one," our guide never fell silent (he was quite a talker and it did not matter to him whether anyone was listening or not), "in our as soon as the Germans arrived, first of all they would take away the stocks, but the sunflower seeds (I do not know why there were so many of them in the warehouses in Bobruisk), it wasn't forbidden to nick sunflower seeds or sugar which had got mixed up with sand; some people were standing in a queue to get it and one of ours from Slutsk looked very much like that bloke with the moustache. A German happened to walk by.

He halted and looked! Everybody waited to see what would happen. He stood there staring and thinking and then he gave him a slap round the physiognomy. Was it for daring to look so like the Führer, or was he himself getting even with the Führer? They even said that he was a Pole or a Slovak, but not a German. Well, all right, old chaps, what shall we bring you this time. Just order it as if you were in the little old cafeteria. I've got some stocks tucked away..."

"You'll soon be choking us with your cold potatoes without salt," replied Styopka the Conjuror.

And the others joined in, "You're enough to drive anyone mad."

"They might have managed to get hold of a bit of bread, but they crawl out somewhere close by and then come back!"

"It's a good thing that they come back at least. In their place, I would have made off ages ago. But nobody needs you cripples much, so I have to stay here with you, waiting till all's up with me. That's right, isn't it, Rubezh?"

Rubezh (my guide) grinned, not the least embarrassed by such an attack on him. Raking around in the sedge with his crooked thin legs, he came over to me.

"Are you going with us, lad? No, you needn't today! You take a rest, otherwise you won't be able even to crawl through the mud. We've got plenty of mouths here, you see, and look what big teeth they have, haven't they?"

The reconnaissance plane flew by high overhead, evenly as if on a string. It was as if it were drawing some kind of invisible lines of its own and that it was not the least concerned with us and the "island". Once it had flown over, we emerged from the bushes and waved to the women and the wounded once again. They were staying there, and we, four of us, were leaving. We were already separated by the path of sunken poles. Glasha was standing next to Styopka the Conjuror. She had asked to go with us, but the commander of our group (the wounded called him the "commandant" had in his turn made the following request of her: "If you insist, I will allow you to. But someone ought to stay with them. This time all four of us are leaving, going far away into the inferno. We need to have at least some kind of reserves. While we still can."

Our "commandant" was a Leningrader. They used to refer to that as if it were a personal quality of his. His polite way of addressing everyone, even the teenagers, his shy taciturnity, his willingness to explain at length and in great detail what other commanders would have resolved with a single "yes" or "no" and the very youthful well-proportioned figure of this slightly grey-haired bearded man, all merged for us into the concept of a "Leningrader", coloured by him and colouring him. In short, we liked the "commandant" and it was therefore to the point that he hailed precisely from that city. Although you had never seen it, just as you had never seen the splendidly mysterious northern lights, you could not imagine either yourself or the world without the remote, unobtrusive existence of that city.

"I wouldn't take him either," the "commandant" nodded in my direction. "It is Rubezh's idea."

We felt miserable as we walked away as if we already knew what was coming. And then there was that Auntie Khramelikha as well! She brought Gleb Vasilyevich puttees that had been washed and dried, although there had been heavy drizzle all the time over the last few days.

"How did you get them dry, Auntie?" Gleb Vasilyevich was amazed. "We don't seem to have any fires."

"It's a secret," said the woman. "Enjoy wearing them."

But a little girl gave auntie's secret away. "Auntie Khramelikha dried them on herself, under her jacket."

Our Leningrader blushed. He even took one puttee off his foot as if he did not know what he should do next. Here yet another woman interrupted us and begged, "Don't leave us all alone here, lads."

"Whatever gave you that idea?" Rubezh flustered.

"Your own people are here, too, the wounded," the woman reminded us all the same.

We crossed the second "island". There was the spot where Glasha and I had encountered Rubezh at that time. The "commandant" lit up a German cigarette, and each of us in turn drew on it several times. I also took a pull, and my head immediately swam and I felt dizzy. Gleb Vasilyevich cast a glance at Rubezh reproachfully and at me anxiously,

"All the same, we shouldn't have taken you with us, Gaishun."

"Never mind, a wolf needs his legs if he is to feed himself," said Rubezh, "and he needs to feed himself, too."

I remained silent because I suddenly had a desire to return to the "island". We pulled the long poles that had been specially hidden out of the bushes and moved along the path. The poles in the marshland slipped away from under our boots and here we were still inhaling mouthfuls of the stench for the cow carcasses were floating right on the top now, even more distended than before. Rubezh was dragging the "führer", Stepan's present, as well ("You can barter it with the Jerries for crackers"). Even while shuffling along the slippery sunken fogs this funny long-nosed, skinny-legged Rubezh never stopped talking. He kept on muttering away, talking for himself, and for us, and for the "führer" and even for the bloated cow carcasses.

"Come on, come on, you clowns! This is not like warming yourself near aunties. Drag me along, carry me, you fool! (This was the "führer's" voice). Phew! Pooh! Get a good noseful of us stinkers! (Now his deep bass voice was supposed in be coming from the motionless cow carcasses.)

...But the main person whom Rubezh was talking to, it seemed, was fate herself, the lot of the partisans. Rubezh continually chatted to her, either with her or on her behalf, just as if he were talking to a shrew. As a result of his mutterings (and we had already been wandering around the district for two days), it began to seem as if there were more of us in the group, that there was someone else next to us, a fifth one, a stupid, quarrelsome woman from whom you did not know what to expect. That was the partisans' fate herself.

"I'll go and bespatter you from above as well, as you haven't got very wet in the swamp," Rubezh promised gloatingly in his cantankerous woman's voice, as he glanced up at the overcast sky. Sure enough, in response to his call, it began to rain down on us. That is what it was like throughout the journey, day and night.

The reconnaissance plane would talk to us, too, "Here I am, buddies. You've been missing me, haven't you? In a minute, in a minute, I'll just fly over you. Not long now and I'll be sending you my little fellow planes with lots of little bombs."

The moon was inopportunely bright. Suddenly it giggled like a foolish woman. "Oh, how round and light I am! How about me sending you a nightingale? I can, if you like, you know!"

"Now he's going to caw as well," Skorokhod, the fourth partisan in our group who looked sickly and pale even under the coating of mud, was becoming infuriated by Rubezh. Right after the first kilometre he limped and tottered, walking bow-legged and swaying from side to side. He was covered in boils, in the most awkward places where it rubbed most. And as if that were not enough, fancy him having such a funny surname as Skorokhod. It was just as if someone was making fun of him! "Well, what did you drag that crank along for?" Skorokhod became angry, as if it were he himself and not Rubezh who had to carry the führer's dummy.

"I am dragging him, perhaps he is dragging me, after all, and you, too?" Rubezh responded. "If it weren't for him, you would not be rubbing your boils, you would be sitting in Minsk like a king. What kind of "fledglings" shall we be if I abandon him? What shall we do without our 'führer'?"

No matter what happened to us on the way; that was supposedly what was to happen for what more could you want from "fledglings". We had to eat wood sorrel instead of the crackers which we had reckoned. They scared us and we ran. Skorokhod lost his tattered shoe in the mud and was left with just one. There was nothing cheerful about this cheerfulness, just somehow it truly did not seem to matter quite so much what had happened to us and what might happen to us owing to this lack of respect for all those nasty things.

Skorokhod alone used to get exhausted, wet and hungry; and he would become ferocious and frightened—everything in earnest, scorning the buffoonery with which Rubezh had infected both myself and even our "commandant".

When we stumbled on an ambush for the third time and raced like elk through the charred coniferous forest ringing with bullets and echoes, Skorokhod ran ahead in his one shoe; then he stopped and watched gloatingly, while he waited for us as if saying, "Well then, are you still having fun?" And, as if out of spite (not Skorokhod, but towards somebody or something in general), the "fledglings" began to choke with laughter, and Rubezh went on to recount in the third person how they had approached the edge of the forest, how they had looked at the well-fed German horses, and Skorokhod was supposed to have howled like a wolf, and how the Germans gave it to the "fledglings", how they gave them it! And how they bolted "as fast as their legs could carry their arses!" Further, he described how the Germans found the "führer" left by Rubezh, and how the dummy would yell at them for letting Skorokhod and the "fledglings" escape.

I took part in that strange merriment, but an inner horror of myself did not leave me and kept on growing, that that was me. I just could not believe it was me.

We were making our way towards the fires and the shots in the night. Everything all around was transformed by the glows of fires, alarming uncertainty, and what had happened to me. I still could not believe, could not come to agree that I was the one whose mother and little sisters had been killed so frightfully, that it was really me. The fact that the war, the Germans, and death were close by no longer prevented me from *being*. But the I who had lost everyone still did not exist in the world. Nor did the I who was there before exist either. I did everything just as they, Rubezh and Gleb Vasilyevich, did; I would act cheerfully, make fun of the "fledglings" and Skorokhod's bursts of temper, but there was now something alien, something strange inside me. Others even noticed it. I heard Rubezh saying behind my back, "What an old fool I am to have dragged that boy along with us. It's painful to look at him."

Once at the edge of the forest, the road across the meadow lay ahead. In the night the field seemed to be ironed out, lacquered over by the light of the fires and the flares leaping up over the horizon. Suddenly strings of tracer-bullets would tear out of the darkness, out to find and gel us. To begin with, they rush along, noiseless, it is only later that you here the "ta-ta-ta", like a metal chain being dragged along, being jerked.

When you are standing in the middle of the field your shadow becomes long and multi-layered: the glow of the fires, the moonlight and the flares eagerly pick it out, arrest it and cast even more shadows of you, doubling, tripling and lengthening your presence. Exhausted and famished, we were wandering about, either stepping on our shadows which were as long as the road, or bearing them along at the side of us or dragging them behind us. We were already tired of throwing ourselves to the ground, of racing back and forth every time a flare went up. Our shadows were doing all that for us. When a flare soared up, your shadow behaved like a frightened dog fussing round your legs, squeezing it up against you as tightly as it could. When the flare descended and melted into the darkness, your shadow would shoot out, taking your head and shoulders somewhere into the field. The shadows from the glow of the fires and the moonlight would stir and move around, creeping towards one another, and then once again they would leave you straight away in a cowardly manner as soon as a flare went up nearby.

Finally, we managed to reach the thickly growing corn: Gleb Vasilyevich had kept a straight course towards it right from the edge of the forest. Beyond the corn was the road that we had to slip across. We had sunk our shadows in the sparse, trampled corn and were roaming about as if in deep yellow water. The moon was shining down on us, large and round.

"Just you look here," Rubezh whispered, "how everything grows during the war. And how many self-seeded cereals there are instead of those planted by people. Everything is growing as if it is in a rage. It is just as if the plants are saying. "If you don't know how to live, then we will! You don't know how to do it as you should, then we will!"

"You must be Spinoza, Rubezh," said Gleb Vasilyevich. He was listening intently to the rattling of the machine-guns, estimating where we should make the spurt across the road.

"They kill a person and the forest immediately grows a couple of inches higher," Rubezh mumbled to the back of our necks.

"If they get you," Skorokhod could not restrain himself, "it will go up a whole foot."

As soon as we stopped for a moment, Skorokhod started to swaddle his unshod right foot in a puttee and bandage it round. He just could not make up his mind to throw away the other shoe.

We were listening to the distant tapping of the machine-guns and the incomprehensible silence of the road bathed in the white moonlight, and next to it a whispering, a muttering and the strange eyes of Rubezh who appeared to be entreating. "Stop me, please, look what's happening to me, not with me but to me." I suddenly thought and apparently understood that this person, Rubezh was miserably afraid, he was almost sick with fear. It would have come out in a different way in someone else, but in Rubezh it took the form of constant chatter, either earnest or jocular, with which he stifled his fear. He was not teasing death itself at all as Skorokhod thought, but quite the contrary. It was terror in the face of his own fear, that fear that depressed him and drained him of his strength; it was this very terror that tormented him and made him be like he was; all the time he was preparing himself, making himself ready to reach a pale that he could always see and that he could not manage to forget as others did.

"Now we'll fish you out of this corn," mumbled Rubezh, "Where are you, my lovelies?"

And true enough a flare made a cracking sound, close by this time. It soared upwards, described an arc and fell about one hundred metres away from us. We hid in the corn, some squatting, some kneeling, bathed in yellow light as if in an aquarium. The flares cracked one after the other, flying upwards and hanging in the air with a trail of fiery droplets behind them, as if they were looking round to see where they should fall, and immediately dived swiftly downwards.

We could have run away but it was pointless to do so. The Germans were somewhere in the vicinity: we had to get closer to them without them guessing that we were there. We wanted to enrich ourselves at their expense with something more nourishing than potatoes and wood sorrel. That was why we had to stay there at the ready and wait for the right moment. All we had to do now was to make out what kind of Germans there were here and where they had what. True, we had reckoned on going further, but if there were Germans posted on this road, waiting in ambush, it meant that transports, herds, would soon be stretching along it. Gleb Vasilyevich was listening attentively, weighing things and kept fingering his goatee as if getting used to it.

"I don't like the look of things." said Skorokhod. He suddenly started unwrapping his puttee and threw it away. He took off his one and only shoe and angrily cast that aside, too. He was getting ready for something.

Yes, it would not be very cozy in the corn when the night came to an end, the night that linked us with the distant forest like a dark corridor. Daylight would cut us off from the forest for a long time, and without the forest we would feel distinctly uncomfortable. We did at least need some little clump of woodland. How could we carry anything off, steal anything across an open field. Here we would have to be careful to keep our own.

When we were still walking through the corn, something loomed black to the right, a patch of bushes it seemed. Our thoughts and our eyes now turned to them. So, we crept quietly towards them in single file. The dew-soaked corn had chilled our knees, and my raincoat (a present from the "island") was sodden with water and felt like it were made of tin-plate. The flares had gone out. They no longer soared upwards and had sunk to earth, and the glow of distant fires was no longer over the horizon, and the night was turning grey, retreating before the breaking dawn. The corn came to an end, and there were the bushes, disappearing behind a hillock. Without looking, Gleb Vasilyevich set out, indicating with a shove of the arm to those standing closest, and we crawled, Rubezh and I. The flaps of the stiff tarpaulin raincoat caught under my knees and got in my way. It seemed as if the tarpaulin was making such a loud rustling noise that could be heard for miles around.

We were already close to the clumps of birch saplings when a flare crackled and lit up right above our heads. Immediately a machine-gun rattled like a landslide, quite close to us. Something had happened, a live, familiar sound overwhelmed me, and even made my hand shudder. Something had occurred, I could feel it in my hand, but I did not understand what. With a hiccupping sound, bullets were boring into the hummock, into the ground round my head, next to my very shoulder; out of the corner of my eye I could see the fiery needle of tracer-bullets spearheaded at us, disappearing and reappearing as if trying to sting us....

The machine-gun fell silent as suddenly as it had started firing. But the flares kept on going up one after the other. We could clearly see the Leningrader and Skorokhod lying on the grassy meadow closer to the corn than to our bushes. Aha, so that was what sent a shudder down my arm like something alive; they had hit the butt of my rifle and smashed it. Rubezh and I crawled deeper into the bushes from where we could see how Skorokhod was beginning to stir, lifting himself up and looking in our direction. The Leningrader lay motionless. Then Skorokhod crept towards the corn, jerking the Leningrader who was either wounded or dead, towards him. That was how what had been until a minute before our group, was broken up. What good were we now and what were we going to do? It is strange but the more tense the state in which a person weighs something up and makes a decision as to what he should do and how, the more aloof he becomes, observing with the incomprehensible curiosity of an outsider and even sort of apathetically to see what the person would do next. It is almost as if you are waiting for yourself, as if you have not yet come on the scene.

"That's it!" Rubezh whispered. "They can't get across here now."

The flares were no longer going up, the Germans had calmed down, but the night with its concealing darkness, did not return, and dawn had broken completely. We looked around, appraising our new position. Now we were no longer what we had been ten minutes previous, and we were seeing things in quite a different light, just as you do after a sudden short dream. There was neither forest nor even woodland here, a clump of little birch trees and that was all. We were in the middle of a bare, open field.

"Now you'll have to wait and see what fate has in store for you," Rubezh muttered.

And, in truth, there was a sensation that the whisps of dawn mist were taking us further and further away from those who were left in the corn and closer to the road where the enemy lay in hiding. We could already see the gravel road, a yellowish grey strip running across the green of the meadow.

Time passed. Time was passing on the road, too; everything was happening and was changing there, but we could only watch and wait.

We knew that in just the same way over there in the corn Skorokhod was keeping an eye on the road and on our little clump of birches, trying to guess what we were going to do. If we were to make a joint decision, we would have to crawl back to the corn and we dearly wanted to do that; that concealing strip of corn was drawing us like a magnet. But crawling now would mean letting the Germans know we were there once and for all. We still did not know whether it was an accident that the machine-gun close by had blindly strafed us or they had noticed us and were now keeping track of us and waiting....

It was not until morning came that we saw how awkward our situation was regarding the road, for everything here was visible, within firing range right up to the forest itself. Now we would have to wait for nightfall, and so much could happen in the long day. We did have a tremendous aversion for "open spaces" which we had developed over the time we had fought as partisans.

In order to overcome our sapping anguish and nausea, Rubezh and I began to have breakfast. In the bags we had with us for the German canned foods and crackers, there was a dozen battered potatoes, and we chewed away at them. I kept trying to see whether I could use my rifle without the butt. The Leningrader's ten-loader was over there in the corn but that was out of reach. Thirsty, we looked round senselessly hoping there might be something to drink, but for the moment we do not say a word about water, we can last out for there are far more agonizing things in wait for us!

"Look," Rubezh whispered.

A German had stood up from behind a yellow mound of earth covered with birch branches probably broken from our bushes. He looked about him and walked out onto the gravel road. It was strange to suddenly see the person who had been shooting at you. Wearing a green waterproof cloak and without his helmet, he moved his arras round in circles. Screwing up his eyes, he cheerfully glanced in our direction. The sun was rising behind us. But the Germans had not guessed we were there, for they would not have been wandering around on the road like that. The German said something. In the morning air the unexpected sound of his voice rang out loudly. The sun was casting a pink light on the soft, wavy outline of the young birches and the gravel road beneath the German's feet. This light fell on the soldier's face and hands, and a taunting rainbow shone from his hands to the ground. The soldier wheezed and strained, and from the dug-out they responded with laughter. He bent down and probably took the tinkling mess-tins from someone's hands. Shuffling his feet, he walked along the gravel road and was concealed by the corn.

"You keep watch," Rubezh said in his place, "and I'll have a good snack meanwhile."

In the sun rays the wall of corn had sort of lit up from within, becoming light orange. There where the forage cap of our Leningrader lay, several completely red, broken ears of corn were rocking back and forth. It did not strike you immediately that it was blood. Was he still alive? The red ears of corn swayed gently and heavily back and forth. The grasshoppers had already busily set about their chirring. One of them, a green one, sprang with a click off the broken butt of my rifle and landed on my sleeve.

The Germans probably had their kitchen-trailer over there. The sound of voices and laughter carried to us, and a machine roared. (Any kind of sound we heard seemed very sudden.) Two motorcycles raced past, rattling along with machine-guns mounted on the side-cars. The time flew by as if it were rushing into a precipice. On the road that was. But in our bushes it seemed to stand still amidst the sultry chirring of the grasshoppers. This swift passing of time there and its standing still where we were made things drag by, wearing you out and you wanted to do something: rash, say, jump up and run across the road before the Germans' very eyes. In order to pull myself out of this state, I started to fiddle about with my rifle: cutting it off with a dagger, I took off the strap at one end of which the severed rifle butt was dangling, and tried to see how I would fire it if need be. That instant had not yet come, had not drawn close, it was somewhere up ahead, but that moment would definitely occur.

"Well, where is he then?" Rubezh muttered impatiently. "With that breakfast."

Rubezh's face with its long nose was frighteningly serious. I wished he would stop that muttering. I was already starting to be infuriated by him, just as Skorokhod was not long ago.

My tarpaulin raincoat was beginning to dry, and light patches appeared on it as it did so. It became stifling in it as if I were in a plastic bag, I needed to take it off. I could put it back on again in the evening, but it was no good in the daytime. You could not run in it, nor did we need to run here for there was nowhere to run to. I pulled a grenade out of my pocket and placed it in front of me: there it lay, a round black German grenade with a light blue pin. They had turned it and packed it full of explosives so that a German soldier could throw it at me, hurled it at my feet. But it did not occur to them that it would be a friend to me, for me a last terrible salvation. All I had to do was to flick back that little bluish pin, pull it out, and press the small black ball to the ground with my own body. German grenades took a long time to explode, perhaps as much as six or seven seconds. Its explosion was neither powerful nor far-reaching, just very loud. After three or four seconds you could still roll far enough away from it or sling it somewhere. That kind of a grenade was dangerous, in doing such a thing. There was too much time to change your mind before it exploded. A whole six seconds you would be hovering on the very brink, and that terrifying moment might destroy your resolve to die.

Even if what was ahead of you was more terrifying than death.

It is believed that people are so little worried about their natural end, about death because they somehow learn not to think about it and do not know when it will happen. But on that unbearably long day I felt something quite different: I lay there, my arms and legs relaxed, conscious how dry the soil smelled, listening to the chirring of the grasshoppers, greedily chewing the last little potato and thinking about the remote happiness of being able to have a swallow of water; yes, I could do all that. I listened to Rubezh's mumbling, became angry or grinned, in a word, I lived as people generally live, but precisely because I could choose to die, and death would shelter me from something even more terrible. Yes, to my good fortune, I was mortal. Although I understood full well about the torture and torment that awaited partisans who fell into the hands of the Nazis alive, it was not that that I imagined to be the most fearful, more dreadful than death. At the moment of taking that ultimate decision, to blow yourself up, the future cruelty of the enemy must not seem quite so close, but hours, even days of captivity away, a whole eternity of life, while the grenade, death was right there. This is the reason why it is not the torture and the torment (which will occur only later) that is more frightening than death, but the aversion to, the unendurable and acute loathing of that first instant when you are standing or lying before them, and they are looking at you. It is not fear but rather aversion towards that alien and complete power over your pain, your life that directs the hand clenched around what is for you the last grenade. Once you have managed to get across that dividing line, that moment when you first have to go against your own will, a person may not even remember experiencing such a feeling later on. But, thank goodness, it does exist, it suddenly becomes part of a person who has to choose his own death, and a person is probably never freer than in those very instants.

Nowadays they write a great deal about and make a real effort to prolong human life. Unicellulars do not die at all, so why must a group of cells necessarily be doomed to aging and dying? It would, of course, be a good thing if we multicellulars could live forever. Only what would we do about life imprisonment then? For people still are imprisoned for life in certain countries. In some places it is being abolished, in others brought back. Or what about the death sentence, that would have to be thought about, too. The long-liver would have to sacrifice innumerable decades or even centuries of life for his striving for freedom and justice and for his and other people's happiness. How much of a Prometheus would he be to decide to risk not twenty but two hundred years of his life? But, in any case, people have had no practice regarding this.

Even today it is true that a person who is ready to meet death is genuinely free. It is not a question of longevity but of whether they would be freer if they were almost immortal? Would they really? In any case, the world being what it is, does it not amount to bondage, this wish to go on living forever?

It may well be so, and yet... if we take seventeen-year-olds avidly claimed by any war, what they sacrifice is nothing short of immortality! For when you are seventeen or twenty your life seems an eternity to you. That is your practice with immortality for you, and age-long at that.

In any case, that Flyora who was lying on the grenade seems somewhat nicer to me than that Flariyan Pyatrovich who later came to take his place, who clings so fervently to his life of blindness, to his painful love, all too reminiscent of a blind man's stick. Look how he had seized hold of Glasha (with his hearing, with his whole being), of Kasach, puzzlingly quiet behind him, and of Seriozha who with his very being, his presence ought to protect him from something, from Kasach....

Flyora lay there on that black German grenade with its bluish head, touching its smooth coldness either with his chin or his cheek, waiting while the happenings on the road (the vehicles were already moving) would suddenly come to a head, and with a frightened and exultantly malicious howl, would swiftly close in on him. That would happen as soon as the Germans found out that Flyora was there, that he could be killed. How they would fluster and rejoice that they could do that! He found it hard to believe that for them, he, Flyora, was so important. But immediately he imagined it all quite differently, that he had stood up, revealed himself, was walking where he liked, while the vehicles just continued on their way, for it was not someone dangerous, but just he, Flyora. He lay there on the black grenade, as if he were spanning a precipice and he knew that the very instant that they started to come rapidly in his direction, he would slip down into it. He even felt curiosity as he watched the road. Rubezh was muttering something, whispering, recounting the conversations as he imagined them, of those on the gravel road, and of those hidden in the corn, and even of the corn itself ("I have strewn my grains of corn around to the joy of the mice!..."), but Flyora is not listening to him. He is watching his own killers.

The vehicles and armoured cars had passed by, roaring and giving off clouds of smoke. Now large covered wagons like those used by Gipsies and ordinary peasants' carts followed them. Riding on them and walking by them were Germans and Vlasov army men in green, and the polizei in black or simply in civilian clothes. They all had an injured look upon their faces.

Flyora and I saw that close up, our eyes fixed intently upon it, and registered in those days that executioners and killers always bear an injured expression on their faces and in their eyes. They were offended at those they had already killed, at those they were killing and at those they were to kill. The physiognomies of the Germans who followed the carts with Alsatian dogs on leads bore an especially injured look; they were not walking along the road, but along the road side, through the grass, only a stone's throw from the bushes where Flyora was hidden. They were driving along a crowd of people huddled into a hot, dusty lump, peasant men half undressed and women and children barefooted. The Alsatians suddenly started to tear towards the bushes, towards Flyora, towards the corn, straining at their short leads; the guards in loose green and black spotted raincoats jerked them back angrily, they urged them on towards the road, towards the crowd. First one guard, then another would rush at the people, making them jostle against one another (growls, children's screams), but when they walked back (even closer to the bushes), the look of injury on those narrow, full, round, thin, pock-marked faces, with spectacles and without them, became even more noticeable, taking on that hue of rage. They walked past, dragging and leading away the Alsatians that were rushing towards the bushes. This made it seem lo us as if the road with the people on it, the side of the load, and the meadow across which the Germans were walking and running with their Alsatians were all listing, about to slip down, to pour down, to collapse on our heads. It was as if we were in some agonizing state of expectation, by now almost willing it to happen....

And then something did indeed happen. Two or three people from that dusty crowd raced towards the corn. Oh, how aggrievedly the Alsatians yelped, how exultantly. Some of them tore towards the corn, pulling their handlers along and being pulled by them, and others sped towards the people who remained on the road. Rubezh and I exchanged glances, "That's it, we are finished!"

There were a few bursts of firing followed by shouts and barking. The Germans had let the Alsatians off their leads and were now afraid they might hit them. Anyway, where could the fugitives manage to go from this patch of corn in the midst of an open field? Two Germans had run up from the direction of the bushes. Tense like huntsmen, we watched their green clothed backs dotted with sweat. The corn was absolutely seething with the barking and growling of dogs, and their heavy uneven panting. Suddenly a regular rattle resounded, five shots from a rifle. Was that our Leningrader's ten-shooter? Immediately there was a squeal just like that of a mongrel. They had probably wounded an Alsatian.

Everything became absolutely still for an instant. The first to come to their senses and race back towards the road were the two Germans who had run up too far from our direction. But those who were by the road, and there were many of them, rushed headlong towards the corn. And everything was drowned in the frightened firing and shouts.

...When you have previously seen dead people alive, you notice that the world does not immediately accept the deceased: everything all around has to get used to his presence. Then when an hour has passed and even half a day, and the corpses are still there lying in front of you, they gradually become part of that same hostile and troubled world in which Rubezh and I were caught. The traffic was moving on the road, the Germans and the dogs were walking along and those who had spent the night in the dug-out were running around with saucepans. Only Rubezh and I kept as still as the dead. The Germans had taken Gleb Vasilievich and Skorokhod away like an unexpected, pleasing gift, a trophy, and before that they clustered together by them for a long time. The men and, it seemed, one woman from the column, who had been killed, were thrown by the roadside. We could see them for they had been right before our eyes for two hours now.

A person had been killed, a person had ceased to exist, and then there appeared that something lying on the grass. Possibly, you yourself would be killed before the sunset, and again something would appear in the world and, just as you were doing now, someone else would be looking at it and getting used to it.

Rubezh lapsed into a strange kind of drowsiness. He only managed to say, "Keep an eye out for the moment, all right?" and fell asleep with his face pressed against the ground. His shabby leather hat had rolled off to one side, and his tangled flaxen hair had intertwined with the grass. I watched him anxiously. There is something dead about the pose of someone who is asleep, especially when he is so completely overcome by slumber. It already seems as if he had been lying there too long and everything all around was starting to get used to it.

Which of us two would see the other like that? Who would be the first to appear before the eyes of the other? I kept recalling a film I had seen before the war where people were walking up and looking at clean, untrodden snow; they waited, and suddenly a person began to transpire, to emerge in it, an invisible man killed by English policemen.

I was ready to wake Rubezh up. I did not want to see him in that stance. I feared it as though it were the ultimate solitude in the world.

Vehicles were moving along the road again, but when a tank came to a halt by the trench, I gave Rubezh a shove. It was amazing how glad I was when I saw his face come to life, that long-nosed face overgrown with fair stubble.

"Have they been here long? Why didn't you wake me before?"

He whispered loudly and just as if he could have prevented something from happening, had he been awakened earlier. A person always wakes up in a world slightly different from the one he left when he fell asleep. When times are good, he is only too eager to catch up where he left off, but when times are bad, he is overwhelmed by the anxiety of not knowing where the danger has shifted to.

"How did I manage to fall asleep?"

He was wide awake once he had caught sight of the road and the dead.

"What happens if they do us in, too, old chap? Back on the 'island' they will say that we ran away."

Yes, there was the "island" and Glasha.

"That will be really bad for them," Rubezh weighed it up.

They were waiting for us there, marking time itself: the past was when we left, and the future would be when we returned. That was surely the only place on earth where they were waiting for us, for me, and what a must it is apparently that a person should have someone waiting for him. Formerly, when Mum and my little sisters were still alive, I never thought about that, just as a person may not think about the sun for a long time, for it will always be there, even if it is forgotten behind the clouds.

Now only Glasha and the "island" was there to remember you, were in need of you and not somebody else.

When a flare plummets down, the ground does, as it were, rise up a little to meet it. Everything that can be seen in the light of the flare cascading down, stretches upwards as if on tiptoe, for some reason peering to see where it had fallen. You also pull yourself away from the ground, lift up your head and stretch in that direction.

Yesterday Rubezh and I spent a long time crawling away from such flares, from that accursed gravel road where we had lost the Leningrader and Skorokhod, where we had left those murdered peasants whom we do not know. First we moved over into the corn and dragged ourselves stealthily along the corn downtrodden by the fugitives, the Alsatians and the Germans. Then we stood up and walked. When we stood on those legs that felt like cotton wool after lying down for so long, the world immediately moved apart and we walked away across the field towards the forest, propped up by our own short shadows, and they joyfully, faithfully confirmed that we were there, that we existed. But two days later the flares were making us flatten ourselves against the ground once more, but this time we were not moving away from them, but crawling towards them. For nothing had changed, and we did at least have to get something with which to return to the starving "island". We had not yet come across anything worthwhile, True, we had espied a cow in the forest, but we could not take it. We did not know what we would find in the village we were creeping to. But we had to do something, give it a try if only like this, crawling along in the furrows of a field of unharvested potatoes, in the direction of a polizei garrison.

"Well, how do you like this after auntie's milk?" Rubezh, who lay two furrows away from me, was trying to cheer himself and me up.

With this remark he probably was referring to that very same cow, imagining perhaps how we would take it back to the "island" on a string, instead of slithering now right into the furnace.

Oh, how the "fledglings" rejoiced, when they, quite to their surprise, caught sight of a cow in a forest glade, half a tonne of meat on its own legs and even with a string lassoed by its horns. It was so amazing that the "fledglings" even sat down on the grass to admire it and probably to convince themselves that they were not dreaming. The cow had most likely run away from the Germans. Rubezh shook the tobacco dust out of the pocket in his breeches, but he did not have any paper. He pulled himself carefully across the grass in search of a dried leaf. He had to have an oak leaf. As he crawled along, he feasted his eyes on the fat sides of our little old brown cow. He set about striking fire. While he was getting himself a light and smoking, he even managed to tell a story.

"There was a family back in our town of Slutsk. There was that fledgling Timokh and he had a house full of girls, a little family similar to my own. My family is in Slutsk now, unless they have taken the older girls to Germany. Anything may have happened. After they took me away in a cart in the spring of 1942, at the time when Slovak troops were fighting against the partisans, and after I found myself with the partisans in that same cart, I have never been anywhere near Slutsk since. I have kept out of harm's way. My little lady knows where I am, and it is better for the children if she has not told them. God forbid that they should let slip that Timokh Rubezh is with the partisans! They are living at home and let them live there while they can. Aha, I was telling you about the "Fledglings", that was the nickname given to that family. They weren't a very bright lot, and people used to say of them in the town that they were like "lard without bread". But what kind of lard was there? It would have been all right if there had at least been bread. No matter what you say there are families for whom poverty and misery is like a scab from which they cannot rid themselves. An amazing thing happened. The Fledglings bought a cow from a gipsy. But if only they had not been the fledglings! Every time they wanted a drop of milk they would pick up a mug and stick it under the row, everyone in turn, just as if it was water coming out of a tap. This was fine for a week or two. They kept milking the poor cow a drop at a time until the supply dried up."

Rubezh had already smoked the cigarette he had rolled in an oak leaf and he set about cutting birch-bark to make a little mug. I dare say the fledglings had given him the idea!

It was then that we saw the woman. She was standing behind the hazelnut bushes, watching these strangers who were crawling round her cow; we realised immediately that the cow was hers.

"Good day to you!" Rubezh greeted her, even pleased to see her,

"Oh, what a fright I got!" the woman walked towards the cow to touch it. "I was looking to see who it was. Then I saw it was partisans, our own people."

She said it as if reminding us. The woman was wearing a long dark skirt, and a jersey, her hair was unkempt, and her feet were bare.

"I'd only just got her out of the pit and let her out to graze, gone a step away and strangers come along!" The woman could still not calm down.

"Where are you yourself from, Ma?" Rubezh asked, continuing to work on the little cup he was making out of birch-bark.

"From the village, we live in the village, that is, lived. When they began to burn everything all around, they came down on us one morning. I looked out of the window and, my God, the courtyard was full of Germans. They entered the cottage and one of them, a local interpreter, asked, "Which village are you from, Uboinoye or Bobrovichi?" That scoundrel knew it all. At one time the hamlets and smaller settlements had been joined up to form villages; only our farmstead had somehow remained on its own. So, that was why he was asking us whether we belonged to Uboinoye or Bobrovichi. I guessed immediately that they had come to burn down Bobrovichi or Uboinoye and slaughter the people. That was why they were interrogating us to find out where we belonged. I looked at him and I looked at my children. I do not know why but I did not want to say we were from Uboinoye. Perhaps it was because they had killed a lot of people from there in the previous war, and my grandfather told me that when the French came we burned as well. What was I to say, how was I to reply? "Are you from Uboinoye?" asked the translator. I looked at him. Was he hinting I should say that or trying to catch me, oh Lord? You did not know what to do, for he just stood there grinning, a man with a moustache. "We're from Bobrovichi," I said softly. How my arms and legs went limp. That man with the moustache went on standing there and kept on grinning. "Well, all right..." I heard him tell the Germans something about Uboinoye, not Bobrovichi, but Uboinoye. I wanted to do what was best, but I myself had stepped right into the fire. But he had told the Germans "Uboinoye!" So, he was human after all! Because they were going to kill the villagers of Bobrovichi. I grabbed the children and the little old cow and went straight into the forest. They set light to Bobrovichi and slaughtered everyone there, and in the evening they did the same to Uboinoye as well. They flew past our farmstead once more and burned it down. There is a family from Uboinoye here with me, a woman..."

A pit like those soldiers make for their vehicles and guns with a smooth slope into it had been dug in a thick fir grove.

This was where the woman was hiding her cow and now she drove it in there as if showing us that this was her place and not anywhere else. Two girls came clambering out of the pit when they heard our voices, one was dressed in a long men's jacket with the sleeves rolled up and the second was barely clothed in a tattered dress. With them they had a chubby, plump little boy.

"Why is it you've left the yellow sand for all to see?" Rubezh reproached them. "Now then, you little ones, go and look for some moss. One can spot your hide-out from a mile away."

"Oh dear, how right you are!" the woman started in her usual manner. "We tried to cover up the sand, but you can see what kind of workers I've got here."

The two little girls ran off to pull up some moss and, in order to take a better look at us, the plump podgy little boy leaned against the woman's leg.

"This is the little son of the woman from Uboinoye.

Where's your Mum, Pavlik? They've got their own pit over thre."

The woman from Uboinoye had already emerged from the hushes.

"Don't be afraid to come out, these are partisans," said the owner of the cow.

"What's going on, lads, what's going to happen?" the skinny, freckled woman began speaking immediately. She and the freckled little girl who was walking behind her looked very much alike, only the girl had a very serious, even stern look on her face, while the woman's face bore a strange kind of smile.

"What happened to you?" Rubezh asked.

"What happened? They just slaughtered us and that's it. They went from cottage to cottage, murdering everyone," the woman said that somehow in such a matter-of-fact manner. "Go into the cottage! Lie down!" And you get shot.

"Why did you stay there then? Surely you must have known what they were doing".

"Some did run away, we fled, you see. Some were afraid to. The Germans told the village elder they had appointed to tell us they would not touch Uboinoye, and that they were razing Bobrovichi to the ground because many of the young men there had joined the partisans. The elder told them people from our village had not become partisans. They said that if they found anyone in the forest they would shoot them. True enough, at first they ordered the men to bring axes and spades and repair the road. Those peasants who did not hide, who came forward, they gathered together and began to drive them to the open space on the edge of the village. Then, with their hands up, they were made to run round and round on the sand, on the sand at that! Those who lagged behind were beaten. We saw what they were doing to our menfolk through the window. The purpose of that was to tire people out, for they knew men would surely offer resistance. This was to make it easier to drive them into the barn. They herded them in and then began to go round the cottages. They switched on some music outside, loud, loud music, and they were ambling around, and shots could be heard. I said to the womenfolk, "You know what they're doing, they're murdering people." We, about ten

families, got together in one cottage, so that it
was not so frightening. They're going to kill us,'
I said. We looked out of the window. They were
not shooting at or doing anything to the people in
the street, just indicating that they should go into
the cottages. We watched three or four Germans
going into one cottage and as many entering the
cottage opposite. They killed the people there
and came out, adjusting their submachine-guns,
and then went to the cottages closer to ours.
They walked up to the gate, looked at us, and we
stared at them through the window and wept and
wept. I don't know what, but they had forgotten
something, remembered it, and went back for it. I
grabbed hold of the children and rushed out into
the kitchen-garden. Music was blaring out all over
the village. Lazy, chubby little Pavlik came over
to the woman who was recounting her story, and
now leaned against her leg. We hid behind the
well in the kitchen garden. I threw potato leaves
and goosefoot over the children and tried to cover
them with sand, but from the street the Germans
were coming increasingly close to the well. They
would drink the cold water, 'A-ah!' That means it
was good. They washed their hands, splashed one
another and laughed. But my hair was standing
on end. The Germans did not hear when he (she
stroked Pavlik's head) and she (she glanced at the
little girl with her fixed stare) whispered to me,
'Mum, Mum, we'll run away, we'll run away, Mum,
they won't kill us!' They had noticed that I was
ready to die. Where was there to go from here? But
they kept saying, 'They shan't kill us, they shan't.'"

The expression on the woman's face conveyed
nothing of what she was recounting. (But all of it

was reflected in the staring eyes of the little girl standing next to her.) It was as if the woman did not believe what had happened, as if she were asking us what she had seen, smiling guiltily and awkwardly. All the time she kept looking round to see where her children were, whether they were here.

"Well, we crawled to the collective farm barns, but they were already on fire, and German bullets kept whistling through the air, whistling and whistling. It was our menfolk they were shooting and burning there. We could hear people shouting and howling, oh my God! How they whined and cried and yelped! We slipped away between the burning walls, among the sheds, accompanied by the patter of bullets on the walls. I covered the children with my own body, raking the sand up onto my legs which were being terribly scorched as we were so close to the fire. My hair was crackling and shriveling up. All the same, Pavlik kept saying, 'Mum, they shan't kill us.' How would we manage not to get killed if we were already getting burnt, and we could not escape for a German was standing in our way. I could see him through the smoke. I could not endure it, I kneeled, got up, so he would kill me and get it over and done with. We did not want to be burned alive? The children were already beginning to whine because of the fire was scorching them. The German brushed the smoke away, bent down and disappeared. We crawled and ran out of the fire, away from the smoke..."

The smile on the woman's skinny freckled face looked ridiculous and strange, but it did not seem crazy to us. It was simply that it was no longer strictly defined when a person should weep and when he should smile. It still seems as if people do not believe that it has happened to them, that such a thing could take place, that it is true and that they are asking us whether it is true or not.

How fearful it is when a person smiles.

...The barking of dogs faded away in the distance at one end of the street and then the other. It was a big village. The flares soared upwards and then everything started moving; long shadows like huge levers were turning the sheds, cottages, and trees they were attached to. A round of machine-gun fire would immediately follow in its wake like the creaking of a dry wooden pulley. The tracer-bullets cut a jerky fiery path away into the field behind our backs. This recurred at regular intervals as if some kind of mechanism was triggering it off. This meant that there were Germans here. The polizei did not operate so methodically. In the day time we had seen army vehicles standing in the village. My raincoat became hard like a shell or a coat of mail because of the dew and the dampness. As I lay there, I freed myself of my piece of tarpaulin and did up my belt with the cartridge pouches over my German military jacket, and I left my raincoat by a wild pear-tree in a potato field. For some reason I kept looking round at it as if at some third and very cunning person among us. Rubezh was crawling along a furrow and kept looking round as well just as if that third person was luring him back. A pungent smell of burning rose from the cold ashes in the night air. It appeared that the village in which we were preparing to acquire something to eat was not as safe and sound as it had seemed to us when we had studied it from the forest in the day time. At that time Rubezh had drawn such a fine picture of how we would load our waiting empty bags with lard and sausage from the polizei's wooden barrels and would arrive at the "island" with them and how we would be welcomed by boys squealing with delight and Styapan the Conjuror dancing on his crutch.

The closer a person gets to danger, the more, after a certain point in time, he throws caution to the winds. It already seemed that the irreparable had happened anyway, that you had been too awkward, and it already seemed somehow immaterial what the outcome would be, so long as it would happen as soon as possible. The deeper we crept into the polizei village, trying, however, to keep away from the buildings jutting out into the field (there were sure to be sentries posted, there or an ambush!), the clearer it became that we were wittingly doing something pointless and dangerous. The first step we made in the village would arouse the whole garrison. True, the dogs barked at the flares and at the rounds of machine-gun fire. But what a howl they would set up when they smelt us.

You crawl through fragrant beds of dill, come up against the hard, cold pumpkin heads, but you get the sensation that you are not pulling yourself stealthily along, but stretching out across the entire field, like a spring with one end attached far back there where the raincoat was left. And you do not know whether you will continue forward in the next instant, or recoil back to where you've started. With every passing metre the spring becomes tighter and pulls you backwards ever more strongly. You cling to the soft soil, digging in your elbows and your knees, and every metre of the way it seems as if you have left something behind just as you left the raincoat; in crawling out of it, you shed it like a skin. You are already creeping across the whole of the field. Already the most unfamiliar, the strangest thing is that you continue to drag yourself forward, to move furtively towards the walls and windows of the cottage. How will he act, what will he do in the next instant, that person holding a heavy grenade warmed through in his hand and a shortened, buttless rifle trailing along behind him?

The inside door in the entrance hall banged!... The iron bolts rattled and the outside door opened wide with a sonorous creak. For the moment all these sounds drowned one another. With surprising agility Rubezh ran over to the corner of the shed and stood there. I quickly crawled over to the hoarded fence and kept quite still.

We heard a man, evidently a smoker, coughing in the courtyard. He spat vehemently and headed for the shed, the white of his undershirt appearing distinctly above me.

"You there, uncle, just come over here."

Surely Rubezh had not uttered those words? It was Kasach who spoke in such a sharp, ironic tone.

"Who is it, who's that? Who's there!"

"Quiet, come over here!... Who are you? Are you from the potizei?"

"And you? Boys..."

"All right. Is the shed locked?"

"I don't know... What is it you want to do, boys? There are Germans here. They've been here for two days now."

"We know. You'll lead us out of the village now, together with the cow. Are you with us, uncle? And no tricks! If you show us how to get out, you can run back."

"Right away, lads, I'll do it right away. If needs must!"

"I like people with an intelligent attitude. Flyora, come over here. Where's that belt? Be a bit quieter. Show us the way, uncle. All your doors creak. You must oil the hinges. How is it that the Germans didn't shoot the dogs? That's gross negligence. And you've got white on you, and the cow. What can we cover you up with?"

"I'll get something in the cottage..."

"A rifle? You can do that with my neighbour. His nickname is Fledgling. Have you remembered that? Here's a sack, put it over your shirt." We were returning to the "island". We had a splendid cow, large, black and white and with a huge udder. There would be meat and there was already milk for the asking. We almost had to carry it out of the village, the owner holding it by the horns and we holding it under its sides. We hurried away through the kitchen gardens as quietly as we could, and then we ran, pressing ourselves against those sonorous sides going pit-a-pat and giving them a shove. We stopped by the forest, out of breath. To celebrate, Rubezh had asked the elderly fellow for a cigarette and he had been very upset that he did not have any with him. He flapped his arms up and down like a cockerel, feeling for some in the pockets of his black breeches. But here he withdrew his palms as if he had touched something hot for the trousers were obviously polizei issue, and his boots were strong, army ones.

"It's a good job we got through!" said the elderly fellow. "I did wonder when the flares went up!"

"Well, be off while it's still dark," said Rubezh good- naturedly.

"Aha, I will be so they don't guess what I've been up to."

"Go on then."

"We don't have the polizei, but self-defence. It's two days since the Germans arrived, they are housed in the school."

"Go on then."

"It's a pity I hadn't got any cigarettes on me."

"Next time."

"I'll be off. I can still get some shut eye."

"Yes, you do that."

We ran on, this time to get away from that elderly man. (Those trousers of his did look too "polizei-like". For all we knew he might raise the alarm and bring his mates in pursuit.)

But we felt cheerful, either because we let him go ourselves, and now we were running to save ourselves ("That is what you "fledglings" are supposed to do…"), and perhaps because we were at last returning to the "island" and not with empty hands either.

But soon our goading and shoves in the cow's soft sides ceased to have any effect and the cow ambled along, its distended sides swaying heavily, and then it stopped walking altogether. It regarded us with its kindly, perplexed eyes as if saying, "There's my udder, there's the milk, what more do you, "fledglings" need from me?" We were tired as well and sat there in a relaxed attitude, the backs of our necks propped up against the pine-trees, listening in them to the humming, restless quietness of dawn. After fumbling about in his clothes, Rubezh pulled out the flattened little birch-bark mug. On bent legs as if he did not have the strength to straighten his knees, he danced up to the cow's udder instead of walking up to it. The cow even mooed at him as if he were its mistress. Rubezh skillfully stroked the cow's swollen udder, wet his palm and washed the cow's nipples, and rubbed his palm dry on his knee. He set about milking the cow into the little birch-bark cup. I could not help laughing for it was just like his story about the Fledgling family.

"That's how my girls ran back and forth with a little mug," said Rubezh. "I've got six of them."

"Your girls? But you were telling me about a neighbour, weren't you!"

"About a neighbour? Perhaps I was. Everyone is a neighbour to someone. Aren't there very many "fledglings" in the world then?"

Here it crossed my mind that Rubezh had been just the same at home, that at that time he had learned to take any failure, constant misfortunes with sombre laughter at himself. And, I dare say, you often had to be cheerful with a family like that.

Reaching with his lips out of the white stubble, Rubezh tried the milk in the little cup.

"We'll get drunk on this. It's a fine drop of liquid that is! Even the 'fledglings' have been lucky!"

We took it in turns to gulp down the warm, foaming milk, smelling of morning and childhood, and true enough, our voices, our words, and our laughter became louder and louder and got more and more out of control as if we were drunk.

"Where's our little old uncle now?" Rubezh suddenly re-remembered. "He had good box-calf boots. But the trousers were from the polizei all the same."

He looked down at what he was shod in, his rawhide sandals and cloth puttees encrusted in mud.

"But perhaps he's looking for us, wants to exchange his for mine. All right, let's get going, for it's true—we've been celebrating before we should."

We rested again while we waited for night to fall. The most difficult part lay ahead. What would be lying in wait for us in the six kilometres of open fields we could only guess at, but there was not much hope that it would be something good. Once again Rubezh was taken with unrestrained muttering. That was a bad sign. Untying the cow which had been thoroughly milked and had a good graze on the succulent grass of the forest, from the tree, this time he was distressed for the cow, expressing its feelings, "It would have been better if I had stayed here as an aurochs. I've got to run around in the forest all the same. Then I would at least be an aurochs!"

We tried to rub and smear mud on the splendid white patches on the cow's sides.

"You can be seen day and night," Rubezh reproached it.

Night was gradually seeping out of the forest onto its edge and beyond it into the field, from the horizon it was creeping towards the sky, erasing all the patches of daylight that remained. But new spots appeared, those of fires spilling into the dark, damp sky in numerous layers like a rainbow, like kerosene on water. Where there were no fires, where it had burnt out yesterday and the day before yesterday, the sky was black as soot with the last sparks of stars on it.

The alarming emptiness of the field sucked us towards it like a pipe; we could not help beginning to hurry and had already started to run. Rubezh beat the cow with a switch. With a belt round my elbow I kept its head up so that its mouth was held as far away as possible from the rape and self-seeded corn. It kept thinking that we had already arrived and it could get busy on the grass. I was carrying my undersize rifle by the barrel. You could fire from it without its butt by holding it against your abdomen as the Germans did with their submachine-guns, but perhaps I would not need to use it. We only had this field to cross.

The field had neither been ploughed nor sown for several years now, but the old furrows were still there, dangerous to the cow. Its legs were now dearer to us than our own. We had already been walking for about an hour, keeping increasingly to the left, but the glow of the fires was also creeping leftwards, right across our path, flowing over the fringe of the horizon onto our field. This was making us more and more anxious, for it was precisely there that there was a low ledge of forest that we were trying to reach. The tops of the fir trees could already be distinguished against the troubled sky. The closer we drew to the forest, the quicker we tried to walk. Rubezh whipped the beast with the switch and I dragged and pulled it by the belt. The cow was run off its legs, its hooves clattering tike wooden ones as it ran.

All of a sudden, something snapped and the cow stumbled. Our first thought was its legs. Had it broken one!

Like a water-fall the dense, harsh light of a flare going up showered upon us. I even made out a hay stack right by the forest itself. I looked round and saw Rubezh on his feet, alive. Immediately fiery needles raced at us, past us and through us. A machine-gun was firing point-blank, spitting fire from behind the hay rick. It seemed as if dozens of glowing needles had penetrated the expanse which was filled with my clumsy, huge falling body. Letting go of the belt, I fell to the ground. I lay there removing those needles from my consciousness like splinters, convincing myself that here I was, still alive and not even wounded.

The cow was calmly chewing at the rape stems. From that faint sound, I realised that the firing had already stopped. It had ended just as suddenly as it had begun. But the nearby forest no longer appeared to offer us salvation. It was menacing, towering over us heavily as we lay there flattened to the ground. Rubezh was lying motionless and patiently not far away from me. Without getting up, I tried to catch the cow by the trailing belt, but it made a smacking sound with its lips, took a few steps to the side and began to sniff the ground. Reluctant to call or shout to Rubezh, I crawled over to him. It was not until I was right next to him, that I thought there was something wrong. He lay there with his mouth to the ground, his winter hat which had tumbled off seemed like an empty upturned bowl. I touched his head with my hand. Rubezh's hair was surprisingly soft and warm (my fingers registered this and remembered it!).

"Timokh, Timokh!" For some reason it was the first time I had called him by his name and it sounded like someone else's. But this was not Rubezh anymore and someone had appeared in his place. Rubezh had left me on my own, all alone with this dead body in front of the forest where the enemy was hidden behind the hay ricks. With every passing moment the body lying by me was becoming more and more dead, increasingly alien. My hands felt big and sticky from touching him. I tried to take away Rubezh's rifle, but his motionless hand would not release it, held on to it tightly.

As if giving the dead man time for something, I let him keep the rifle and began to rake the cartridges out of his pouches. Rubezh had a German rifle so his cartridges were needed as well. I stuffed the cartridge clips into my pockets, loaded myself up and again began to pull the rifle out of that dead hand. The hand trailed after the rifle and finally let it go.

I moved over to a hummock overgrown with grass so that it would be easier to crawl away or shoot when they came this way from the forest. I remembered about the cow and sought it out with my eyes. It was swiftly going away from us. At first, it appeared white against the dark background of the forest, and when it had the glow from the fires behind it; it looked as black as coal. I could even see my belt jumping backwards and forwards as it dangled down to the ground.

The cow's legs were still immersed in the darkness, while the torso and the head stood out against that sky all aflame. Withdrawing further and further away, pulling its legs out of the darkness as if out of mud, the cow was rising higher and higher, growing all the time. The fact that the cow was moving away, made my thoughts return to what was most important, made me think about the "island". But that person who lay there close by was demandingly expecting something of me. I crawled over to him again. Having pushed my arm under that dead weight, sticky with blood, I attempted to drag it along after the retreating cow. I even managed to heave it along a few steps until I realised that that was not what I wanted to do.

The cow stood out increasingly black against the light hovering above the horizon and grew larger and larger as it pulled its legs swiftly and cheerfully out of the darkness. I set the rifle on one side, I piled some soil up against Rubezh's legs with my hands, sticky between the fingers. The dead man became Rubezh again, for I had already become accustomed to the reality, to the thought that Rubezh had been killed, was dead. I raked up some more earth just as if I had been told by the man to do so. Our cow was disappearing, absorbed by the light and, as if it were melting away, its legs no longer made contact with the flickering outlines of the horizon. I rose to my knees and hastily set about heaping the moist sand closer to Rubezh, but was not yet covering him with it. I was shifting the sand with my hands, my knees, my chest itself, almost with my face as if I were covering myself with soil and all the time I expected that my jerky, incautious movements would cause us to be spattered with another shower of machine-gun fire, But the more aware I became of my imprudence, the more carelessly and hastily I did everything, as if on purpose, as if to spite something or someone. I had sand in my mouth, under my collar and in my hair. Finally, I made up my mind to shove the heap of sand onto Rubezh, prostrated on the tussock, at one go. I did it, trying not to look and not to think, rapidly, hastily so as to complete the job before I became fully conscious of what I was doing. After a certain moment I ceased to feel that I was taking in what was happening; it was as if I had reached saturation and the rest of what was taking place was spilling over somewhere. It is fortunate that man is capable of shutting himself off that way. There I remained all alone, out in the field, wet, dirty and sweaty with sand grating between my teeth. I had been in such a hurry to pile up the sand and cover the dead body, to get away from this spot, to crawl after our cow, but now I had finished and I lay there motionless. Suddenly everything seemed quite unreal and I simply wanted to wait around until it all faded away of its own accord. I watched aloofly as the cow retreated, its slender legs no longer touching the ground at all; it was moving swiftly on them as if pushing itself off from the light that was flickering as if evaporating above the horizon.

(To this day I cannot understand why those who fired at us from behind the hay rick behaved in such a strange way. Possibly it was a German or polizei listening post and not an ambush, and they were simply playing about, because a listening post should only observe and not give itself away. But we had been really exposed to their machine-gun when the field was lit up—it must have been quite a temptation for them!)

At last I managed to crawl away from the forest, from Rubezh, from the endless nightmare in pursuit of the cow whose little thin legs began to wade through the blackness, again to become submerged beyond the line of the horizon. I was dragging along the dead man's rifle, creeping forwards with sluggish, blind indifference, doing the only thing that I could, although I was no longer reckoning on anything.

The cow suddenly stood stock still on the spot. It inclined its head, sniffed the horizon, veered off sharply to the left and back towards the forest again. I crawled in that direction as well to intercept it. The cow ascended the vanishing line of the horizon once again, and because I was watching it from below, as if from a dark pit, it seemed huge to me and completely black like some kind of lone aurochs. Sweat was running down into my eyes, becoming mixed with the sticky blood smeared on my neck, with the sand in which I had been floundering; I looked like someone who was drowning, making those last hopeless movements. The cow was approaching me, but when it was about a hundred metres from me, it turned once again and moved away to the side. It was heading straight for the forest where the hay stack was, where the Germans were lying in wait, and I could do nothing about it. I could not make a single movement more. Tears mingled with the dirty sweat on my lips and trickled down onto my sticky throat, I picked up a clod of earth and slung it pathetically after the cow which at close quarters had white spots again, became quite real, cheerfully swishing its tail from side to side. Now, however, it was more unattainable for me than when it was going down beyond the horizon. My belt dangled tauntingly around its front legs.

When the cow suddenly stumbled, having trodden on the belt and stopped to sniff the ground, it seemed to me that my sense of grievance and hatred of the cow were to blame. I eased myself rapaciously towards it for some of my strength had returned. Fatigue made me grit my teeth in an unbearable way as if the top ones were pushing the bottom ones out of line.

I was crawling along, grating my teeth, now coming out in a sweat, now bursting into tears, dragging myself towards that repulsive creature, towards my own killer in order to grab hold of the belt and lie still like someone who has attained salvation. If only I could lie quite still for one single minute, could lie there motionless, knowing that there was no need to go anywhere, to run away, that it was possible not to stir.

I frightened the cow by creeping around it and crawling in front of it. It stopped cropping the grass, looked and listened, turned and moved away again, trotted off. With my mouth and ears full of sand, wet and weakened, with my salty lips I whispered, "Daisy, daisy, there's a good little cow..." and for some reason, "tut, tut, tut..."

To me it did not appear to be a cow, but a cunning, mocking killer, in concert with those who are lying in wait behind the hay stacks by the forest. If it moves forward, starts to go away, I shall jump up. Let them shoot me! I was stretching towards the belt as if it would pull me out of the precipice, if only I could grab hold of it. The cow, which had got slightly used to my being there, was chewing again; the belt was quivering on the ground itself some ten metres from me, I could see its eye shining darkly and I was afraid to look, fearing that I would frighten it with the greed and maliciousness in my own eyes. There was already a smile on my wet face, I was whispering some words, stock still with tenderness and hatred. I gradually crawled up to it, smiling and whispering all the time.

I grabbed the belt so suddenly that the cow tore away in a fright, dragging my tired, happy body along the ground. No matter what now, I would lie there, and keep on lying and lying. I lay there for a minute or two, my face turned towards I lie sky smeared with light, listening attentively to the silence of the forest and inhaling the close breath of the cow. The moon was right above my face as it cooled down. Visible on its round disc were the shadows and silhouettes familiar to me since childhood looking as if they were behind matt yellow glass, and they did indeed look like human features, like the figure of someone falling, and of someone recoiling in horror before what he has done....

Now we were moving forward like this: I was behind the cow, lying on my side, pushing myself off with my elbow and the rifle; frightened by my pose and my movements the cow would either shoot off to the side or suddenly drop behind, straining at the belt and going round in circles. If the Germans were watching, they were probably surprised by this circus. But what if they were advancing along the fringe of the forest to that end of it, towards which I was crawling and dragging the cow? Or were they lying in wait for me there? And I with my back towards them would fall straight into their hands!

I did not know what to do so I lay down again and waited. The cow stood over me, startled and pulling at the belt. The distant glow of the fires was casting dark shadows on the convex mirror of its eye. Suddenly a flash was reflected all over the rounded surface of the cow's eye, and it glinted. After crackling, the flare hung over the spot where Rubezh had been left. Another one came in our direction, followed directly by a thin stream of fire. Several bullets pierced the cow's body with a squelching noise. It's body shuddered as if having a big, awkward hiccup as it swallowed them. I darted towards it to help it as if there was still something I could do, something I could alter, and the cow lurched towards me as well and collapsed on its fore legs that had broken under it. It shook its head loosely and horribly from side to side, almost like a human being, and then its whole body slumped to the ground and remained quite still. Its legs began to jerk unexpectedly and sharply once again, striking me a painful blow on the elbow and thrusting me away.

I kept on holding the belt, flattening myself to the ground.

The round bulging eye reflected the distant glow of the fires which played and flickered in its black depths. But the eye was already dead. From the cow's neck which was flung back, glistening like resin, a fountain was spurting, sometimes failing on the sparkling mirror of the eye and extinguishing it. There was another flash as a flare went up. I pressed myself against the cow's belly, trying to hide, and suddenly I made out the white veins of milk on the udder. The flare had faded, but I went on seeing the trickling white threads on the black resin-like blood. I do not know why but precisely these little white streams which seemed like someone begging someone else for forgiveness had an incredible effect on me. I did not simply weep, but screamed inaudibly as if from intolerable pain. Stained with blood, soil and sweat, completely and utterly exhausted, I looked at those pitiful, clear childish thread-like streams and cried in a way that I had only cried in early childhood, with all my being, sighing and sobbing. I felt such an infinite, childish sense of injury at the whole world that I could protect myself only with it, desiring solely that my situation would deteriorate and that things would get really bad for me and that I would die, to spite them all or to their delight....

The huge fixed eye of the moon hung over the still field, over the black rampart of the forest and over the horizon which was all afire. And reflected in that eye as if in a mirror I could see two people doing something to one another, perpetrating something terrible....

"...And you, Flariyan Pyatrovich, are you going to go on trying to convince me? No, if I had been supervising our planet, I would have drawn my conclusions long ago."

This time, after flinging his heavy brief-case stuffed full of books on the sofa, Boris Boky began to talk about Khatyn which he had visited, about the cemetery of five hundred Byelorussian villages.

"Yes, you saw it as it really was, Flariyan Pyatrovich! Come on, now, explain to me how such a thing is possible. No, I don't mean about fascism as a system, I can still fathom that out, although I would not take it upon myself to elucidate all the metastases discovered on the most unexpected continents. But what about the individual performer, as it were, a human being borne of human being, who actualizes the system? No, there wasn't. There wasn't anyone in isolation. Since ancient times it has been the everlasting 'we': 'we, the Germans', 'we, the Aryans', even 'we, the heirs of Schiller and Kant!' Yes, yes, that same 'we' without which man's collectively made history would have been unthinkable, but here it has a minus sign to it. It is devoid of the awareness and the feeling that above all other kinds of 'we' are the most general and the most important, 'we, people!', 'we, human beings, mankind!' All other 'we's' serve this supreme 'we'; they don't, even the pride at being the 'fellow countrymen of Kant and Wagner', is tinning into savagery and barbarity. Such complacent 'cultural savagery' already appeared especially dangerous to Tolstoy. It leaves no room for thinking about one's close and distant neighbours and not doing to others what you would not wish done to yourself, for others are not 'we'. Their clothing, the colour of their skins, their customs, language, standards and conditions of living are quite different! Tolstoy cites the following example: cannibals despised their victims and regarded them as savages precisely because they only ate fruit and vegetables. For the very fact that they were not cannibals! Likewise, those who organised Oswiecim and Khatyn looked down on those they exterminated. I feel sure that our villages, being different from theirs with their tiled roofs, was one of the reasons why 'Khatyns' occured. To a rational person, the difference between nations, races and people is a cause for joyful surprise and reflection, but for a 'hairless ape' it is only a reason for despising and biting those who do not look like the Aryan ape it is."

"'A People chosen by itself,' this is what it says in 'Thus Spake Zarathustra'."

"This was particularly evident in their treatment of prisoners. First they reduced people to a terrible, almost inhuman state, by starving them and keeping them in the cold, and then some good-natured lout would drive them to the pits to shoot them and would perhaps sigh, 'No, no matter what you say, it's true, something about them makes them not like people at all!' The whole question, it seems, is that of whether man's ability to feel the pain and suffering of others is heightened by the given idea. Or is the most human of all abilities, that of being able to share another's pain, to be aware of it as if it were one's own and to sense it even more acutely is lessened and dulled. If the edge is taken off it, then it is a narcotic differing in no way from heroin, with which the members of the punitive squads in Vietnam lulled their consciences. Well, technology has helped. They want to install electronic monitors and set up a network of mechanical spying devices in the rice fields and on the forest paths. When something warm, something living passes by, a patch of light appears on the infrared screen at the distant air field, and immediately aircraft packed with death-bearing weapons take off. Not only is any sympathy lacking, but there is not even hatred any more either. What kind of feelings can a blob of light on the screen evoke?"

"There you are then, dear Flariyan Pyatrovich! What do we end up with? Formerly, for millions of years the 'we's' roamed around in herds on the cold plateaus, after leaving our blissful abodes in the trees; for some fifty thousand years 'we' have been rational beings, so to speak. But as soon as we became such, we rationally scattered to the most distant corners of the planet, as far as possible from the others who were for us no longer like ourselves. Then we discovered each other again, recognised each other and were pleased, at the same time colonising those who were weaker and simpler. Homo sapiens became more and more rational until he came upon nuclear power. And what of it? Aren't we going round the second spiral now? Isn't it the same reasonable reflex that is pushing us into and egging us on to scatter once again, but throughout the Milky Way now? No matter what you think, I'm in favour of that. Let's disperse now and get together some time later, eh?..."

"All the same, Albert Schweitzer was right when he said that his knowledge was pessimistic, but his hope and belief were optimistic."

...If I managed to crawl away from that field bathed in perfidious light, managed to get to the forest itself, and in the daytime to the "islands", it was probably that unbearable childish sense of injury that led me, that guided me out, those tears within me that I seemed to be bearing to someone. I brought them back to the "island", knowing how pleased they would be to see and expecting it, how they would hasten to welcome me and how I would tell them about everything. What would happen after that, somehow I had not even thought about it, not even tried to look into the future. And what was I bringing them besides the news that everyone had been killed and I alone was still alive? Everyone had perished in whom they had placed their hopes of not wasting away with hunger.

As I ran I ate whatever I happened to come across: sorrel, berries.

The same smell persisted in the forest near the first "island", but that was a sign that I was almost home. I fished around in the bushes. All the poles were in place. I even counted them a couple of times as if believing still that Skorokhod or Rubezh might have returned ahead of me. I had already reached the water's edge when someone called to me, "Are you back, lads?"

A woman sat there leaning against a marshland pine. Her legs were stretched out feebly but straight and on her knees lay a dirty bundle. The eyes in her exhausted, wizened face shone penetratingly. (I once heard a prisoner of war telling how he had been smitten by that *death* for the whole of six months, namely that of hunger, of dying of starvation). Those dying of starvation always have that inquiring, penetrating look in their eyes.

"Well, that's good, isn't it... You've come..."

She was too much out of breath to be pleased. The woman sighed deeply and pointed to her bundle, "I've been gathering sorrel... It's good that you..."

She looked around, her eyes seeking out the others, eager to see what we had brought her children. It was not until that moment that I realised what my return meant for the "island", what despair and hopelessness I was bringing with me.

"Yes, we're here... in a minute... yes," I muttered something, pointing behind me just as I had done that time in the woodland cemetery and retreating, drawing away from the woman and still holding my pole. I stumbled, fell and grinned (I'm falling over my own feet, see), but the woman's penetratingly burning eyes full of terror had taken a hold of me, kept me back and yet urged me on.

Already I was almost running after hurling my staff aside. I was returning. Where to and what for? I did not know the answer. All I knew was that as things were I had no right to appear on the "island" empty-handed. I could not. I just could not look, in the eyes of those women and children, not to mention the wounded. They all had that same look, suffering as they were from hunger, dying of starvation. They all had those same eyes and protruding lips. Once the first hope had faded, was lost in a flash, they had livened up to see me, I would have seen those eyes that I had deceived with my appearance.

Everything had fallen silent in our coach, except for a woman's monotonous, endless tale about a trip she had made to the south and with what fun and alarm they had escaped quarantine, and someone was uttering the name of the village or locality.

"Soon we'll be at Kozlovichsky Woods."

"And then we'll get to Rudnya."

"Yes, Rudnya."

Once again conversation gradually began to fill the coach, but about Perekhody now.

"They should have attacked in the village."

"Even I can be Napoleon after the event."

"I said it at the time."

"What's that?" Syarozha's voice tuned in. "Is it a cemetery?"

"That's Rudnya."

The coach braked slightly. The window of the driver's cabin made a shuffling noise and a young voice sounded, "Look over there! From afar it looks just like an ordinary village."

"It's just crosses and pillars, Dad," Syarozha told me softly, "instead of houses. And birch trees."

"Here everyone was exterminated," the driver explained, "just as in Khatyn."

"And no one was left at all?" Syarozha asked almost in a whisper, as if talking to himself. He probably told himself that that meant that he would not have been left either.

"That sort of thing doesn't even happen in dreams!" said the driver loudly and youthfully and pushed the window too.

I did not even have to close my eyes to dream it, to see what happened. I could see it anyway. With every passing year my eyes hurt more and more as if an unbearable light were concentrated on them. The light did not come from outside, but from inside, from my memory.

I was walking away, running away. It occurred to me that they might kill me, but the woman would tell everyone on the "island" that she had seen me. I was running away from the wounded, from the children! And Glasha was there. I could see it all before me, I kept on imagining that elderly man from whom I had heard the story in the detachment. There had been a blockade as well. At that time he had been living in a civilian camp, one for families. The members of the punitive squads had driven the inhabitants all over the forest, and he with a three-year-old girl. When the little girl got the "runs" from eating raw mushrooms and berries, the father, or grandfather came to a decision. He climbed a primitive ladder made of a tree trunks with pegs in that he had found near some empty hives and first lowered her legs into a deep, wide hollow in a maple tree and then pushed the rest of her in. The little girl cried when she lost sight of him. He asked her to show him her little hands. Her dirty little fingers moved in the hollow. He took hold of her hands and lifted her up to the opening of the hollow. "Well, can you see me now? That's how I'll pick you up when I come back. What shall I bring you? A little bit of bread. Well, there's my clever little girl!"

He climbed down to the ground and hid the ladder. He listened but the little girl kept obediently quiet. "Well, I'm off now, I'll be ever so quick!" and off he ran. Just like me, so as to return more swiftly. Suddenly the thought struck him as if he had walked into a wall, "If they kill me, she will stay there for two or three days, crying and dying of hunger and thirst!" He raced back. In his fright and anxiety he became lost. He kept banging himself on the tree-trunks like a blind man, weeping and calling. "I howled, chaps, like a wolf until I found that tree!"

They will kill me, and the woman will tell them how she saw me and how I ran away, how I fled.

The village that I finally arrived at slumbered in the chilly mist which spread across the meadow and through the kitchen gardens in patches like sheep in a flock. After a night when I had collapsed under a fir tree from hunger, partly in a fever and half asleep, there was something strange about me. I caught myself mumbling and humming and humming the Georgian song "Suliko", precisely that melody for some reason. I felt some kind of unnatural lightness, emptiness within me, as well as a careless forgetfulness. I headed straight for the village and it was not until later that I remembered to check whether my rifle was on my shoulder. I had no idea who was in that village. The village was quite whole. There were the roofs. Above the floating back and forth of the mist, the roofs looked like the bottoms of capsized boats. There was such a clear, fresh sky above everything and above myself. To the right, beyond the mist, the high embankment of the road showed up darkly. Was it perhaps that same gravel road that stretched here by which they had killed the Leningrader and Skorokhod? Half way to the village, in the midst of the meadow several young birch trees grew out of the gloom of the mist as if out of water. I walked straight towards them. My feet became caught up in the unmown hay which the rain was causing to turn brown. I stopped by the birches and looked around. It was a single birch tree, but with three trunks, like three bent, petrified movements. It made a comfortable seat for shepherds. But what was I thinking about. I raked the hay to one side with my foot and thrust my rifle under it. I had quite forgotten for the moment that I had another belt round me with cartridge pouches and a German bayonet on it. I burst out laughing maliciously. Well, come on now, sing "Suliko" again. I shoved the cartridge pouches and the bayonet under the hay and then I realised that I was wearing a German military jacket and my trousers were German as well. But the trousers had so much mud on them that you could not really tell what they were. I hid the jacket under the hay and was left in my grey shirt with white buttons which my mother had sewn on for me. I put the grenade in my trouser pocket. Well, that it seemed was all I had to do and now I could go on into the village. Or was there something else I had to do? "For a long time I wandered about and sighed..." Well, go on then, sing it then, you silly fool!

A sudden sound up ahead of me made me cautious. I did not move away from the rifle, trying to divine what those recurring knocks in the little hollow bathed in cold mist could signify. (It turned out that I had to learn to walk on earth again without a rifle.) The sounds were those country noises like knocking on wood, mutterings, shouts at horses. As if pushing myself off from the shore, I tore myself away from the spot where I had secreted the rifle and headed in that direction. First I saw the horse and cart. An elderly man, panting away, surfaced from a dense patch of mist, pushing along a heap of hay with a rake. He shot a glance at me and, as was usual at that time, looked around to see whether I was alone or whether there were others with me. The old codger was sweating. It was obvious that he was in a hurry and that he was nervous just as if he were stealing the hay.

"Good morning! Which village is this?" I uttered these words and was amazed how different my voice sounded when I was not carrying a weapon.

"Perekhody."

"Oh!" I acted as pleased as if I had been looking for it. "How nice and quiet it is here!"

"It's not quiet anywhere these days, is it? It's like sitting on hot coals. Some have taken to the forest, others elsewhere. They've already been here, they didn't touch anyone, they just seized the horses. And they shot three families from Bolshiye Borki who were living in shanties in the forest in hiding. They said they were bandits because they were in the forest and shot them. But where are you yourself from?"

I named a village far away.

"Did they burn your village down?" the elderly man asked immediately.

How strange that old fellow was with his eyes clear blue and sincere and timid like those of a child, but his bearded mouth kept stretching into a cunning grin.

I knew what his question meant, whether I had come from a village that had been razed to the ground. If they had set fire to my village and destroyed it, then for the villagers of Perekhody I was a dangerous person. The Germans sought out inhabitants who had survived or managed to get away, persecuted them like lepers and killed them wherever they might find them. In their eyes, these survivors were on a par with partisans and this was why it was dangerous for such a person to be caught in Perekhody. I understood what the elderly man had in mind and hastened to allay his fears, "No, everything's all right in our village."

I could see from that bearded mouth that he did not believe me.

"Aircraft set fire to us long ago," I corrected myself. "An aunt of mine lives here."

"Who's that?" the old fellow hurriedly tossed the hay onto the cart.

"Ganna... Ganna Perekhod..."

I just made a guess at a name. I knew that in some villages nearly everyone had the same name as the village. In Losi they were all Losis, in Nikitki all Nikitkas.

"Our village here is full of Perekhods," the elderly man agreed and, tidying up the hay in front of the horse's muzzle as it champed away, he ran back. His heels were black although they had been washed by the dew. "For a long time I wandered about and sighed..."

I set off for the village. Perekhods? In our detachment there were two or even more with that surname.

The sun was already rising beyond the forest. The mist had become lighter and acquired a pink hue. I did not like the gravel road creeping out of the mist from the right, becoming longer with every passing minute. When the elderly fellow said that they had come, he had waved his rakes in that direction. But the mist was as thick and dense as a forest. It stretched right up to the houses, and the roofs looked just as if they were floating on it. That made me feel easier. I did not have a bag with me so I would have to ask for one, in addition to the food. Like those cheeky smokers back at camp used to do, "give me a light... and a fag while you are at it!" But who was I without my rifle? Who would give me something and what would they give me? I was like some kind of beggar. I had not thought of that until then. But I was ready to beg for I could not return to the "island" with empty hands.

Some sort of noise shook the forest and faded. It shook it again. It was a monotonous noise, coming from afar. Was it perhaps a German plane? We had not seen any for a long time.

Still, I stopped and began to listen. No, there was nothing. It was far away in any case. There was so much dew that it squelched underfoot. I squatted down and, gathering its pure coolness in my palms, I wiped some of the dirt from my face. And, as if I had washed away, rubbed off something else, that strange, unconcerned nonchalance finally disappeared, I got rid of that sensation that everything that had happened was not real. I got up and looked around with a feeling that something had happened. But no, everything was just the same.

But then I saw the elderly fellow following me, that same bare-footed old chap with the rake and in a shirt worn outside his trousers. He was not walking but breaking into a run all the time. And he kept on looking round. Behind him rose a wall of pink mist, but now it was concealing something. I was not yet alarmed, but was already weighing up whether I should run and where I should take refuge.

Ahead of us, immersed in the mist, a shed without a roof was showing up darkly and murkily.

I cast a quick glance at the gravel pad. Just as before there was no one there, but suddenly. Further to the right, where the birch with its three trunks stood, where I had secreted my rifle, the mist had grown darker; it began to move apart and the floating figures of people began to take shape in it; they looked larger than life and had the same equally long heads. They wayed as they moved forward as if coming out of a dream, out of a nightmare....

I was already lying on the ground. But I jumped up and hurried over to the shed; the elderly fellow and I were going to the village, to our village. Fancy getting caught like that, no, stupid and unnecessary! I could have been in the forest at that moment, could have lingered and waited another half an hour in the forest, but there I was, and that was the end, and it could not be rectified. I was aware and I felt with the whole of my being that there was no escape, but still I eagerly sought that one last possibility, the chance that might save me yet. I headed for the shed. The old chap followed me. We were both looking round. The helmets, shoulders, and figures separated, broke away from the pinkish wall of mist. Now they were black and real enough. There were already a lot of them over there by the gravel road. The Germans were slowly moving towards the village in a long line.

I felt the grenade in my pocket. Should I throw it away or keep it? I was only supposed to be a villager from Perekhody, but a grenade made me a partisan. It meant death for me, but it was death at my disposal and not the one that would face me and calmly scrutinize me as much as it cared to before killing me....

Beyond the shed on a high mound there were some kind of boats, sinking or half submerged, with their sterns torn. Why were they there? Or was this in truth a dream, a nightmare, a delirium and I had to force myself to wake up. They were cellars, just cellars in the ground covered with a structure of boards nailed together. That was the place to hide! I rushed over to one of the rounded structures, but there was a lock on the door and on the next one as well. I pulled at it and the lock readily gave way. The door creaked perfidiously, allowing me into the darkness which smelt like a pit, reeking of mould. I took out the grenade, but immediately put it back in my pocket, trying to fathom out what I wanted to do. The grenade meant the end. Somewhere there must be, there still must be a last chance! I had to manage to slip out before they reached the cellar for they would hurl a grenade into it straightaway. I shot upwards just as hastily as I had plunged into the pit a minute before,

The elderly man had already caught me up and looked with white eyes, "Germans! Oh dear, we're for it now, we're in a right mess!"

Immediately we saw people running towards us out of the mist where the dark outlines of the village could be seen. In the distance, beyond the village a machine-gun pattered away resonantly for a long time. Those who were running towards us caught sight of the Germans coming from our direction, rushed back and forth, began to fall down and crawl and raced off back to the village.

Looking round wildly, the elderly man ran over to the cellar just as I had done a little while before. I pressed myself against the wall of the shed to have time to decide what to do. I could not get rid of a feeling that if I were to get away from the Germans for a moment, just to have them out of my sight, the situation would return to that when something could still be changed, when all this had not yet occurred. The fact that I had a grenade in my hand (I kept it in my pocket all the time) was speeding up and driving on what was happening to the last pale. I could not resist peeping out from round the corner. The faces under the helmets were distinguishable now, they were holding submachine-guns. Vehicles were creeping along the gravel road. Time was passing as if it were rolling down a steep slope towards the line of Germans, taking in and whisking away with it all the air, making it hard to breathe just as when you are running but no longer have the strength to do so.

Down at the bottom of the wall there was a hole where a log had rotted away. I fell on my knees and peered inside. I heard someone in a hurry behind me. The elderly fellow was running over to another cellar. I crawled into the shed. Over my head there was a long rectangle of blue sky without a single cloud in it. Several poles, the remains of the ceiling, lay by the wall itself. In the far corner stood a heap of notting black straw.

When the walls shut me off from what was happening it was just as if the sound had been switched on for the shouts and barking of the dogs became louder. I got out the grenade and watched, as if waiting to see what would happen to me next. I just had to climb up onto the poles. That would give me an instant more.

A man ran in through the wide open doors of the shed. It was that elderly fellow again. He glanced at me and the grenade widely. His eyes swept over the walls and around the corners. He hurled himself at that pitiful heap of straw and began to do something clumsily, raking up and sprinkling over himself the dusty rotted straw, which looked like smoke in the sun-rays and squeezing himself against the ground and the wall.

I clambered up on the poles. There were cracks in the wall wide enough to put your hand through. Once again I espied that approaching line of punitive expedition members, I made out several Alsatians racing forwards, straining at their leashes. I quickly lay down on the poles so that they would not notice me. Then I heard the village howling horribly like a captured animal. The voice of Germans, even abrupt commands, not like ordinary everyday real ones. I even heard someone laughing among the Germans.

My disobedient fingers had unscrewed the blue head of the grenade. My eyes perceived the white twisted cord being pulled out. Just one pull, and there would be an explosion. I squeezed the head and the cold body of the grenade so hard that it made my palms hurt.

The Germans were already right by us. Through the chink I could see two, one holding a machine-gun, running out of the line and stamping swiftly in the direction of the shed. No, towards the cellars. My hands felt as if they were clasped by handcuffs; the white silk core protruded from the body of the grenade about four centimetres. So, this was the joyless, compelled right that man had to die, to become free even if it was only in death itself! Death gripped me like handcuffs, but it was in my hands as well. That was the only thing that made me stronger than myself, trapped and helpless as I was before the imminent.

Cut off from what was happening by the endlessly depressing feeling of the closeness of death, as if seeing it through a glass partition, I watched the black and green members of the punitive squad running towards the cellars and the shed, the whole line of them encircling the village in the distance. An explosion thundered right close by, they had thrown a grenade into the cellar. Presently, someone would hear a similar explosion, that of my grenade.

I saw women running backwards and forwards across the kitchen gardens, falling down and jumping up again, crawling and dragging children. The German line was coming slowly and implacably towards the kitchen gardens, towards the village. A woman in a bright coloured cardigan, which seemed incongruously pink, ran over to the bath-house and, looking round on all sides, beckoned to her little ones. Two, no, three ran towards her, stumbling and helping one another up. The woman pushed them under a covering of blackened potato leaves. Once she had hidden them she herself ran away, fell down by the fence, but raised her head and, probably, said something to the children. From above I could easily see her bright pink cardigan.

Howling noises kept resounding over the village, but I could not see where they were coming from, it seemed as if people were doing everything in dead silence, without uttering a word, as if the sounds were separated from them hovering over everything and everyone....

An old man in linen trousers, which looked pure white from a distance and a shirt was walking down the straight village street, slowly, even ceremoniously, as if on his way to church. All around him people were racing back and forth, but he kept walking as if there was still somewhere for him to go.

But then it all disappeared, only those close footsteps could be heard and voices rebounding off the wall of the shed. They were coming this way.

"Mister, heir, mister," said the dutiful voice of someone running ahead, "We must look in the cellars. They went in there."

"What's it to you where they went?" came another morose voice. "They'll give us orders where to go, don't you worry."

"I'm not worried, but you always know what's best."

They were going to enter any moment now. There was nothing more frightening than waiting for people to enter through a door or gate. That was going to happen right now, I pressed myself against the poles, glanced at my hands with a white cord wound round them and felt how enlarged my body was, how noticeable from everywhere. They were sure to notice it as soon as they walked in and would immediately splatter it with machine-gun fire. And I would not have time to. I did not manage to figure out what I would not have time to do. Perhaps I was afraid that I would not have time to die, to kill myself with my own grenade.

It turns out that if a person is capable of getting used to the idea of a certain type of death, then he is only prepared to die that definite death. If something changes, then he is completely at a loss. (I remember a woman in the rail car told us that when the Nazis had killed everyone in the village and walked over to the shed where her family was hiding, people were prepared to be burnt to death in the bay rather than come out to face their killers and be shot. They stayed there in the smoke and the heat rather than die by the bullet. Finally, the woman alone could not bear it any longer and tore out through the smoke, but her husband and sisters were burnt to death, kept back there by their fear of another death, although it was a less agonizing one).

Now they would hit me from below and I would not have time to rip out the cord, and the grenade would not have time to explode while I was still alive.

"Aha, there's some here!"

The voice was cheerful and amused and this restrained my hands, gave me time to recall, to realise that I was not the only one hiding in the shed. Keeping my head down, I watched two men in the black uniforms of the polizei heading for the corner of the shed. The elderly man jumped up, covered in rotted straw. A smoke-like pillar of sunlight in which the dust played turned white. He stood up before them.

"You should have hidden yourself better, shouldn't you, old chap?" the cheerful voice of the polizei man rang out. (He was probably the one who had shouted to the German about the cellars).

"I'm not going anywhere," shouted the fellow.

"Come on now, let's check your pass and then home you go, old boy. There's going to be a meeting."

"I'm not going anywhere. We know what those meetings mean."

"Oh you, bandit's mug!" the cheerful man was becoming angry.

"Just kill me here, I'm not going."

"So, you don't want to go in a civilised manner?"

Blows and groans followed. There were only two of them grappled there. The sullen polizei man was calmly observing the scene as if it were nothing to do with him. The elderly fellow flew into the middle of the shed, then as if being dragged, he rushed back and clung to the wall, pushing his fingers, and palms through a chink between the logs.

"Just kill me here, I'm not going into the fire!"

"What fire, you bandit! And you there, what are you standing there for watching? Come on, help me!"

"Don't be obstinate, Grandpa," drawled the voice of the second polizei man, "They're just going to check you and that's all."

"You go into the fire yourself!"

There were sounds of a rifle butt striking a log and something living at the same time. The cries were almost like those of a child. I probably moved because the morose polizei man immediately said, surprised, "Oh-ho, there's another one! Come on, climb down now, jump down!"

He leveled his rifle at me. I moved a little, raised my backside, indicating with my body that I was not intending to do anything, that I was doing as I had been told. But all the while I was looking at the grenade, at white cord in its opening. I felt a faint, summoning resistance to death on the end of the taut cord hidden in the grenade. Now I was infinite, like a never ending sigh. It was painful to burst your chest, but that deep breath kept lasting, I kept lasting, becoming huger and huger, and thinner and thinner, weightless like a balloon. Suddenly something happened down below, and the cheerful polizei man and the elderly fellow flew out of the door.

"Well, how long do I have to wait?" the remaining polizei man asked. I raised myself onto my knees, keeping my hand with the grenade in it resting on the poles. I moved towards the wall, giving the appearance of climbing down. There was another explosion somewhere outside.

"They've chucked a grenade into the cellar," I told the polizei man.

"How much longer do I have to wait?"

I was no longer the person who was just going to blow myself up a minute ago. Something had changed and a cunning person had arrived in the world, with a silly smile as well. He was crawling along, holding onto and hiding the grenade, and I was watching him and the polizei man as well, waiting to see what I will do. The I that was waiting and observing, was amazingly calm, as if all this was happening to someone else.

"Jump down now!" The polizei man had an inkling that something was wrong. His voice was startled, betraying alarm. I got up hurriedly and submissively turned my back to his rifle and, without looking, I pulled out the chord as if ripping it out of myself. The click in the round body of the grenade seemed deafeningly loud. "Dead men don't get toothache!" It seemed as if someone else was for some reason counting out the seconds aloud, reiterating the words of my friend Fedka, and he, that sly, malicious, deft person did not wait to finish the count, but raced outside to my surprise as if throwing himself overboard, leaving the grenade to fall on the polizei man in the shed.

Pain surged through me from the ground, the explosion and the darkness. The well of the shed breathed smoky stench at me, which got into my eyes, screwed up with pain, and my nose. I jumped up with a dislocated or fractured shoulder to run anywhere, to anyone, just to get away as far as possible from what I had done.

"Halt! Komm her!"

The pain in my shoulder subsided, my eyes had not suffered. The German was standing by the cellar, pointing his submachine-gun at me. I walked towards him, even quickened my pace so as to get as far from the shed as I could. Two Germans were semi-recumbent by a machine-gun mounted on a tail bipod.

Another two were standing over some old woman. She lay with her face to the ground waiting with her skinny, angular shoulder blades for a shot to be fired, but the Germans just stood there smoking. They found it amusing that all they were doing was smoking and smiling and a person was getting ready to die!

"Nach Haus, Ma," a German with thick-lensed glasses that looked as if they were beaming, touched her with his submachine-gun.

I was relieved to note that no one was bothered about my explosion. Now another German would throw a grenade in the cellar. He hurled it in and sank down below the sand-covered roof of boards. "My" German had lowered his submachine-gun and was awaiting the next explosion. Afterwards, he headed towards the spot where the old woman was lying. He indicated that I should walk over there, too.

I had immediately ceased to be a partisan who had thrown a grenade and killed a member of the polizei. Now it was a country lad in need of a haircut, wearing dirty boots and a grey shirt over his trousers. Only his trousers were made of Italian, yes, yes, some kind of yellow cloth, not German, simply out of a blanket. It was evident that scouts had swindled me, the trousers were made of a blanket and there was nothing German or soldier's about them at all!

"Mutter?" The German pointed at the old woman. The thin country lad smiled wanly, his mouth wide open (for the first time I liked my stupid smile) and touched the old woman's shoulder.

"Let's go, don't be afraid."

The old Woman hastily rose to her knifes, looking but seeing nothing, her lips moving ever so quickly.

"Weg! Nach Haus! (Be off! Go home!)," The German with those beaming glasses pointed in the direction of the village, I helped the woman to get up, and we hurried away, making for the kitchen gardens.

The first line of the punitive squads was already ahead of us, moving more slowly near the sheds. The second line where there were fewer people, was driving us on. A German and a polizei man were heading towards us from it. The polizei man was obviously an urban policeman decked out in a black uniform with wide grey cuffs and matching collar. Both the German and the polizei man were smug young men and looked very much alike, although the German's head was covered with the steel cap of his helmet, and that of the polizei man with a black forage cap.

They shoved me and the old woman and explained in turns who we were and why we had to be chased.

"Schnell, schnell, Rus!"

"Come on, get going! Stalinist, bandits!"

The young German walked in such a way that he could keep an eye on the polizei man as well.

"Schwein! (Swine!)"

"Bandits!"

These were not simply swear-words. These swear-words embodied the whole of their conviction, their explanation of what was happening and what they were involved in. Weapons must be rapid firing, ideas briefly formulated, so that one would catch up with the other.

"Schwein... schnell... Stalinist... russkies... bandits... schnell... get moving... schnell, schnell! Get moving, come on now!...

It is strange that all the time they were driving me along, while I was walking to the village, I remembered the shed and the phlegmatic polizei man on whom I had thrown the grenade. At first I was scared that they would find him. But another feeling, one I was already familiar with, flared up to replace this one. Once we fired on some German cyclists from a sparse pine grove right near a town. The wheel still kept spinning round, glittering in the sunlight, over the body of the soldier I had knocked off his bike, and we had already jumped to our feet to run away. Germans in cars unexpectedly appeared. We were stunned, pursued closely by dum-dum bullets, the Germans were already surrounding us, and there was dry, quick sand like flour underfoot. You could not run, but were helplessly jogging along in one place. What is more important is that it suddenly ceased to matter; you became unquestioningly indifferent to yourself. The fact that I had killed someone a few minutes before was responsible for that in part, simplifying everything, my own death included.

The first line of the punitive squads had already reached the kitchen gardens. Suddenly they hastened their pace and shouted. German commands, the shouts of the polizei men, the howling of dogs, the cries and weeping of women and children swept through the village like flames. The executioners looked in every doorway, every pit, overturning the heaps of corn that were all over the kitchen gardens. Once again I caught sight of the woman in the pink cardigan about whom I had already forgotten. She kneeled up near the fence, showing herself when the German went over to the bath-house and began to root around in the hanging potato tops with the barrel of his rifle. When the German saw the woman getting up off the ground, he went straight towards her. But a second German (neither in a helmet nor a forage cap, but wearing a green cap with a very long peak) walked up the bath-house and flung the pole with the potato leaves on it down on the ground. The children, two of them older, were kneeling, pressing their faces up against the wall and covering their eyes with their hands, but a boy of about three years was staring at the man with the strange peak surprised and puzzled as if he had just woken up.

The woman gave an inhuman cry and crawled and then ran over to the bath-house.

"Schwein! (Swine!)" The young German with the submachine-gun shoved me.

"Bandits!" stumbling, the polizei man explained to himself and to me, and also gave me a shove.

The shouts, weeping and howling which had flared up in that instant, raced through the village like a fire and did not cease throughout that day, right up until that very last moment. They pushed us out into the village street—the old woman and me and the woman in the pink cardigan who did not have enough arms to gather up and press to her little ones. Just as the weeping and cries had been sparked off in that instant and did not stop, that crazy drive, that chase started at that very moment. They pushed us out into the street along which they were already driving people, people were already rushing back and forth, and more and more women and children and men were being pulled out of the cottages and courtyards, thrust through the gates and hurled into the street. They kept driving them forward to somewhere at the end of the village. They herded the swelling crowd amidst cries, wheezing sounds, blows of rifle butts and the snarling and menacing rushes of the Alsatians. At first, the procession advanced slowly, only in its midst was there continual movement like the shouting and the weeping, bustling, rushing hither and thither, leaping away in fright from the dogs on leashes with which the punitive squads rushed the crowd so that the animals bit the people. But the commands, shouts, blows, bounding of the dogs, the howling and the sound of people weeping became more and more abrupt and the growing crowd was moving along faster and faster to something ultimate that was waiting for it at the end of the street. And the more rapid and insane the run became, the crueler the executioners became, the more frequently they pushed, struck, yelled, and growled.

The red, sweaty mugs of the executioners looked more and more aggrieved, their physiognomies betraying suffering, agony, and a sense of insult. For we were such slow-witted and undisciplined people. We were making no effort to comprehend what they wanted of us, screaming and resisting, not desiring to have our *ausweise* (passes) checked, to have our documents examined, not believing in something quite ordinary and necessary.

The members of the punitive squads especially loosed their sticks and their dogs on children. When a boy of about ten slipped his mother's hand and flung himself into the wheat field, the German groaned with irritation and set the Alsatian on him. The woman raced after them, and another German flew at her. Oh, how furious he was, how aggrieved at the lack of order, and what a look of suffering he had on his mug.

Once again I spotted the old man in white whom I had espied earlier from the shed. He had already managed to walk right through the village and now stood as if waiting for us by something black, attached to the wall of a collective farm barn. By this big black piece of rag, not a local one, not from the village, which was some kind of ominous sign for the executioners, people were gathered who had been driven in here earlier. (It was not until later when I thought back on it that I understood why the old man in white had stood by the panel and held his head like that; he was blind).

Germans in officers' service caps were crowding round to one side of the barn, and there vehicles and motor cycles standing there. Two mounted machine-guns were pointed at the barn.

A corridor of Alsatians and punitive squads was awaiting us at the open gates. Two rows of people with Alsatians were standing there in a calm business-like manner as if what they were doing was the most simple and understandable occupation in life. All this (as well as the red board on the opposite wall of the barn) I discerned later, many days after, when I turned everything over and over again in my inflamed memory.

But at that moment I only had the sensation that they were pushing us, me, off a cliff to our deaths and I was clinging on with my hands and legs and my stomach, refusing to give up and not wishing to believe that this was the end, but simultaneously realising to the point of terror that this was inevitably going to happen. I might have been, could have been somewhere quite different now. But is it possible that there is something else on Earth, when this is happening here?

The living, writhing file of the punitive squads and their Alsatians began to swallow up the crowd and push them into the dark void beyond the open doors in lots of five and ten people. Someone indistinguishable among those who were shoving and beating us in the back, on the head, shouted, "Get your documents ready, your passports, birth certificates, school certificates, get your documents ready!.."

But no one was examining any documents or asking for them. Probably the plan, the scenario for the horrific spectacle, had been changed by someone's order in the course of the operation, and the crier was already playing a part that was no longer needed.

"Get your certificates ready!.."

The moving file of SS-men and dogs which bulged and closed in on us swallowed up more and more groups of people, tearing them away from the surrounding crowd, which was squashed on all sides, and pushing them on into the gaping depths of the shed. The faces, the mugs of those who were jostling us, flinging us along, striking and stinging, bore an infuriated, maliciously insensitive expression, and yet looked offended. We were behaving so badly, so stupidly, not wanting to understand what they wanted of us, were demanding of us. We were deafening them with the screams of the women, the crying and whining of the children, we were so difficult to deal with, and all we had to do was to go into the shed and have our passports and birth certificates ready.

Two members of the punitive squads set the dogs on a tall young man who was bracing himself against the door post with both hands, preventing people from entering the gates. The dogs' leads had been let out too long and at first they went for him, but finding that they had enough leash, they unexpectedly sank their teeth into one another....

They had already shot the man and dragged him over to the barn wall, and were packing the crowd together more and more closely, but the file of SS-men wound round even tighter so that they could no longer pull the dogs apart. With their teeth at each other's throats, the dogs became still, bracing their strong legs. They were pushing and kicking them and dragging them apart. Other members of the punitive squads were pulling along and thrusting us towards the gates....

A person is ugly when they kill him! You can always read that in the offended faces of the executioners. How I remember those physiognomies and the vengeful feeling of the person who is being killed: it serves you right, you thugs, that's what you deserve! I evade them, bite them, squeal repulsively, am prepared to release a polecat's stench in those mugs on which the executioner's sense of offense flickers.

I was once struck by a photograph in the Partisan Museum in Belgrade. It is probably still there. You start walking towards it from a distance, and hardly have you glanced at it you seem to be drawn by its light. What an amazingly beautiful smile! But when you get right up to it, you see that there is a noose round the neck of the happily smiling youth. And behind him stands a Nazi preparing to knock away the support from under his feet. At whom is he smiling that young man with a white turned-down collar round his clean, slim neck, and such an open student's face? For whom is that smile? To spite the executioners? But there is not a shadow of challenge, of scorn, no tension at all! It is as if his bride is standing before him and not his executioner. If it were not for the business-like figure in the uniform behind the youth, one might decide that these were students simply amusing themselves in an amateur performance, acting out an execution in a youthfully frivolous and cheerful manner, in something that could not possibly take place, and the person to be executed was seeing around him the smiling faces of his friends, and not the mugs of killers....

For whom is that human smile? Is it for the last people whom he sees? For there will be no others, no better ones whom he shall want to see even more. Never again. Still, these are the last ones....

No, no, I could not agree with that. Nor could I go away from the smiling partisan. I finally understood. The man had noticed the eye of the camera and through it has been able to look behind his killers, at friends, at his fiancée perhaps. He could see the people whom he was leaving alive in his place. The executioners themselves had offered him that opportunity....

It was only the executioners that we could see, only them who wanted to drive us into the barn so that it was easier to make a single torch of us, turn us into corpses as soon as possible so that we presented no danger to them, were quiet and disciplined. I rushed back and forth with everyone else along the wall of dogs' muzzles and executioners' mugs; I was furious, helpless, irritated, dirty, ready to stuff their traps and eyes, which looked hurt and enraged, full of something foul-smelling.

Once when I was a student, I saw a group of people in a book bound and ensnared by serpents; it was Laocoon. (My memory keeps drifting away from the barn, even my memory cannot linger there long!) The serpents wreathed themselves round human arms and legs, tense with chilling horror, and the faces and heads were thrown back. The desk at which I was sitting seemed to tip over, the windows went crooked and I hardly managed to get to the rubbish bin before I vomited. The other students in my year found it funny that Gaishun reacted to art like that. It was just that I saw something I had already witnessed before but not in a reproduction. That happened when I was with the partisans, right at beginning. The Germans and members of Vlasov's band had caught one of our scouts, and afterwards we went to bury his body which had been left at the cemetery. The partisan had fired at the Germans for a long time from behind the stones and fences, but they still managed to capture him alive. Horrible dark-blue plaits from the man's own innards were twisted round his arms and neck. And looking at the dead man you could see how he had torn at them in his blind terror and pain....

Squeezed, bound and ensnared by the snake-like files of soldiers and Alsatians, the crowd writhed in horror, despair and fury, while at the side the implausibly calm figures of the officers in their tall service caps stood stock-still. I noticed them and then I saw them again from the little window of the shed. That impossible, frosty, fixed calm had its own centre, and it was he—my main enemy.

But it was not till later that I discerned him, and picked him out.

All the same, when they had pushed and thrust the people into the shed, and the howling darkness had swallowed us up, I found myself right by the door. They closed it and nailed it to with dull thuds like one hears at the cemetery when coffins are sealed. With the obstinacy of a mad man I began to look for a way of being saved, a last chance. That was something of a partisan habit in me. But I was part of the screaming, the tearing around, the rushing back and forth under the roof of the shed lined and cut by narrow strips of sunlight. (Which meant that on that day, even during those very hours and minutes, the sun was shining brightly and all around.)

The strips of sunshine, the columns of light falling from above, were hazy with dust. Children's cries resounded in all corners of the barn: "Mummy, look, smoke!"

"Oh, they've set fire to us!"

"Mummy, will it hurt, Mummy, will it hurt me?"

In that fearful crowd I already imagined the pleading eyes and the tiny faces of my little twin sisters. All the faces, all the eyes of the children here had that same expression. I was already looking for my mother and afraid I might recognise her (I began to imagine that this was happening in the barn where they were burned to death). She would see that I was here, that her son was here as well.

Most of all the light from outside poured in near the door through two little window-like holes cut high up in the wall. They attracted people towards them, so it was especially crowded there. One man could not bear it any longer, pulled himself up by his arms and peeked out. Immediately his head was given a sharp shove, and the man fell on us. (There was such a racket in the barn that we had not heard the machine-gun fire). The bands of sunlight on people's faces and shoulders were immediately stained with blood. It splashed me on the forehead, all sticky and warm. But we were so lightly packed together that I could not raise my hand to wipe it away.

Then I saw how the grooves between the logs and the hoards of the doors had become wet and black, and a pungent smell of petrol filled the air.

Laocoon with his many arms, his many heads, and his many voices and huge women's and children's eyes writhed and tore himself away in the semi-darkness, and I was a part of that picture, too.

Somewhere there was a field, tranquillity, humming with the chirring of the crickets, a road across the field, and a man calmly going somewhere.

Suddenly the little window above us was covered up from the outside. Someone's eyes were watching us from under the long peak of a cap, as if they were looking for something. All silenced down a bit. And only the children's sobbing persisted, like the little streams left after the breakers.

"Come out without the children," said someone speaking with an accent. "You can come out. Those without children. Over here, through the window. The children must stay behind."

It became quiet, but in that quietness the world moved from the spot where it had stopped, probably like the planet's axis had imperceptibly shifted and become inclined before the Ice Age. The women were the first to realise and to understand what this meant. I had not heard such a human moan throughout the whole of that terrible day. No, I had not heard such silence. People became silent as if taking full stock of what was about to happen. Before that last pale, that final minute something had still bound them for they were the people in the nailed-up barn and the others were those outside its walls. Just people and people. Now there was no one to appeal to. For almost a quarter of a century that mute human moan would not fade away and above it all there resounded a bewildered, unbearably monotonous voice: "Sonny, my little boy, what have you put those rubber boots on for? Your legs will take a long time to burn in rubber boots."

It was not until then that I realised what people were doing, hastily in that mute outcry: they were undressing themselves and their children, tearing off the clothes as if they were already smouldering on them....

But someone had already stretched up to the little window which was now free and had looked out. They gave him a push up and helped him. The man turned his face and his head away from the light as if it were intolerable heat, awaiting the round of machine-gun fire. He could not bear it any longer, wriggled his legs and climbed down. Then I indicated that I wanted to pull myself up, and someone's hands and shoulders eagerly lifted me. First I saw the vehicles and those who were farther away from the barn, the officers. In front of the barn soldiers stood in a semicircle, their helmets pulled down over their eyes, their submachine-guns at the ready. I was being lifted up and not my face, but my knees and legs were on a level with the small window. I pushed one leg through the hole, saddled the wall, bent my head down and squeezed a shoulder through. I saw the green grass below me and the straw scattered along the walls. Practically shoved out, I fell in a heap on the ground, and the pain shot through my dislocated shoulder again. They seized me and hurled me away from the barn as maliciously and abruptly as they had flung me in through the door before that. They shoved me and pushed me until I found myself right near the vehicles.

Then I saw him close up, my main enemy. He was bald with a shaven, shiny head (among the officers he alone did not have his head covered), wore gold-rimmed spectacles and was observing everything as if from the side-lines; he looked like a doctor or an official attired in military uniform.

I possibly began to stare at him immediately because a little monkey with round white patches round its eyes and a fat tail, long like that of a rat, was fidgeting and pulling faces on his shoulder. He picked it up affectionately and stroked it. Our eyes met, mine, his, and the monkey's. He examined me curiously (so it seemed to me), while the monkey had an empty, sorrowful look.

That same young polizei who had driven me to the village was standing by me. I did not recognise him straightaway for his face looked wan and pale, not like it did before. Evidently, the narcotic effect of those nice little ideas about "Stalinist bandits" was no longer working. It was probably the first time that he had seen such a thing and had been involved in it.

People were already elbowing their way through the holes of the small windows; a man was stuck in one, hanging there, jerking his leg up and down, unable to pull his head and shoulder through; the distorted face of a woman appeared and disappeared in the second hole. Then a child's head appeared, followed by the woman's face again, questioning and hesitant, twisted with torment, fearfully, dumbly crying out. But then a girl, almost a little girl, appeared at the hole. Her slender arms, legs and head were sticking out. Bare and defenceless as they were, it seemed to me that they were crying out. She tumbled down onto the straw, but immediately sprang up to catch a child that had been pushed out and was being handed to her by four or more hands simultaneously. Straightaway, as if something intolerable for them had happened, the officers' military caps flinched in protest, the whole line of soldiers and Alsatians heaved in indignation. Two or three of them carrying submachine-guns rushed over to the girl and began to pull her away from the child and the child away from her. The barn echoed horribly with screams, rising to the heavens. It was only then that I began to tremble, tremendous cold shivers running clown my spine. The young polizei who had driven me to the village was trembling as well. But over there where my main foe stood, once again all was motionless or just smooth gestures; there was a lack of haste that was emphasised by the frenzied antics of the white-eyed monkey, as it jumped from shoulder to shoulder, peeping out either from behind a cap or from behind the shaven head. The girl and the child were torn apart into two screaming bodies and one of them, the smaller one, now without a stitch of clothing, quite naked, they began to poke back into the hole. They hurled the girl over to the vehicles. She ran as far as the well where they were standing guard over me. No one has ever seen eyes like those of that girl, like those of an old, old woman, when she ran towards us as if begging for help. When she reached us, she fell face down and did not rise.

The man with the monkey cast his curious glance at the girl; he did, apparently, understand everything and those surrounding him understood everything. Only the monkey with its doleful eyes wide-open had a perplexed human expression on its black and white furry little muzzle. Those who threw themselves out of the window were herded over to the vehicles, to the well. Our numbers swelled, and the fewer people there remained in the barn, the more unbearable and the louder their screams and howls became.

A little boy tumbled out and got up, frightened. People in helmets rushed over to him and seized him. They held both his arms stretched open wide and looked at the bald officer with the monkey. He lingered for a moment, but waved towards the well, permitting the boy not to be regarded as a child. An old woman was already squeezing herself through the hole, awkwardly and taking a long time, her face dark with wrinkles betrayed terror and bewilderment.

Something was happening that was clear to the people in the caps, the people in the helmets and especially the shaven-headed man. He watched what was taking place calmly, studying it, but he himself was more interested in the monkey, waiting for it to return to him from someone else's shoulder, to stroke it and pull its tail.

Another boy was thrown out through the hole. This time the shaven-headed man winced as if something unpleasant had been done to him personally. Immediately the people with Alsatians set up a howl and an officer ran over to them. The boy tore himself away from the hands of the soldiers, who were trying to catch him, but they did not carry him, they threw him back to the window-like hole, dropping him on the ground, but not letting him go. A woman, probably his mother, was hastening to climb out. She was being pushed through the hole, but she herself was looking for the boy, where he was and what had happened to him. But they had already dragged him to the other little window and were cramming him back into the barn. The woman wanted to get back into the barn as well, but helping hands ejected her. She toppled to the ground while the boy had already disappeared into the black hole. The woman jumped up and ran over to the hole, dark, huge with terror and agony as it was. They seized her, dragged her along and shot her. Then they flung her on the straw against the wall.

With an expression of displeasure and disgust on his face, the shaven-headed man headed towards the open-topped car. Now I saw his back, round-shouldered with age, across which a long thick tail was moving back and forth like a pendulum.

This was the sign to end things. A young officer ran over to the barn. The Germans lying by the machine-gun made ready and the line punitive squads withdrew from the barn walls. Like a scream the flame leapt up from the straw, along the wall. It hurt the eyes just as it had that time on the "island". I kept looking: how they threw the children out of the little windows and how they fell right on the burning straw....

Iosif Iosifovich Kaminsky (village of Khatyn, Logoi district, Minsk region):

And they drove me into that barn. My daughter, my son and my woman were already there. There were so many people there. I said to my daughter, "Why aren't you dressed?" "They tore the clothes off u s , " s h e said, "They ripped the fur coat off my shoulders, undressed us..." Well, they herded us into the barn and shut it up, herded more and more in and dosed it each time. They had driven so many people in there that you could no longer breathe freely and you could not even raise your arms. People were screaming like children. It was natural when there were so many souls and they were so terrified. Hay and straw lay there as fodder for the cows that were still kept. They set light to it at the top, set fire to the top. The roof was burning, and the fire was falling on people. The hay and straw caught fire, it became stifling and people were suffocating. As people were squeezed together, they could no longer breathe. No way. I told my son, "Press your legs and arms against the wall, keep yourself strained!..." Then the doors opened. The doors were flung open, but people did not go out, they did not run out. Why not? They said that they were shooting them down in the doorway. There was such a din that the firing and the tapping were not audible. Of

*course, when people were being burned, when the fire
was falling onto their heads and those of the children
there should be such a screaming. I told my son, "Over
the heads somehow, get out over the heads!" I hoisted
him up. I myself made my way down below, between
the legs. And the dead kept falling on me. The dead were
collapsing onto me, I could not breathe. Moving my
shoulders—I was physically robust at the time—I began
to crawl. Only as far as the threshold, then the roof fell
in and the fire engulfed everyone!... I still crawled out,
and a German ran over to me and smacked me in the
teeth with his rifle butt—and gone were my teeth. My
son also managed to run out. He only had some slight
burns on his head, and his hair was frizzled. He ran some
five metres and they mowed him down with a machine-
gun.... Mowed him down.... Our neighbour had also run
out of the fire and had fallen on top of me. He sat there,
burning like a tree-stump, all red, his blood spurting out
all over me.... "Save me," he cried, "save me!" Then the
Germans drove off. I started to drag my son away, but as
I pulled him along his innards trailed behind him.... He
just managed to ask whether his Mum and sister were
still alive.... God forbid that anyone who lives on Earth
should see and hear such grief....*

*Avdotya Ivanovna Gritsevich (village of
Kopatsevichi, Soligorsk district, Minsk region):*

*I hid behind a plank-bed under a heap of bast in the
loft. The staircase creaked—they were coming up. I could
hear somebody breathing heavily, here, right next to me.
Footsteps—he was going to the plank-bed. I opened my
eyes and he was looking at me; we were looking at each
other. Then another one came up the stairs. He took a
wreathe of bast and placed it over my face, covered me
up....*

Ales Adamovich

Yakov Sergeyevich Strynatko (village of Shalayevka, Kirov district, Mogilev region):

It happened in the summer of forty-two. Not a lot was heard about the partisans in our parts at that time. There were polizeis here in Borκi. Suddenly the Germans surrounded Borκi. They did not leave those they came across in the fields or among the bushes, but drove them before them into the village. I was going to Borκi because I had been promised to be sold some barley. I hail from Shalayevka which is five kilometres away. The devil himself must have been responsible for getting me mixed up in that. I wanted to turn back, but they did not allow me to. They did not beat me up, I have to admit that. They just indicated that I should continue on to Borκi. Then I whipped my horse on and turned off into the courtyard where my acquaintances lived. They had also seen the Germans closing in from all sides, but they did not know why. Grandfather was criticising the lads from Borκi for going to visit girls in other villages at nights. 'All they've got on their minds is girls and parties, but the Germans think they're going to the partisans!' The owner of the house and I went out into the yard and began to saw up some firewood. You do not feel so anxious when you are doing something. His wife could not bear it, she wanted to call on the neighbours, but the Germans would not let her, 'Nach Haus, woman.' It is quite true though that they did not touch anybody in the street or kill anyone. They just sent people home, 'Nach Haus'. Our neighbours daughter and her friend could not bear it: they went out into the street but Were driven into someone else's home, We were sitting in the home, looking out of the window. 'Don't let's worry, let's have a bite to eat'. "When they go away, then you can have a drink," said his wife. Soon there came banging sounds in the yard'. One entered holding a submachine-gun, followed by others and immediately hurled the owners wife off the threshold and riddled her with a machine-gun burst straightaway, I jumped up from the table and sat on the bed, I remained sitting there, only my vision was blurred and a humming filled my head. The owner of the house stood up front the table and they got him, too. I managed to see them pushing the old man out of a room at the side. That was when they let me have it and I collapsed on the bed. When I came round the grandfather was lying dead right on the threshold....

Anna Nikitichna Sinitsa (village of Borki, Kirov district, Mogilev region):

They entered the house and without a word they shot at Mum. Before that we had heard the noise of guns as they shot at the neighbours. At that time, Mum had told us they were shooting chickens. It did not even occur to us, but we were afraid to go out into the street. If anyone did, they asked them to go home (Nach Haus, woman). When they fired at Mum, she managed to run into our room, shouting, "Children!" I immediately flew up onto the stove, and the girls followed me. I was right by the wall, that is why I survived. One of them stood on the bed so as to be higher up and shot with a rifle. He fired once, then loaded it, then again. My little sister lay right on the edge and I had friends on top of me, our neighbours. I heard how they killed them. The blood was dripping down onto me. "Oh, Mummy, Mummy!" but I way stained with blood. Then I heard them talking and laughing. We had a small gramophone and they began playing it and listening to our records. They played it for a time and left. I crawled out from the stove, that red, red stove. Mum was lying on the floor. Through the window I saw the village burning. Our house was burning and the school as well....

Ales Adamovich

Maria Fyodorovna Kot (village of Bolshiye Prusy, Kopyl district, Minsk region):

They surrounded our village in the morning. We gathered in an adobe house, about twenty of us, neighbours. We could hear that they were already coming.... How they shot at the doors and the windows. My youngest daughter cried. "Oh, Mummy!" I glanced down: she had been hit in the bridge of the nose. She just snorted. My elder daughter was already sixteen. I was lying there with my children. They had killed us, and yet I still had an inkling of how they were finishing up the neighbours behind the stove. I opened my eyes. A woman was kissing his left hand, stopping him from moving the bed for that was where the children were hidden, and he was hitting her on the head with a revolver. They kept on pushing those children zealously with the bed and, oh my God, how they squealed. Another one saw that I was watching and ran over to me and fired at me. I can still see. That dark blue revolver, as blue as blue can be, and the fire in my face, right in my face. He pulled me away by my legs from my children. But I was still alive. I heard them walking about again. I thought it was those Germans again. But it was my son. Zhora, spattered with blood and unable to see anything, walking towards the threshold. "Oh my boy!" He said, "Mum, I thought you were no longer with us. I wanted to go and get killed." "Lie down, son, in this very place. Perhaps it's a lucky one." I do not know whether they heard or not, but one came running in: "Get up!" He stood there for a moment. Then he threw a grenade under the stove. Smoke came billowing out for the adobe house was already on fire. They had doused it with something. The ceiling was burning overhead. They hadn't slaughtered us yet. It was even more bitter if we were to be burned alive. I jumped up. The bed was standing by the window.

I knocked out the frame and called to Zhora, "Help me carry them out." I lifted the elder one, so young and so soft!... I could not do it for she was heavy and my hands had gone dead, but I did not want them to burn as well. Somehow I dragged them onto the bed, onto the window, and Zhora and I tumbled out, and pulled them along to the potato pit. The whole of the village was on fire, people were being dragged along from all over the place, whining and screaming, but the Germans were just walking across the kitchen gardens, whistling, and here the pigs were grunting noisily around their charred owners.... They came closer and closer with their whistling and squelching. I was already sorry that they had not killed us there; they would find us and torture us again and we would scream and whine....

Tatiyana Fyodorovna Kravchonok (village of Britsalovichi, Osipovichi district, Mogilev region);

It happened after Stalingrad. I remember because my brother came from the forest, to see us, and was rejoicing about the victory. He said that the Germans would be infuriated now. The next day a commander came and advised us that if we got wind of the Germans being around, we should hide in the forest. Then he asked us to give him some sheep and people decided that that was why he had frightened us. We knew about the Germans ourselves, but it was winter, the weather was frosty, we had children, but did not have the clothing to keep them warm. At that time of year it was hard to spend a long time in the forest, and thus they caught us in the village, They ordered us to assemble in the school so they could check our documents, our Ausweise. They locked us in without anything for the children to drink, nor were we allowed to go out. They took several people and put them in carts; someone led the Germans into

219

the forest to an empty partisan camp. They returned even more infuriated, slinging the guides, unmercifully beaten, at us. They had been the victims of an explosion at that camp. First they sent our own villagers into the partisan dugout. The latter entered, stood for a while but did not touch anything. Neither the guitars nor the greatcoats. Then four of the Germans, went in and touched something. The explosion threw them way up, right into the pine tree.

They began to drive us out at the school and into a collective farm shed, First they drove us in groups and then in families. Me last, I was the last, and with me my four children. They gunned down my eldest right there on the threshold; I fell down on the dead and my other children with me. They hit me here in the neck. All I heard was how a German sat down on my legs and fired that... submachine-gun.... The smoke and fumes were so awful that it was impossible.... When I stood up, I looked at everyone and thought, "Are all going to get up, to stand up, or am I the only one?"

Yulian Rudovich (village of Dory, Volozhinsky district, Minsk region):

They told us all to go to the church and pray to God and they would let us go home. In the church a German came up to me: "Give up your kid to the woman," and he grabbed hold of my collar and pushed me away. He shoved me away. If you left the children behind, they would let you go! Let you go! This applied to women and mothers, too, but not every mother could do it. Well, my woman did not abandon the children, she did not desert them.... I don't know.... But all the same someone ought to remain among the living, oughtn't they? But my wife did not wish to, she stayed with the little ones.

The Germans set fire to the church. All those of us who were outside in the street could hear the people rushing about inside. They mowed them all down with machine-guns and the fire duly....

Nadezhda Alexandrovna Neglyui (from the former village of Levishchi, lives in Krasnaya Storonka, Slutsk district, Minsk region):

They came here several times, but we hid in the forest. At that time they came and stayed. They did not touch anyone or anything. They ate their own food, and their chief played chess with the teacher's son. The SS-man had a real live monkey in little trousers on his shoulder. He truly did. It was a lively little thing. Well, some started to go home. They did not make them stay and even let them leave again. But it was frosty, and you know what kind of clothing people had before the war, so people made for their homes. In the evening they counted how many windows there were with the lights burning, and all of a sudden they stopped letting people leave the village!

First, they rounded up all the livestock on the pastures outside the village. And the most healthy men as well. I sent my husband away. He did not want to go, he wept, we all wept, I persuaded him that they would kill us all. And the children kept asking, "Are they going to kill us, Mum?" Oh Lord!... I would leap out into the yard and run back, otherwise they would have killed me, and they were there on their own. A German entered the house and looked at us as if he was counting us. He indicated that I should follow him into the cattle-shed. I did not go. He ignored me and went out. Immediately another one ran in and flew right at me. When I came round, all the children were lying there dead, the ceiling above me was burning. For some reason I kept snatching up the cast-iron pots and carrying them out, I don't know why, but I kept carrying the cast-iron pots out....

Maria Alexandrovna Likhvan (village of Borki, Maloritsk district, Brest region):

"All men between eighteen and forty come out!"

Between eighteen and forty.... My husband was holding my little girl; he let her go, kissed her and went out. The German took a staff. He led out so many men, he stood them in three rows, the older ones, those who were younger and the very young ones. Then he took the staff, the sort of poles they used to carry bundles of hay on, and evened the men out so that they stood in a nice straight line. He made them stand upright, and we were already weeping, crying our eyes out. The children were crying, too. There was not a dry thread in our handkerchiefs.

They were driving them, hounding them along the road, the wide road. They were driving those men along. And the Germans, who were chasing them along, they each had already pulled a small bottle of vodka out of their pocket and kept taking a sip, wrapping their raincoats around themselves. And they drove them on.

Our one got into his car, wheeled off to one side and climbed out. He kept running round the houses, running round the houses and collecting all the spades. People had not yet realised why. They thought that perhaps the Germans were preparing to swoop up the partisans or something else. We did not know anything... But when he had collected the spades, we said, "It's a bad sign for us that he's collected those, it'll be to our own misfortune." And he drove off, in the direction of the graveyard....

They took one group of people, then came back for more. They took the men once more.... I forget, three or four times. They made them go there and dig pits. They had to dig pits. For all of us.... And not even very far away.... They began to murder the villagers from our Borki....

REPORT (7)

The destruction of the village of Borki from 22.IX through 23.IX.1942:

22.IX.42. The company was given the order to destroy the village of Borki, situated seven kilometres to the east of Mokrany.

During the night, hours of that same day the company platoons were instructed about the coming mission. The respective preparations were made.

There were sufficient vehicles to take all the platoons and ti reinforcement platoon from the 9th company to the assembly point in Mokrany on 22.IX. The journey took place without incident.

The carts needed for the coming operations were prepared well beforehand, so that they reached the destination of the march, Borki, by the time indicated. Several obstinates were discovered during the selection of the carts, the company demanded that they should be duly punished.

The operations took place in a planned manner but not always according to schedule. The reasons for this were the following: an enclosed group of houses clustered together was indicated on the map of the village of Borki. In actual fact, it turned out that the village stretched for six-seven km in length and width. When day broke, I paid attention to that fact and therefore extended the encirclement from the east and surrounded the village in pincers while simultaneously increasing the distance between posts. I thereby managed to envelop all the residents of the village without exception and deliver them to the assembly point. It turned out to be a favourable factor that the purpose of assembling them was kept from the population right up until the last moment. Calm reigned at the assembly point, the number of control posts was reduced to a minimum, and the forces released were put into action. The detachment of grave-diggers were only given spades at the site of the execution. Thanks to this the population remained ignorant of what was going to happen. Light machine-guns inconspicuously mounted suppressed the panic that started right at the beginning when the first shots rang out from the scene of the execution situated 700 metres from the village. Two men tried to run away, but they fell down after a few steps, hit by machine-gun fire. The execution began at 9:00 hours and ended at 18:00 hours. The execution took place without incident. The measures prepared turned out to be quite expedient.

The grain and implements were confiscated in a planned manner but not on schedule. The number of carts was sufficient since the quantity of grain was not large and the place where the unthreshed grain was stored was not far away.

Kitchen utensils and agricultural implements were taken away on the carts with the grain.

I hereby state the numbers executed. Seven hundred and five people were shot, of them 203 men, 372 women, and 130 children.

The head of livestock rounded up were only determined approximately, since they were not counted on the spot: 45 horses, 250 head of cattle, 65 calves, 450 pigs and piglets, and 300 sheep.

Of the implements the following were collected: 70 carts, 200 ploughs and harrows, five winnowing-machines, 25 chaff-cutters, and other small tools.

All the grain, implements and livestock confiscated were handed over to the bailiff of the state estate of Mokrany.

The following were expended during the operations at Borki: 786 rifle cartridges, 2,496 machine-gun cartridges.

The company suffered no losses. One sergeant-major with suspected jaundice was sent to the military hospital in Brest.

"Müller".

Signed: lieutenant, on behalf of the company commander.[*]

At dawn the elder in Borisovlca (Malorita district) gathered all the population together. After checks had been made on the population with the assistance of the security police from Divin, five families were resettled to Divin. The rest were shot by a detachment, specially selected for the purpose, and buried 500 metres to the north-east of Borisovka. Altogether 169 people were executed, including 49 men, 97 women and 23 children.... The death sentences were only carried out from midday till one o'clock because of the preparations (digging of the graves).

Commander of the 9th company of the 15th police patrol regiment,

"Captain Kasper".

---

[*] *USSR Central Archive, folder 7021, file 148, unit 1, sheets 225-227.*

Fyokla Kruglova (urban-type settlement of Oktyabrsky, Gomel region):

I lay there and lay there and thought.... I'll go to Rudnya, I've got friends there. Perhaps they will hide me. Perhaps people have remained alive there....

I got up. Nothing stirred. There was not even a cat or a sparrow, nothing at all. How quiet it was, how silent. Perhaps I was the only one left in the whole world? Then I thought, let these Germans shoot me or do something. For how shall I live all alone in the world. Then I thought, I'll get to Rudnyti". There were no Germans, no one at all. They had already left here, left Oktyabr, they had razed it to the ground and left....

I had only just arrived and gone aver to a little shed, close to a small house. I stood there and heard someone screaming. There was such screaming there, dear Lord, such terrible cries. They had already taken people from that end and were driving them from there to this end near the state farm. They were already rounding up these people, all the women.

I was standing right by that little shed and thought I would take a look what they were doing there and why there were such screams issuing from it, I peeped round the corner, just as a German was looking in this direction. He flew over to me, "A-a-ah!" How he hit me with the butt of his rifle.... My mouth was full of blood. I had to get rid of that blood somehow, scooping it out with my fingers so that I could breathe!

This is what happened to us after. They brought along a box and put it down. On the box they mounted a machine-gun. On a box like those they bring potatoes in. A German came over to that house and pushed out so many people, three, four, five souls, from there. Who wants to go to their execution? Well, the mother got her family together, putting her arms round them and falling down because they were shouting 'Lie down!' The mother and children and whatever other relatives were there, embraced each other and threw themselves down. And they ridded them with machine-gun fire....

I stood there at the back right till the last and did not come out,

The people could see everything, were looking through the windows into the house and saying, 'There's my daughter burning and my granddaughter is burning to death!'

And what do you think, nobody was crying.

From the archive:

The company was given the task of destroying the village of Zabolotye (Mafarita district) situated to the northeast of Mokrany and of executing the population. Attached to the company was the. From platoon from the 9th company and 10 men from the armoured car unit of the 10th regiment. On September 21, 1942, at approximately 02 hours 00 minutes the company approached the first isolated farmsteads in Zabolotye. While the main forces were moving further into the village, towards the territory with a cordon round it, the individual farmsteads were surrounded by a detachment selected for this purpose, and the inhabitants were brought out of the houses.... The entire population headed by the village elder was driven into the school, and one detachment immediately set off for the settlements located seven kilometres from the village, to round up the inhabitants there.... All the rest were divided into three groups and shot at the place of execution.

The outcome of the operation was the following: 289 people were shot, 151 farmsteads were burned down,

700 head of cattle were rounded up, as well as 400 pigs, 400 sheep and 70 horses.

The execution was carried out in a planned manner and without particular incident, except for one attempt to escape. Most of the villagers retained their composure in meeting the fate they fully deserved and which did not come as a surprise to them owing to their guilty conscience.

Commander of the 11th company of the 15th police regiment,

"Captain Pels".

...They were pushing us, jostling us somewhere away from the well, from behind near the barn. The machine-guns were pattering away resonantly, but even they did not muffle people's screams.

Something was happening to me. I kept pulling senselessly and furiously towards the open-topped car where the stooping back and smooth shaven head of my enemy rose stiffly, and around whom the creature bespectacled with white fur, pulling faces and teasing, was racing back and forth, flicking its fat, rat-like tail. The polizei shoved me away, but he himself seemed as if he was sleep-walking. When I had almost reached the vehicle, it suddenly shuddered and tore off. I did not know what I wanted to do and what I could do. Perhaps I was urged on to him by an unbearable need to take a look at him and vindictively remember him. To see what that frisky monkey was covering with its tailed backside, hiding something or bidding one to take a look.

To a certain extent this was mixed up in my memory with the time I was in a cellar at the Louvre, examining some medieval Romanesque gravestones. I peered up into the faces of the aged nuns carrying a dead night. (I kept on travelling, looking at everything, as if building up my stock of memories, as I knew I would soon be at one with darkness). The knight, petrified, was stretched out alongside his long sword with its cruciform hilt; his feet were trampling a lion that appeared submissively small; and the old women in black were stooping in a life-like manner under the weight of his body, their faces hidden under their deep funnel-shaped hoods. You just could not help bending down and peeping under the black hoods for it seemed that concealed there were noiseless, satisfied grimaces of laughter!

I did not know what the hunched back of my enemy, submissively bent beneath the dancing monkey, was concealing and hiding, and taking away, what sort of expression contorted his face. It was that same cruel look of gruesome curiosity. The conviction of yet another victor that it would always be like that: "them" under us and "us" over them. A most short-lived, narcotic idea, but one tenacious in history, that strength means right, purpose and justice.

And, of course, there was that grimace of cannibalistic scorn for the uncivilised behaviour of the victim whose features were contorted with inhuman torment!

The only thing that occurred to me was that he drove away from the shed, all ablaze and filled with howling, without even thinking that everything might suddenly change today. And that even before the sun had time to go down, everything might appear to him in a completely different light. And would be quite different.

"...Flariyan Pyatrovich, I always listen to you... It did cross my mind that people slander animals. They're always talking about 'animal instincts'. Animal instincts would not be a bad thing! This year I lived on the Belovezhskaya game reserve for a month. How simply, I would say by means of moral approaches, do the bison and even the wild boar establish their supremacy over their fellow creatures. For the most bloodthirsty wild beast seldom fights to the death with one of its own species. At any rate, the struggle against representatives of its own species is not of an exterminating nature. This is precisely what animal instinct is—an instinct to preserve its own species. There they go again, they never get tired of saying the same old thing! (Boky banged his palm against the sticky leather of his briefcase which gave a squelching sound.) They say that nature is to blame for man being aggressive and cruel towards his kind. If Mother Nature is to blame for something, then it is only because she has let him go too far away from herself. And he has got too far outside nature's sphere of attraction and has almost lost his main instinct, that very instinct of survival of the species."

"There you are then, colleague. After that the 'second nature' or culture begins. It all depends what kind of culture it is. How humane, how human and considerate it is. And as for fascism, it defames both human nature and humankind's culture. It is the most malicious defamation in history!"

"But what of history itself? Is that a calumny too? The wars, the inquisitions, the crusades, the massacre of St. Bartholemew and all kinds of other 'massacres', the wars of the 'roses', the innumerable Tamerlanes and Chinese emperors who embellished the planet with monuments built of millions of human skulls?"

"All the same, fascism is a defamation of humankind. Even our prehistoric forefather in his animal skin, even he does not deserve such an insult as to be the ancestor of a fascist. No, you just imagine him, our poor forefather, without fangs and swift legs and not strong at all amongst the wild beasts, his whole body bare of hair with his sweat-drenched efforts to survive! There he was, the only mortal being, so alone in the world, because no one else knew that there was such a thing as death. It was a good thing if a fellow tribesman was killed by a wild animal, if he perished during the hunt. But what if he died without reason, from illness? How could they fail to be terrified, not explain it by the witchcraft of their neighbours? The animal feeling of immortality came up against human experience, the realisation that death might overtake one. How could it overtake the immortal? The only way it could do that was by witchcraft. One of 'ours' had died, that meant seek out your neighbour, the sorcerer, and kill him. That was not vengeance, just a preventive measure, the medicine of the time. Our forefather was not savage, he was touching in his infantile helplessness in the face of the fanged and incomprehensible world..."

"Well, there you are then, it was at that time that man's awareness split in two like the blades of scissors, departed from the instinct of survival of the species. Awareness restricted that instinct, withering it down to a tribal level: another tribe was no longer 'us' so they could be killed and could be subjected to cannibalism! Well, since you could murder a 'sorcerer' from another tribe, why not look for one amongst your own people, amongst your fellow tribesmen, if that one was quite far away. That did not take up so much time and was more convenient. 'Look for the sorcerer!', surely this is how the manipulators of all times and peoples have operated, haven't they, Flariyan Pyatrovich? And you mark my words, it never fails to work. 'We' are the Aryans, 'we' are the Whites, 'ours' are far, far superior, 'we', 'we'!.."

"Yes, but without that 'we', there is no resistance to all this. 'We' are the revolution! 'We' are the working people! 'We' are humankind! I am talking about the 'we' that nourishes and promotes man's ability to realise and feel the sufferings of others, to feel their pain as if it were their own, and even more acutely than their own. After all that has floated down the river of history, with its lower reaches quite befouled, and its waters all soiled. And yet its source is always pure. But it is a must that as many people as possible do at last realise the mortal threat that is posed by pollution of not just the natural environment alone but of human souls as well. Naturally, we are quite accustomed to toxic effluent being released into rivers and lakes. It is quick and cheap. We are even more accustomed not to have citizens nor people, but crusaders filled with the slops of fanaticism, storm troopers, hungweibings and supermen. With their assistance affairs of state and other matters are resolved cheaply and rapidly, using the most efficient method. That is how it seems to some people. The only thing is that that may cost the whole of humankind and the planet dearly today and tomorrow. That has to be realised unless the world wants to perish. It is like the words of the poet, 'Humankind, beware! The word 'hatred' has been switched on!'"

"Ha, if it doesn't want to perish! Just say it! Your world has an eye like that of a hen: it only sees separate grains, those which are closer to it. And in general you count on my long-suffering too much. This when we've got the present bomb? Don't be late, Flariyan Pyatrovich!"

...It burned and howled as if in a red-hot pipe. They drove us down the street of the blazing village, and we herded the cows. It was evidently because this job needed to be done that they allowed us to escape, to climb out of the shed, as if saying, you can go on living for the moment. Or maybe the one with the monkey wanted to see how people would clamber through the last crack remaining to them.

They did not give us any sticks. We beat the cows' sides and bones with our palms and our fists and grabbed them by the horns. We pushed the crazed beasts along the fiery corridor, followed by the punitive squads with their sticks and rifle butts. Some of them were wearing strange clothing that we were not familiar with, yellow and green uniforms and round green caps with very long peaks on their heads. They were yelling at us and at the beasts not in German but in some language we could not understand.

Now I too was to go along that accursed gravel road for we had come out onto it. All ablaze, the village stirs mutely and terribly behind us, like something alive, in a baggy tar-black sack of smoke.

I eagerly looked at the forest ahead. That was where it was going to happen. It was even somewhat odd that the Germans and those in the caps with the long peaks were just as sure of themselves, just as furious, bawling at us, concerned that no cow should lag behind and that no peasant's harrow, no plough or sack of grain should fall off the cart, rather than with the fact that they would die in the forest, they would choke on their own blood! I could see just as well what was taking place in the forest: how people were running up to the gravel road, how they were mounting machine-guns and looking out from behind the tree-stumps and trees into the woodland glade, into which the German vehicles and strings of carts would drive out, into which the punitive squads would come out. The Germans were still not getting into their vehicles. Each group, each party was walking behind its vehicle in an extended line. That was bad. But it meant that they were afraid, that they knew they would not get away with it, they knew it! I kept looking round, seeking out the car with my main enemy in it. I could see so well everything that was going to happen now. I could even see the eyes of the partisans. And I was begging them, demanding that they should be there, that they should appear. After all that had happened, they did not have the right not to be there, they were obliged to be there! I made sure my eyes did not meet those of the polizeis, so that I did not give away the fact that I knew. I ran behind the cows more eagerly than anyone else, picked up the stalk of a sunflower that had been cut down and herded the cows to the road, shouting loudly and yelling at them. At my heels ran the little boy whom the women's hands had pushed out of the window and who had not been killed. I told him to keep with me, and he obediently followed me, but he kept looking round at the huge, black sack-like cloud of smoke billowing over the village as if it were alive. We also had with us the little girl who had so tightly clutched the child from the shed and had not surrendered it for a long time, tears kept running down her pale stern face; she did not notice anyone or anything but just went on weeping as she wandered among the herd of cows. The old woman here was the same one with whom I had gone from the shed to the village. She kept lifting her blackened, wizzened hands to her mouth one after the other, in turns, either biting them or trying to stop her wrinkled lips from trembling.

In the movements of the men, the peasants who had escaped and been allowed to come out (of whom there were no more than five or six), there was a senseless haste and some kind of common bewilderment as to why they were there and where they were going.

The members of the punitive squads suddenly became anxious, commands resounded in German, and they ran towards me from the vehicles. I was even frightened that they had guessed that they had become aware of what was known to me. But I wanted to see their anxiety and disquiet, for if they were afraid, it meant that something really was going to happen.

Now the Germans were also helping us and the polizeis to round up the herd on the road. Perhaps they feared there would be mines and had decided to use the cows to check the road? I looked round furtively, my eyes seeking out the open-topped car.

Finally, as we walked along, we reformed into the order the Germans wanted. At the front was the herd of cows, then we, the herdsmen, followed by the polizeis and those in the long-peaked caps, and then behind them the Germans, those on foot, with the vehicles and carts bringing up the rear. The polizeis kept glancing round at the Germans like dogs at their master when they sense there is a bear around. You curs! You're in for it now, you're in for it!... We were almost right by the forest. Once again I spotted the young polizei who had driven me and the old woman so angrily to the village. I suddenly called out to him, "What are you lagging behind for, get moving!"

I gave him such a fright. He started as if a tree or a dead man had barked at him. Here, close to the forest, we perceptibly changed places, although it was he who was still holding the rifle. It was apparently a French rifle, long like a rake and awkward to carry. It would have been better if it had been a submachine-gun. The only good thing the polizei had was his boots, not short, hard ones like the ones the Germans wore, but our army boots....

The Germans were again catching us up at a run. The polizeis immediately became bolder and cheered up.

But I could see them, you know, I was already talking to those who were lying in wait for them, those who were ahead of us, some ten or twenty minutes ahead.

The road narrowed, gripped by the forest on both sides, the deep ditches lining it were crammed with alder thickets. Having inhaled the smoke and blood, the cows kept huddling together, mooing, sniffing the ground, and butting one another. The

Germans who had been sent to assist the polizeis, had decided, it seemed, to hide themselves from the partisans' bullets amidst the herd, behind the cows' backs and flanks. This mooing, butting maelstrom of cows was now buffeting them about and bearing them along. It was sucking us all in, so that we bumped against each other, and then were dragged apart straight away. Such clumsy helplessness even seemed funny. One German thought he glimpsed a grinning, offensive look on my face.

"Are you a bandit?" he asked. The German was very short, even his pot-like helmet did not boost his height. "Are you a partisan?"

"Schwein?" a polizei helped out. In their fear in that whirlpool of cows they had not apparently noticed how languages, heads, and their short-lived ideas had replaced one another.

"Nichts!" I shouted, carried away to the side. "I'm a Schuler. The bandits are there. (I pointed to the alder thicket close by). We are Bauer. Well, you, carrion, be off with you! Schuler, peasant collective."

I myself could see my own face, exultant and maliciously joyful. I knew that I was going too far and could not stop myself. At a distance, from behind the cows' heads, lowered as if in drunkenness, our eyes, mine and those of the squat German, met and became locked. He tried to get to me. I knew that he was ready to fire at me if he had not been afraid of raising the alarm. I should have averted my eyes, but I could not force myself to. Now, no matter where I was carried, I felt the gaze of the infuriated dumpy person fixed upon me.

Banging on the cows' horns with his submachine-gun, he kept trying to draw closer to me, but I distanced myself from him in that mooing, butting whirl. Was I to rush off into the forest? Or should I wait for the first shot and the ensuing panic? It was strange how sure I was that an ambush was awaiting us as if I could actually see it. I never gave a thought to the fact that the bullets would not distinguish who was who. But for me it was not enough that it should happen, I had to be there when it did. Only if I were present would the day be complete, otherwise that day would never end for me....

What had happened? Was the forest coming to an end? It was as if the ground had been torn away from under my feet. That malicious tubby person in his pot-like helmet had already extricated himself from the herd and had stepped into the glade. He was walking along at the side, his eyes were seeking me out. No, all this was merely a large clearing which became a field on one side, but ahead there was forest again.

That was where they would be waiting, from whence they would strike! That shortie again squeezed himself in amongst the herd; for all that he felt ill at ease and chilly out there in the open. This meant that I could make my way to the outside, walk along at the side, knowing that he could not get at me.

The herd of crazed cows driven wild by the smoke and the smell of blood, like a whirlpool in a river, drew on shoulders, heads, helmets, forage caps of the Germans and the polizeis, and was already thrust itself out into the clearing, already creeping across it. A few men from Perekhody and I, as well as the polizeis with sticks, herded the cows towards the road, towards the forest again, shouting at them. The vehicles had already appeared and were moving across the clearing. I could see the open-topped car and even the monkey jumping up and down there.

I know what a column like this looks like from an ambush (I had twice lain in ambush myself), and now I was looking at the clearing as if down a rifle barrel, taking aim, my sights trained on the shaven head over which the monkey was scampering about. (I kept glancing round at the car, even forgetting to keep my eye on that dangerous squat fellow to see where he was.)

The vehicles and the Germans were now in the clearing already, the herd and the polizei patrol were quite close to the narrow opening of the road into the forest that awaited us. Any moment now, any moment now! I called the boy from Perekhody over to me and held his shoulder so that I could shove him to the ground in time. I did not walk any further but allowed the herd to pass me and waited for the car, so that I would be closer to it when the action started. I achieved along the cows with a stick, ready to round up the punitive squads and the cars. The words, "Hurry, hurry, now, now!" raced through my mind....

"Down, straightaway!" I whispered, trembling with joy, to the lad who did not understand what it was all about, but was also trembling. "Where's that girl, we must get her here."

But nothing took place. The mooing, butting herd carried the polizei patrols and the Germans along into the forest, moving deeper and deeper into it and stretching out, and nothing happened. The quiet of the forest was not disturbed by thunder, it did not open up into a rumbling abyss under the feet of the punitive squads.

No, but it did happen! The most dreadful thing happened! No one ran or sped here when children were falling from their mothers' arms onto the burning straw under the barn walls, and these frenzied arms stretched out, cried out, entreated and summoned.... How I scorned myself, how I hated myself because there was no one there, because no one came running, no one came hurrying here, now at least, to wipe these ones, these creatures off the face of the Earth!... I flailed the backs of the poor cows which were in no way to blame, drove them towards the road, shouting swear words at myself, not giving even a thought to that vicious dumpy person who was probably on watch for me again.

"Aha, aha, you're in for it!"

Suddenly machine-guns vengefully set up a deafening howl, not ahead of us but at the back of the column. The fiery whining of the bullets densely and extensively riddled the clearing. There where the vehicles were, broad like the whole world, an echo was already thundering, burning, shrieking over the forest (or was it in me?), chuckling and crying out of malicious, vindictive happiness. Aha, aha, you're in for it! That's what you deserve, you're getting what's coming to you! I ran up against the sides, the horns, the muzzles, the cows, against the members of the punitive squads whom the awkward cows were preventing from lying down and firing. I saw the polizeis fleeing into the forest.

Where was that lad of mine and that stern, weeping little girl from Perekhody? And where was the car?

Then I saw it, racing straight at me, the car bouncing up and down on the hummocks and ruts in fright. Still not really aware of what I could do, of what I was going to do, I flew towards it. I even managed to catch sight of that shaking doll-like dark glossy head of my enemy which looked as if it were being torn off, the eyes goggling as wide as the lenses of the Hold-rimmed spectacles, and the terror in the little face of the monkey. The car had almost been blown up....

And so had I. The forest, like the wings of a huge bird, burst forth with a deafening black flapping over the road, over the burning vehicles, carrying everything away with it. In the whole world there remained the very simple and very calm surprise: "Is that death? That is death, isn't it?"

...In the beginning I sensed my return, light as an acute pain in my eyes. I lay there, immersed in a monotonous whistling silence while hard, cold drops were falling on my face. They were yellow as well. I could see them, they were yellow. No, those were birch trees standing over me, serene and wet in their autumnal garb. There were some people next to me as well. My eyes were steeped in pain and swimming with tears. I was not lying on the ground but on something high. It was something white, it was a horse. I was on a cart. There were some other people as well. My tightly screwed up eyes detected a broad human face, a man's face, floating in a rainbow and next to him a woman's face, a laughing face. It was such a long time since

241

I had seen a human face laughing. How strange it was to hear voices in a quiet conversation:

"And yet you betrayed me, Natasha."

"But why?"

"If I had known why."

"You all ask too little of me. That's what it is, Alyosha."

"But I..."

"Wait a minute! Heh, boy, you're falling off!"

I had already tumbled off and was lying on the ground. I had got up from the cart so easily as if taking off, but then I could not stand on my legs! My legs felt like cotton wool. And there was something the matter with my eyes.

"Oh, look what's happened to you!" a woman's face ho-vered really close to me, now appearing, now fading in the rainbow. They helped me get up. No, it was all right, my legs were becoming firmer, they were just shaking terribly.

"Let me bathe your eyes for you. Give me my bag, Alyosha. My bag, I said. Get your hands off. I'm not going anywhere, Alyosha dear. Never mind, dear, your eyes are intact. You just caught the blast a little and got some soil in them. Are you from this village? Your people went off, they ran back to the village. Why didn't they say anything, did they forget about you?"

"No... yes... did they get the Germans? There was one in glasses, the one in charge. He had a monkey with him."

"They killed some, but others escaped. They took some prisoner. They took a whole crowd of

242

them alive. Wait a minute, don't flinch like that. Does it hurt?"

The woman's hands were touching my eyes with something smelling of a chemist's, soothingly cold.

"Put up with it a bit. Until you marry..."

"Where are they? The one in the spectacles with the monkey!"

"Wait a minute now! Where are you off to? Here you are, put this over your eyes..."

Pushing aside the trees that came flying at me, I ran through the forest, then along a cutting in the forest packed with carts on which wounded partisans were sitting and lying, and weapons and German blankets were heaped.

"Where are they? Where are the live ones?" I asked the partisans. It was as if my dash for the car as it raced along in fright, interrupted by the explosion, was being continued.

"The Germans? They're over there."

"You want to see the monkey, do you?"

Once again a rainbow hovered before my eyes and they were watering once more. I had lost the little piece of cloth and now I tore off rough, wet, cool hazelnut leaves, attempting to nib away the pain with them.

There they were, the Germans! In their helmets which looked so out of place here, they sat, huddled together, on the ground right there in the cutting with a large crowd of partisans standing over them. I perceived that vicious dumpy fellow straightaway. Only he was not vicious at all, he was the kindest, quietest, most subdued person on earth! And he was so low in height. And the uniform seemed not his own, it was like a sack on him. Someone had put the helmet on his head like a pot to make fun of him....

I rushed over to him, and to them with a bunch of hazelnut leaves clenched in my fist and pelted the squat person with their own words like stones.

"Rus, schwein, bandits, zuruck, los!... Ah, you!..."

No one understood. The partisans looked at me in surprise. The dumpy fellow obviously did not remember that these were his very words, and that not very long ago they had expressed everything that he thought and did. He looked at me from under his pot-like helmet, bewildered and genuinely terrified, someone quite different, another person altogether.

"That's them, they're the ones!" I shouted, frightened that people had already believed their surprisingly doleful, meek eyes and faces. "They're the ones!" I shrieked, rubbing away that floating rainbow, the pain that was bothering me, from my eyes with my dirty hands.

At last I made him out too. Everyone was looking at him. No, not at him but at the little monkey that was on him. A young jester-partisan, (this voluntary post exists in every detachment, in every platoon) hung about with belts and weapons, was pretending he wanted to take the little monkey, was touching its tail. The monkey raced around, scampered away, made funny movements with its little paw, wizzened like the hand of an old woman, but its little face, the eyes of the monkey looked like an expressionless, motionless mask from close up.

"It won't let me get at it, the pest!" the contented partisan laughed, and the others smiled as well. But my enemy seemed to be ignored, as if he was just a stand for the monkey. That shaven head was the same, only dirty and sweaty, just as were the big ears and the uniform; only the gold-rimmed spectacles were missing. The expression he had in his eyes formerly had disappeared, his face looked different. His face and his look were those of another being, quite another. He bent his head down so that the monkey could not hide behind it to avoid the hand of the jester-partisan and so that he himself could see from below whether he was holding it right, whether the partisans liked it. Without the spectacles his eyes were blind and anxious and betrayed no meaning like those of a newborn baby. The monkey's features were set in an expression of fright. While his face bore an idiotically subdued, disciplined, dolefully obliging assiduity, which called out to everyone, even in spite of everything, "I'm the one, here I am, do what you like with me, you have the right to, you yourselves decide, but this quiet, smiling, submissive old man, that's me, he is me, that man here, that's me!"

It was as if he and the little monkey had exchanged roles; it was not he who was in charge of it, but the monkey that was in charge of him. It was written all over him: "Am I behaving all right? Can everyone see? Or is it better like that? Or how else should I hold it?"

"He's the one!" I said. I was no longer shouting, but talking. They did not appear to hear my shouts, to understand them. "He's their main one."

The partisans looked at me strangely, distanced and even surprised. It was as if they really did not understand the meaning of my words.

Then, you know, I felt and saw that one can be afraid of one's own hatred, as if it were pain petrified inside one: a person begins to restrain it, to grip it within oneself, awaiting and fearing the moment when it cannot be held back any longer.

But at first I swooped at those deaf ears, at those bewil-dered reluctant looks, as if at a wall.

No, I knew that the punitive squad members would be killed just as the partisans did and they themselves too. What frightened me was that they were permitted to die, to depart like that, like, such kind chaps, amazingly doleful, subdued, as if transferring some burden on us. They had certainly made it out to us that someone else was to blame and not them! No, these were the ones who should pay, it was they precisely!...

Of the eleven members of the punitive squads taken priso-ner only two or three had blood-stained faces and hair; the rest were not even wounded. Four of them were not wearing helmets but caps with long, long peaks. Although those in the long-peaked caps were sitting right next to the Germans, they showed by their whole appearance that they were here by themselves and should not be mixed up with the rest. The tallest of them all, his neck distorted by a huge Adam's apple, regarded his neighbours, the Germans, especially disapprovingly and scornfully:

"The young man is telling the truth," he said suddenly, catching my eye. "That is the German commander of the whole unit. He gave the order. He made the report to Berlin as to how the execution should be carried out, how to perform the military operation best..."

He turned towards my enemy and the three sitting next to him swung round as well. The Germans who did not understand what the man with the Adam's apple was saying looked startled and huddled together more tightly. The shaven-headed man even stopped the monkey's antics, grabbing hold of it, as it were.

But was not that the voice (such a high-pitched, shrill voice with an accent) that had shouted out, "Get your documents ready, Ausweise, passports", by the barn.

"Oh, so you can sprechen Russian then!" the jester-partisan was surprised, and forgetting about the monkey, he turned to the man with the Adam's apple. "Well, did we give you a good battering then? What makes you wander along without looking round? You're not at home, you know."

"Yes, you certainly did. The Germans roam about as if they were out for a promenade. You gave them a jolly good thumping!"

"Where do you come from then?"

"We're not Germans!" The man with the Adam's apple was even offended.

It was then that I saw Kasach. Wearing a military cap and his dolman jacket trimmed with fur, holding a submachine-gun under his elbow, he was walking along the cutting and with him was our detachment! They were just partisans like the others, like those surrounding me. To a stranger they looked the same. To me they were special for they brought closer my own world, returned that world without which nothing remained at all. I tore myself from the spot, ready to run towards them, to see them all, to dip myself in and return myself to that world where everything was so sound and so reliable!... But Kasach was walking ahead of the detachment along the narrow overgrown cutting. And, although it was precisely to Kasach that I had to tell something important to him and to us both, I restrained myself. How could I run towards Kasach, fall upon him from God knows where, meet that ironic stern look that would not recognise me?... I was so afraid of it now, after all that had happened to me. I quivered inside like a string that had become soundless with tension.

Chatting away to a partisan with a moustache who looked like a commander, Kasach stood about a hundred paces from us. The detachment stopped, too. No, not all of them. They were walking round Kasach, slipping past him in twos and threes, and quickly coming this way. The little girl who had walked with me from Perekhody jumped out from somewhere and ran towards them. She was still crying, from that very moment when they tore the little child out of her slender arms by the barn.

When the little girl reached them, she grabbed the big, heavy partisan in a stiff tarpaulin raincoat, who was striding resolutely along, by the arm, by the elbow, and I recognised this partisan. It was Perekhod. That caused my thoughts to return to those who were sitting at our feet, to the members of the punitive squads.

"Hey, neighbours!" exclaimed the partisan who never tired of his voluntary role of cheering people up, of being the jester. "What did you hatch out on that road? Look what we found on the gravel path! A monkey!"

(The punitive squads did not usually leave along the road on which they had come. This was probably why they had set up two ambushes, and our people were waiting on the other road. The partisan in full military uniform with binoculars hanging on his chest, with whom Kasach had stopped to talk, was probably the commander of that detachment.)

Perekhod who appeared huge because of the wet sticking raincoat rapidly and abruptly came over to us. He began to disengage the skinny hands of the weeping, stern-looking little girl who was hanging on his elbow. While he clumsily pulled away her clinging, thin fingers, a second Perekhod, his nephew, ran over to the Germans and stopped. The younger Perekhod had a very pale, thin face, his eyes looked like the big eyes of our little girl from Perekhody.

They made way for them as if understanding immediately who they were.

Once again I saw that the extreme intensity of feeling suddenly paralyses a person, taking all his strength and his will, as if fettered by cramp. The younger Perekhod stopped three paces from the punitive squad members: his sweat-co-vered forehead and pale cheekbones had stiffened, his look was fixed, and the lower part of his thin face was trembling, becoming distorted; sounds were forcing their way out of his throat which could have been taken for laughter had it not been for the look on his face.

The older Perekhod who resembled Kasach in some way, but was more angular and more cumbersome, went into the very midst of the punitive squad members sitting on the ground as if plunging into water, pushing aside with his knees anything that happened to be in his way. He stood over the heads of the Germans.

It was as if a sky full of rain clouds had descended heavily, low over the earth. It became stifling. All that could be heard was breathing, as if we had raced away from the spot and were rushing somewhere in silence.

"Well?" Perekhod asked quietly. "Was it you?"

"We are not Germans," the translator with the Adam's apple corrected him. "You're just the one I need. Come on, get up now! On your feet, all of you!"

It is hardly likely that the man knew what he was going to do. He raced back and forth like someone on fire, flinging himself about in search of something cold, a position in which it would not hurt so unbearably; this huge strong man rushed about, seeking refuge.

And this burst forth in others.

"Drive them into the glade! What is there to look at!..."

"Do them in! You, just you wait!"

"They're sitting there like little Christs!..."

Quickly, hastened by the shouts, Kasach and the commander with the moustache came over. When the punitive squad members saw them, they apparently interpreted, understood the shouts and shoves to mean that it was demanded of them that they show military respect for the commanders for whom the partisans made way. Their fear was immediately replaced by assiduity and standing to attention. Only the poor old führer was tormented by awkwardness and uncertainty: he could not make up his mind to throw the monkey off his shoulder, to offend the monkey that had pleased the partisans, and to stand to attention with the monkey was somehow disrespectful, not correct.

It was written all over him in huge letters that he so much wanted and was trying to salute the commanders. Even the more so as they were dressed in military uniform like himself. But what about the monkey!... He was afraid to get rid of it. It was like coming out from under a shelter. But what kind of form would that be with a monkey, what kind of respect? The führer of the punitive squads stood to attention and stooped, looking smartly and disciplined, hesitantly and inquiringly inclining his shaven head. Perhaps the partisan commanders would in fact be interested in his little monkey and not in him?

Kasach scrutinised the punitive squad members with that familiar cruel and ironic grin, but how opportune it was now. How I understood and loved it at that moment! I ought not to have run and shouted, but should have approached them and looked at them like that!

The commander with the moustache stood next to Kasach, admiring his trophies, the prisoners, with obvious pleasure. But Kasach suddenly espied me and quite unexpectedly re-cognised me. (It was hard not to recognise me when everything about me was crying out that it was me, that I had to say something to him, had to tell him...)

"Is that you? Well, how's things?"

"Comrade commander, they're on the 'island'," I tried to get through to Kasach from behind the backs. "There are wounded there. Rubezh and I went on an operation to get some food. He was killed, so was Skorokhod and the 'commandant of the island...'"

I still had not uttered the word "Glasha", I myself did not know why I did not mention that name,

"How did you get here? Never mind, what happened to your eyes? Go and see Filippov."

Filippov was our detachment doctor.

All the time it seemed to me that Kasach knew that I had been with Glasha, but did not want to mention her name either because everyone would hear....

"Commander, do you want these for souvenirs?" the jester-partisan handed the man with the moustache a bundle of photographs. "I found these on them: 'Love me as I love you!'"

The good-natured moustached commander passed on the photographs, and they did the rounds, Kasach being the only one not to take one. I got one of a soldier on his own. It was one of them wearing a black raincoat, his hands on a submachine-gun, with the barrel pointing straight into the lens, into the face of the person who would be looking at it. I scrutinised the live punitive detachment members in order to determine whose photograph it was. But no one had a face like that, a look like that. The photograph had established the moment when the thought had not even crossed his mind, not even a hint of a thought that a situation might arise when he himself would not understand and would not remember how he could have wished for anything else, only not a submachine-gun aimed at his head, that they should not kill him, but to live, to stay alive!...

"What are we going to do with them?" an old man asked the partisans. He was obviously one of those posted to guard the captive punitive squad members. "Soon they'll be asking for something to eat. As I see it, they appear to be people, if you did not know what they'd done."

"They themselves know what they deserve," said the commander with the moustache calmly. "Does anyone speak Russian here?"

"That tall one over there".

"Well, what about it? Why did you give yourselves up? Surely you did not reckon that the earth would allow you to go on living after all that?" The moustached man spoke in an even tone, firmly, but good-naturedly as before. Probably everything is quite simple when you have such a commander with you. The partisans addressed him with a customary smile, and their smile was one of pleasure.

"We're not Germans. Those are Germans over there," the translator with the Adam's apple reiterated stubbornly.

"Haven't you got anything else to justify yourselves?"

"What is to be done then? Kill them?" the older Perekhod suddenly cried cut. Protesting, disagreeing, he shouted out, "They should be... They should..."

That almost senseless protest, but a protest that we immediately understood, was against the fact that they would depart, taking refuge in death, while the village of Perekhody, and what had taken place there, would remain with us. Perhaps this was the reason why we had driven them further and taken them with us alive. For our burning hatred they were instead of the cold that I had once sought, had grabbed in passing and carried in the reddened, swollen palm of my hand....

Two hours later armoured cars and a chain of submachine-gunners had already come in pursuit of us. Aircraft flew over the edges of the forest. We had retreated into the marshes, to Chertovo Koleno, taking with us the captured punitive squad members.

From the blind, furious artillery shelling and the aircraft, we felt that the Germans, who were closing in the ring of the blockade, had been extremely worried when they discovered active partisans in their rear. (Kasach's men and the detachment of the moustached commander had managed to escape from the pocket of the blockade about five days before Perekhody was burned down.)

For the moment our ambushes were keeping the Germans back, but both detachments withdrew, taking the wounded with them. There were numerous wounded and most of them had sustained injuries of late, during the blockade. There were not enough people and hands to carry the stretchers although our numbers were quite large, about three hundred. We also used the captive punitive squad members, making them carry stretchers of blanket and poles. They carried them diligently and got very alarmed and lost their self-possession when a wounded man began to groan because of the jolts.

Night fell when we were right at the marshes' edge. The pursuers called a halt, and German flares danced about some two kilometres from us. From time to time the Germans would fire shells into the marshes, believing that we were already there. It was damp and cold underfoot and we had to support the stretchers by putting our knees under them. People gathered in groups, chatted quietly and smoked.

I was looking for Kasach. Several times I walked past the squatting punitive squad members. The partisans who had been picked to guard them were evidently nervous and becoming furious. In darkness like this, when we ourselves were surrounded, the German divisions were standing guard over us, the punitive squad men were naturally weighing up how they could make a getaway.

At last I caught sight of him. Kasach was talking loudly with someone near an aspen or white birch which appeared to be gleaming. I waited until he was alone and approached him. Kasach was sitting on a tree-stump and smoking in a tired manner. I breathed out, "Comrade commander," and again I blurted it out in a hurry, "the 'island'... there are wounded... Rubezh... we could get there through this same marsh... Glasha's..."

"Which Glasha? Wait a minute! Glasha?! How did she manage to get there? So, you've come from there, were you there with her?"

"When the fighting started I was in the glade, looking for Goering. I met Glasha, we could not get to the camp".

"Where is she? Is she alive?"

"Yes," I replied like someone caught out.

What is it, what happened? Why could I not talk about Glasha with him? I never managed to talk to Glasha about him of late either. Once again I mentioned that we could make our way across the swamps to the "islands", although it was a long way....

"They're forming a new pocket, a stronger one," said Kasach after a silence. We watched the rockets which were quite near. The shells kept falling in the marsh. There was a patter of firing, reiterated by an echo, then it would rend the darkness and the echo would confirm it. My eyes really hurt me and went on watering; everything around me melted, diffused in that tiresome rainbow. Then there were different coloured rockets leaping up and down, flickering, quivering blue, red and yellow light streaming down the damp white bodies of the aspens, the stubby, gloomy face of Kasach, and my hands. I seemed to be half asleep. And the conversation with Kasach, and our solitary silence were still so unreal, as if not happening at all, impossible. I had got the shivers although I was dressed in a soldier's jacket once again and had a sweater on, a German one too. (I found it when we seized trophies from the German carts under fire and then had to abandon carts.) I kept drifting away from reality and only remembered that I still needed to tell him something about the "island".

I thought that I had not told him all properly, that I had not explained myself very well and Kasach had not understood.

"Was it frightening?" Kasach suddenly asked. The blue light thrown across his exhausted stubby face was replaced by a white one and a red one, and I kept talking about the "island", not able to realise that he was asking me about Perekhody.

"In Perekhody," Kasach reminded me of his question.

"The women were throwing their children out of the window, and straw was burning, down under the wall, and that's where the children fell... Hands stretched out of the window, like this. Mothers and women were stretching out their hands....

Like a blind man, I stretched out my hands with the fingers spread wide, and the changing, flickering light played over them. Kasach looked at me, at my fiery coloured fingers, and for the first time I saw in his face uncertainty, a question.

"I should never have listened to them! They begged and persuaded me not to touch the punitive squads in the village, so that people would not be burned. The Perekhods themselves, the old man and the nephew came to ask me. They said the families would be burned to death if we attacked the village. Well, there's your 'if' for you!"

It was as if Kasach was trying to justify himself to me!

"It's already a mania they've got. They can't just kill you, they have to either burn you alive, or freeze you to death or starve the life out of you. That cross-eyed maniac of theirs had prescribed them that rite, has he? No heaven has been brought so many sacrifices as they now make to earthly idols—some lance-corporal with a moustache. They set fire to you and they tried to freeze me to death in Forty-One. Right to the very last little tear, old man. The ground was as hard as iron, a bare field fenced off with barbed wire and in the middle there was a burned-down brick shell of a building. It must previously have been a small brick works. There were smashed kilns and pits. And many thousands of us. Frozen bodies were scattered about, in the pits and in the frozen kilns, lying in heaps of two and threes. If you do not share your warmth, you will not get warm! Those who could still crawl packed themselves into the brick shell of the building, piling themselves up right to the top. Those closer to the bottom kept warm, but those who kept warm immediately suffocated. Both the living as well as the dead had ice-covered beards from their last breath. Their last tear was one of ice as well. Yes, old boy, a person can become frozen deep down. Right to the last tear. You can. But then don't you go and whine later on!..."

He even stood up when he said, "...don't you go and whine!" He got up, looked at me surprised and suddenly grinned as if shutting himself up, as if shielding himself with his grin of non-recognition.

...And would he now have that constant smile for no one in particular? It was in his voice when he greeted me. If only I took a look at him, just a look. At Glasha. If I could see Syarozha just once. I remember my Syarozha as having blue eyes. I had dreamed of him being blue-eyed and fair-haired many times. From what Glasha said I knew that he had dark hair and his eyes were dark, too. If I were to see the real Syarozha, if they cured me, I would lose that blue-eyed, fair-haired one. You could even lose things like that.

I wondered how they looked together, Kasach and Glasha. In their world people were changing and growing older. But for me they were still the same. (That is apparently the only advantage of having a husband like me.)

My Boky is a bit like Kasach, you know. That has only just occurred to me now. I have never seen Boris Boky's face, but I imagine that it has on it that smile of Kasach's, constantly directed at God knows whom. You could feel it in Boris's voice and his words.

So, that is what it was all about. That is why I kept recalling my arguments with Boky on this bus, why they kept coming to mind. So, that is what the matter was!...

Glasha had met Kasach after the war, in Forty-Six after she returned from Germany. Kasach worked in the district executive committee in the same district where he had been a partisan.

Many years later, in Fifty-Three Glasha told me about their last meeting. She could never explain (and that tormented, surprised and even angered her) what had staggered her so about the new post-war Kasach and what had forced her to go away and leave him forever this time. Just as in Pushkin's "Blizzard", he was not the one, not the one! She had rushed to him, she had dreamed so much about the day when she would see and meet him again, even when she was in the concentration camp at Ozarichi where she lay on the snow, sick with typhus, and in Germany where the Germans had deported her. But when she saw him, she realised that he was not the one.

But, to judge by her stories, it was precisely that same Kasach that had been before, only in quite different circumstances, and she was already seeing things through quite different eyes. It was one thing when a war was being waged, everything was unsteady, you came across death and cruelty at every step, and among all this someone was the firmest, the most confident in any word and deed, so masterful and slightly mysterious, looking down on everything from some kind of incomprehensible, even scornful height. On everything, both the bad and the good. On everyone and on himself as well because he had seen, knew and remembered himself in all kinds of states. With the partisans and before the partisans, in captivity and perhaps in the prewar times: those times left a mark on him too.

Possibly I had made Kasach more complicated, imagining him to be a more involved person than he was. I even perceived his resemblance to Boky! But Glasha was an eighteen-year-old, still a girl really and she was in love with him. Naturally, she made him out to be even more compli-cated. She simply refused to understand and just loved him and tormented herself. She used to run to the glade to weep. She would think of anything she could to console herself, she indulged in fantasies, she even made up, that time in the glade, that she was going to have a baby.

Then it turned out quite differently when they met in Forty-Six. That period had responded differently in the various localities, although there was famine everywhere: half the country had been destroyed, killed, burned down, and then there was a terrible drought as well. But in what was previously the partisan zone where Kasach had remained to work, all that had a special tinge. All that remained of the villages were the birch trees, the maples, and the little benches near the sites of the fires overgrown with goose-foot and the occasional adobe houses in places. There were neither vehicles nor horses. People hitched themselves up to the plough and did the ploughing and harrowing.

But they had already become used to that during the war.

What people could not, and did not wish to become used to and what they did not expect was the fact that what they had experienced and suffered in the war would not be re-membered.

It was only afterwards, later on, that everything was re-called again: people came to reunions, erected monuments, wrote about it, and awards were made.

In Forty-Six, when asking for your tax, few people were interested what village you came from, whether there was a village, whether it still existed, whether there was a house. At times it turned out like the proverb that a husband loves a healthy wife and a brother a rich sister.

What did Kasach look like in a situation when personal bravery, a cold readiness to subject himself to mortal risk were no longer required of him, and he still remained ironically aloof from people with all their constant and harsh troubles, I could only guess at that. But it was precisely in this locality and to this Kasach that Glasha came.

"A person was standing before me, sitting at the desk, talking on the telephone or with a woman who was crying, shouting or grinning, and I had the feeling that I had not come to the right place, to the right person. Everything was just as it was, the face, the hands, the strong shoulders, even the jacket with the high collar was the same, only more threadbare. But we both felt awkward. Well, just imagine: it was night and a person saw one thing and then all of a sudden it was day, it was light!... I can't explain it. He was just not the one and that was all! But what hurts most is that I don't know, I don't remember what he, the real one, was like. He's not there in the past either. There is a cumbersome, strange person. That I remember. I remember my feelings. But the two are separate. There was something permeating the air itself, surrounding him, us, uniting us. When that air was dispelled there was nothing left.

You keep talking about someone else's pain. It would be very simple if it were the way you say it is. If he who had himself experienced a great deal could understand another person better. Sometimes, you know, quite the contrary is true, quite the other way round! A person finds himself drained. Kasach hit the nail on the head when he said that of himself, only it is amazing and even hurts me now that he never talked about anything serious with me and for some reason he suddenly did so with you.... You see, so try and understand us women. No, it's true, frozen to death. A house with its windows and doors torn out. During the war you counted yourself lucky if you could warm yourself in a house like that. But to live like that for the rest of your life?! That's frightening. I ran away. I did not look at the fact that there were twenty million fewer of you men and that same twenty million more of us. It would not be true if I said that I could not help thinking about you at that time. I remembered you and wept when they said, when the rumours went round that Flyora Gaishun had died in some military hospital. I often dreamed of you and how we escaped amidst the fires. But all the same, for me he was the pivot around which everything centered. Then I packed my things and left. I said that my mother was sick (it was true, she had lost the use of her legs). How he understood mention of my mother, I don't know. And she never told me anything. I don't know. I'm afraid to know everything. I felt such an old woman, so tired. The only time I felt at leisure was when I remembered our glade, and I healed my wounds with those memories. At times I wanted to meet him very much, but as a lonely, old, uninteresting person. Well, that's just a women's silliness..."

Why did I have such a desire to see Glasha and Kasach next to one another now? What did I want to convince myself of? That nothing passes in a woman? And nothing in general? Surely I must know that from my own experience! Look how you feel it all—as something long dead and withered. It begins to hurt. That is the way frozen fingers begin to hurt in the warmth. The more feeling you lost in them before being in the warmth, the greater is the sensation of pain when they start coming to life.

This is how Glasha found me. In Fifty-Three she came to get a place at an institute on an external course. After being confined to bed for a long time, Glasha's mother died, and Glasha arrived. Suddenly she spotted Flyora alive near the dean's office. Possibly, if she had not thought that I had passed away in that military hospital, she would not have cried out like that, to the amazement of the entire corridor, she would not have thrown herself on the neck of a joyfully blushing young lecturer. The years that had passed since that day when I had departed across the marshes and she had remained on the "island", sorrowful as if she had a presentiment, would not have been erased immediately like that. What happened on the "island" afterwards, I learned from her in that very institute corridor.

Five days later, the punitive squads managed to reach the "island". When they crawled out on the bank, wet, stinking and furious they began to gun down everything that was hidden or ran behind the bushes. Styopka the Conjuror (he was the only one of the partisans who could move about on his crutch) defended himself by firing and then hopped over and sat down among the wounded and dragged towards himself the kitbag containing the tolite. Glasha and three small children lay in the swamp outside and saw exactly what happened. He ran over, threw away his crutch and his rifle and sat down. The wounded crawled up to him, and he laid their heads against himself, on the bag of tolite. Glasha also wanted to run over to him for the punitive squads were just about to come out of the bushes. She already heard their voices. But she was so terrified, she could not get up. Especially when the wounded crept over to him as if he were a saviour, and he carefully put their heads in place. In the end, her eyes met with those of Styopka the Conjuror. He looked (every time when Glasha was recounting this, she burst into tears at that point) and somehow smiled in a strange way.

"But perhaps I just thought he did. They were crawling over to him, and he held the grenade to the bag of tolite, watching me as if he was begging me for help, not to look away, not to hide, not to be afraid, smiling at me... I could bear it no longer, hid myself and immediately there was an explosion!...

When the Germans dragged us across the 'island', drove all those they had not killed, I once more saw the place where the wounded had been..."

Just before we were married, Glasha and I went to the Braslav region to visit the lakes. While I was putting up the tent, she went off somewhere and then called me, her voice changed and unfamiliar. Startled, I ran over to her, but she was sitting calmly, her arms round her sunburnt knees, and gazing down at the still beauty of the evening lake framed by yellow birch trees reflected in the water, which seemed to be still alight with the day, and the dark, completely nocturnal fir trees.

From the beauty of the visible world I had always experienced a feeling that was agonising rather than joyful. It was as if you were a narrow-necked bottle into which they were pouring a wide stream of thick sticky honey. Some of it ended up inside, but more trickled down the walls of the vessel outside. (But, on the other hand, now I could strain it in a thin, economical trickle, saving every single drop. What has been collected inside the dark vessel has been enclosed there forever. That is all that remains to you and there will be nothing new. Pour it, strain it, from yourself into yourself...)

Glasha interpreted my silence in her own way.

"You'd better say: don't interfere, if you yourself do nothing!"

She smiled guiltily, joyfully and submissively. That was something new and unusual in her that had appeared after the war, she would put the words in my mouth, while always making it easier for me, but reproaching herself. ("You'd better tell me, I've got enough to do without those women's tears. You'd better tell me: you can work things out with your Kasach yourself...")

Once she suddenly started telling me what happened to her after the "island", about the typhoid-ridden concentration camp sited next to the frontline near Ozarichi, in Polessye, about a five-year-old boy who died on the wet snow.

"He kept consoling me, I was keeping him warm and he promised, 'When I come home, I'll make three stoves, for Mum, for me and for you!' His mother had been shot and was already lying by the barbed wire. She had wanted to gather some twigs to warm up... There I go again... You have seen war..."

It kept on seeming to Glasha that she was imposing her memories, her tears, her past on me. I tried to make her understand, believe that that was my past as well and my memories, that it was all ours. Gradually she believed it, but once she had been convinced, as often happens with women, she immediately went further. Now it seemed to her that she had not been in love with Kasach at all but with me, and it was only my foolish love for the commander and my conviction that she could love only him, only someone like him, had prevented her from sorting herself out. On the whole, I could have been more like Kasach, only not so lacking in feelings.

I could not bear it—the sincere way she reproached me, with such an awareness that she was right and I was to blame—and I began to chuckle loudly. Glasha became angry and was even more hurt: "Well, what are you so cheerful about like that Flyora on the machine-gun cart! I've been through so much because of you. And who was the cause of it then?"

"Aha, you're getting muddled up again, Akulina Ivanovna's eyes with Nikolai Fyodorovich's figure this time, is it?..."

"It's impossible to have a serious conversation with you!"

What was she feeling at this moment when both of us, Kasach and I were there? The initial tension when she probably did not know herself how such a situation would be perceived, had receded. She was already sitting differently and talking to Syarozha in the ordinary way she usually did at home. Her face probably bore that naively tranquil expression with which she had fallen asleep, leaning against the tree, at that time, during the blockade, which seemed to say, "You yourself can sort out all this about war and death!" She was tired of it. Sort it out for yourselves, if you are like that... But what were we like, Kasach and I, to see things with her eyes? Time and again I detected in her signs of irritation with us both, already with us both. Yes, Kasach supposedly did not exist for her. She was even surprised at what had happened, that anything at all could have happened between them, but she was often annoyed by things about me, about Flyora.

"It's good to be Flyora, but not to such an extent! You're not seventeen now. It's time you stopped being so humble. Are you going to go on like that for the rest of your life?"

It was no longer Kasach that I had to be jealous of, but of someone else who was not like Kasach, but not like Flyora either. Of her feelings in the future. Those "feelings in the future" are always there in women. As tomorrow's and not just today's measure of humankind, of the humane. And for that there is no reason why women themselves have to be better than us. They have simply been given that quality to preserve. No matter in which direction life is surging, we measure ourselves, make checks, love or scorn with a woman's view all the same....

At night the detachments moved into the depths of the marshes. The glow of the burning forests to which the fires had now spread cast yellow reflections of the low clouds scurrying to meet us, lying on the water, under our feet, imparting to everything an even more hasty, troubled tempo. If you lagged behind, they would catch on with you, if you ran ahead, you would bump into them! We were going away from the punitive squads while advancing towards them. And the more distinct that feeling became, the more obstinately we headed to the other edge of the marshes where battalions and ambushes were probably moving and spreading out, lying in wait for us. The squelching noise on the mud, the splashes, the infuriated or awkwardly cheerful cries, the heavy breathing all seemed to go on forever; no one knew when it had begun, nor when it would end. Yours and someone else's hands came together, grabbed one another, clung to one another or pushed one another away in fright, for you had to keep going. We were carrying the wounded, on stretchers and blankets, six or eight of us to a stretcher, clutching the cloth or tarpaulin until our fingers and nail hurt. They had to be held as high up as possible, but sometimes the bottom would disappear under your feet and then people would fling themselves to one side and the other, keeping the stretcher in place and clinging onto it, as it were. Those who were close would hasten to assist and something like a skirmish would start, a struggle amidst grunts, shouts and swear words.

The faces and eyes of the wounded in the midst of all this struck one by their fixed stare, even indifference which disguised despair and shame, helplessness, and a feeling of hurt at their own failure. But even among the wounded there were their own "jesters".

"Pull in the fishing nets, chaps. We'll have some fish soup."

I was replaced at the blanket stretchers, but immediately Kostya Chief of Staff caught sight of me, did not recognise me, of course, but commanded:

"Help the guards. For some reason we're dragging those Jerries along with us! The devil only knows why!..."

We were driving them ahead of us for some reason and we did supposedly understand why, but we were amazed in turns, "The devil only knows!" I found them there where the voices were louder and sterner. The Perekhods, the old man and the nephew, were there. They were the most tacit of the guards.

It was odd to see those thugs trying not to step in the swamp, wallow and stretch towards the stunted trees and tussocks, grabbing onto the partisans, even onto the Perekhods, onto each other as if they did not understand that they were already dead men. But no one obviously believes that while one is still alive. This is why people do at times behave very strangely and awkwardly, if you observe them from the side. The prisoners had become so drenched in the swamp that I did not immediately recognise my shaven-headed enemy, and he was like a blind man without his spectacles. (He no longer had the monkey with him.) We found ourselves next to each other a few times. But strange as it may seem, it was as if I was ashamed of something. I did not want him to recognise me now when we were on our own together and not in a crowd of partisans where I would seek to attract his attention to make him see me, and recognise me as the one who had escaped from the village he had massacred. There was a reason why I protested like that, so hated their helpless submissiveness, their obedient assiduity right from the start. They definitely knew beforehand, expected that awkwardness would arise in me from the awareness of having complete power over someone's life and death. It was an awkwardness from which they themselves, I recall, did not suffer.

I was keeping track of my main enemy as if attached to him, I watched for him as if from ambush, but kept at a distance for I did not want our eyes to meet.

Suddenly the deceptive surface on which he stepped rocked menacingly in the yellow darkness. He immediately fell, squawking like a woman and waving his arms about. At first the fingers appeared, spread wide, stretching out, then the head came into sight and remained still as if severed, on the shuddering surface of the firm moss, a head without a face, without eyes, intermingled with the slime as if it had just been overgrown with it.

"Heh, help that fellow over there. Can't you see him!" they shouted to me. Holding shakily onto a low snag, I thrust forward the barrel of my rifle, touching his moving fingers. They snatched at the barrel at once, and I nearly drew it back. He was already hanging on, weighing me down and dragging me off tin rocking tussock as well. If that had been a stick and not a rifle, I would already have let it go. Now it was as if we were fighting over the rifle, tearing it away from each nilior. I pulled towards me the head entwined with water-weed and the mire, the jerking shoulders, the arms of my enemy; he seized at the snag, at me eager, terrified, blind. I was already pushing him away, ripping him off me, and shrieking wildly, "So, you're going to keep trying, are you? Be off with you, you vermin!"

The mud swam round the shaven head, and I could already see those eyes close to me and crazed with the terror they experienced. And they appeared to recognise me.

And then, jerking my rifle to one side, I loaded it, but I could not stop myself grabbing hold of his shoulder. I crabbed and grabbed at him and, looking into those eyes reflecting the yellow glow of the distant fires, I cried, "You, fascist, want to look and climb out, scum, to live, yes, to live, isn't it?"

I was shouting his sentence at him and could not get through those senselessly frightened eyes of an old man with mud all over his head. Those eyes were in front of me and, since we were so close to each other, and I would kill him, I wanted to see the one who had stood by the vehicle, sat in it....

Evidently, realising that he was about to die, he screamed and flung himself aside, sinking into the mire up to his waist again. I rushed after him, right at him. Now I was pushing him, driving him, rubbing my watering eyes. It was precisely him that I was hounding, and he knew it was me, that I was here, that all the time I was going after him. He looked around shortsightedly as if seeking me. Now he knew who was his boss, who was in charge of his life and death, and somehow that had a strange effect on him; he became even more assiduous, as if saving his life already specially for me.

At last we managed to clamber out into a flooded meadow on the edge of the marshes. The morning drizzle fell on our burning faces, our necks and hands from which the steam was rising.

We tried to pour the yellow water out of our boots without taking them off. To anyone watching that must have looked like strange morning exercises: a huge, worn-out crowd of people, standing in the middle of a wet meadow, each engaged in holding on to their neighbours and picking up his leg backward like a bird and then stretching it out in front of him. Those who were not wearing boots, but rawhide sandals or even bast shoes, tiredly praised their footwear in which nothing gets caught. You've got something on your feet and are barefoot at the same time. Who's for doing a swap? But no one was eager to neither exchange their footwear with them nor even keep up the weary banter.

Some three hundred people were standing in the shallow water in the meadow, hopelessly soaked, on their very last legs, and holding stretchers. Gazing at each other as if at their own reflection, they washed the mud off their clothing, their faces, rinsing their caps and forage caps in the water. They tried to clean the black dirt off the faces of the wounded if the latter could not do it themselves.

The punitive squad members were washing themselves hesitantly, without saying a word.

Huge willow bushes were ensconced on the water like hay-ricks; you could even sit on them. While there was some hold-up ahead, many tried to take a rest, to sit down but they were unable to, and there was no way that you could sprawl on your stomach or your back. Tired, dejected laughter was already ringing out.

We assembled the punitive squad members by one large willow bush, and they leaned on it as well though it rocked and crackled. Already the faces had that morning look, rather than a night one and that was quite a different matter. After a difficult night the morning emphasises the fatigue in any person as well as the relief that it has ended, that it has passed. The punitive squad members were already washing themselves more boldly, more diligently, and if they had the means, they would have cleaned their teeth: scooping up the water in their palm, with one hand, over and over again, and all this not without purpose. They were preparing to live yet another day and it was as if they were cautiously asking us, standing there opposite them with the weapons, or were convincing us....

My enemy was meticulously washing his head, which was again smooth and blotchy like a badly painted Easter egg; his short-sighted eyes were seeking out someone; I could not help thinking it was me. He seemed to place some kind of hope in that quest. Amongst the faceless hatred, he had sensed my own, although it was animosity as well, but for a definite person. Instead of fearing me even more, he was looking for me, if you please! For all that, he had acquaintances here! I did not allow his helplessly swimming eyes to become fixed on my face, I would walk past him without showing him any sign of recognition. It should indeed be the last straw for me to be shy in actual fact, to stand to sternly and mercilessly before him, all covered in mud and meek! Don't look, you won't find it, you won't....

Among the "non-Germans" who definitely kept themselves apart, the most prominent was the interpreter with the Adam's apple. Not only his height attracted attention, but the expression of some kind of constant, senseless cunning on his face as well. He lost his cap with the long peak which distinguished him from the Germans, and that worried him greatly; there was even a moment when he took the cap off his fellow countryman next to him to keep his head warm, as it were, but the latter suddenly remembered it and took it back. He kept on trying to talk to us.

"Oh, we're tired. You've got some real marshes here!"

He looked somewhat startled, perhaps he had said the wrong thing. And he reported that this was not a good time for rain because the harvest was about to be taken in.

"But, on the other hand, it will give us a wash."

How craftily he stressed that common "us".

"Shut up! You over there!" Someone could not bear it any longer, and the interpreter, startled, shrank away, but immediately translated it to his own people, evidently passing that on as a general command. After shuffling about, the punitive squad members fell silent.

Partisans were still coming up. Something was attracting them here. Kasach, in his dolman jacket brown with caked mud, with straggly, wet fringes round the edge, gripping a submachine-gun with his elbow, walked over and grinned sullenly at his neighbour, the moustached commander: "Are you going to be humping your trophies about for a long time?"

"You've got some people here from Perekhody, so take them and decide what you're going to do with them."

Kasach looked at the punitive squad members in a supposedly calm manner, as if from a distance, but the interpreter could not help reminding him, "We're not Germans!"

And he pointed to the caps (and to his own uncovered head as well).

"Is that so?" Kasach was surprised. "Well, what should we do with them? With your bosses?"

"They deserve to be executed," the interpreter said loudly and clearly.

"That's precisely what you will do to them now, since you serve them!"

Kasach glanced several times at the elder Perekhod who was standing stock still in front of the punitive squad members. The look was a nagging one: was that right, what Kasach was doing or preparing to do? For this reason it was I unlike Kasach to have such an inquiring look. Yet there was something very characteristic of Kasach in that look, wickedly testing, when he knew the answer beforehand.

"Come on then, give them rifles."

But still we did not understand him.

"With the locks removed," Kasach explained, instantly irritated.

We snapped the breech-locks off the rifles. At these sounds the punitive squad members shifted, crouched, and the bush behind their backs heaved and cracked. But terror, stark terror contorted their faces and showed in their eyes when the German punitive squad members saw that the rifles were being handed to their neighbours in the strange caps.

Staletaw ran over from somewhere as if afraid of missing something. He had not seen what had occurred here, and his eyes squinted in fright and eagerness. He did not understand why the punitive squad members were holding rifles. He stepped from one leg to the other, pushing himself closer to the "non-Germans". On his back he was carrying a kitbag that was squirming and wriggling as if it was alive. I did not understand what was in it straight away, but when I did, I forgot about Staletaw and his kitbag directly and only recalled and thought about it for a long time when it was all over. So, that was where the monkey from the shoulder of the murderer-in-chief was. Staletaw had got the job of carrying it. It seemed as if it had happened on purpose. He was the chronicler. The live, wriggling, breathing sack, and Stataw himself was squirming, bobbing about from foot to foot....

Someone shouted, "Go on then, slaughter them if you're butchers!"

The four "non-Germans", as if bewitched, listened to the soft, whispered commands of their interpreter and leader. Taking the rifles by the barrels, they stepped back from the other punitive squad members who were squatting and pressing themselves into the willow bush, which was moving, heaving and rocking. Those with the stick-like rifles were also gently swaying back and forth as they kept watch, stepping from one foot to the other and cocking the truncheon-like weight of the butts. They drew level and kept quietly and swiftly talking to each other in their own language. With an abrupt cry, the interpreter suddenly raced towards my enemy. The butt flew over the shaven head, and the hollow crunching sound that the blow made, was immediately muffled by the completely hare-like cry of the dumpy German at whom two had thrown themselves together!...

Then came a round of submachine-gun fire! Unexpected, abrupt, it came like deliverance, like relief.

Two of the punitive squad members with rifles and several Germans, clumsily trying to grab hold of the bush and of one another, began to slip down into the water. The round of fire had rung out, the echo had faded, and they were still holding each other tight, continuing to fall. There was a relaxed look, one unfamiliar and undeceitful, on the interpreter's face. He stood, leaning low on his rifle and suddenly butted head first steeply into the water and the mud.

"The devil take them! The devil take them!" Perekhod shouted. He was the one who had fired. "The devil take them all!"

At this point there was a despairing cry from behind the bushes.

"Stop it! What are you doing? You there! What are you up to?"

We raced in the direction where the cry had come from. Behind the bush the younger Perekhod was kneeling down and seemed to be looking for something in the water, scrutinising the mud, inclining his head and his face lower and lower. The partisan who had cried out was looking at us furiously and stretching out his hands towards him, either pointing him out to us or wishing to grab hold of him and lift him up. A dark red spot with a tinge of blue was floating in the blackness, in the mud, rapidly dispersing. The hand of the younger Perekhod that was pressed against his jersey on his stomach was terrifyingly aflame with blood. Perekhod the elder looked at him stunned. He strode over to the punitive squad members, seized two of them, a German and a "non-German". From his heavy hands they collapsed in a heap, but he jerked them up onto their limp feet and struck one of them with the other, and again and again, each time more feebly, but all the time with ever greater despair, shouting, "Curse you, curse you, curse you!"

...We moved on, heading towards the German flares hardly visible in the morning light. We kept hoping we might manage to slip through into the big woods which the block-ade had not cut off. That striving of hundreds of people towards an exit which had already been shut off or was about to be closed was at the same rapid pace away from (but also towards) what had happened by the rick-shaped willow bushes and seemed to be still continuing. As soon as we made a halt, it would happen again, it would come back. But where could we flee to, escape to, if the same sort of punitive squads were laying await up ahead of us like the four survivors whom we were driving along with us?... The reconnaissance plane was already flying over us, now soaring upwards, now losing altitude. The sparse bushes could not hide us from that eye in the sky. We already sensed, as if seeing their shadows, that ahead, in the direction we were fleeing, German battalions were moving, ambushes were being laid, and they were lying in wait for us.

The water underfoot came to an end. In its place there was old, dried-up mud-like tar, and finally we were on dry ground, in a surprisingly waterless peat bog. It seemed as if there had not been any rain there, it had just sprinkled a bit for the sake of the glinting sun and the waxy, spicy smell of the peat and the ledum. We did not have the strength left to brush away the short-backed stinging horse-flies. On the other hand, we no longer had to deal with the clouds of mosquitoes in Polessye. Autumn had whisked them away, although it was still not cold. You would sprawl on the ground and your whole body would feel how soft and light it was, all grasses and fragrances. The tall, dried-out tussocks of the bushes were growing dark deliciously and enticingly with late berries, large dark blue bog whortleberries. People were so worn out that they just looked at the berries, licking their dry lips, reluctantly exchanging remarks ("Those whortleberries make your head ache if you eat too many!", "Come on, give me some!" "Straight away!"). But the partisans were already arranging themselves round the appetising bushes, just as if they were getting ready to sit down at table. Some were crawling up to them and some rolling up like a log. It was good in that position, you did not even have to get up. The most heavily laden bushes had already been taken over; the partisans pulled German crackers out of their bags, some talked of water.

"Wouldn't you like some tea?"

"You should have drunk your fill when you were neck-deep in water."

They gave some of the berries to the wounded who were well enough to eat. There were many of them, far too many wounded. Some had lost consciousness, they were in a fever, and cried out, and those who had their eyes open scanned the low skies where the importunate airplane continued to whine. The wounded knew where we were taking them, into what battles, helpless as they were and completely dependent on the hands, feet, braveness and weakness of others....

Among them there was also Shardyko, our commissar. When the detachment had breached the blockade, the Germans had riddled him with machine-gun bullets across his waist. But he was still alive although he was unconscious. Several times I saw Kasach and Kostya Chief of Staff going over to him accompanied by our lively, round little Filippov. The detachment doctor guiltily mentioned some medicines and injections he needed but did not have.

It seemed that only Perekhod never sat down on the ground and never rested. Huge in his stiff tarpaulin raincoat, he stood by the stretchers on which his deathly pale nephew was breathing heavily. Perekhod would look at the wounded man with a strange, somehow aloof surprise. There was something very alarming about his stance, the stance of a person who was about to do something unexpected and terrible. At his feet a little girl sat over the delirious young Perekhod, her mouth crammed full of berries, her lips stained, and tears rolling down her cheeks. The little girl from Perekhody was crying again.

Something had changed about the punitive squad members who had survived. They sat tightly huddled together with their eyes lowered. There was something reproachful in their posture, in those injured looks cast downwards. The partisans had not appreciated their disciplined behaviour and humility—now they had become convinced of it. But, no matter what happened, they seemed determined to remain the same, as a reproach to us. Perhaps that was not what they had in mind, but their posture and attitude seemed to belie this intention. Now they did not take sides against one another, the two Germans and the two "non-Germans". Perhaps because so few of them were left. But it was still strange that what had happened near the bushes had not parted them completely, but had even brought them together again....

In detachments and platoons, with people whose hands were taken up by the wounded at the back, we moved across the arid marshes, ready to go into battle immediately. There seemed no end to the old ditches overgrown with yellowish-brown sedge, the dune-like heaps of peat fragments, rusty-black and only covered with green grass in places. Before the war peat was extracted here. The ground was springy underfoot, giving you the feeling that you were walking on a suspended bridge. There were not centimetres but metres of peat in the depths of the bog. A young partisan (he had not been in Perekhody, his eyes did not hurt or water like mine) suddenly jumped up as if he had been bitten and landed on the ground on his knees.

"You Byelorussians, it's like a mattress, you fellows!"

Some looked in amazement, others disapprovingly at a person who was still ready for a game. Such remarks were passed as "If fire strikes, it will burn for six months".

"It's already burning over there, you can see."

A soft light blue cloud of smoke, gently being dispelled into the low damp sky, was hovering over the distant peat mounds.

We spotted people. First, it was little children running among the peat dunes. A bare-footed woman came out quite close in front of us from behind a black-and-green heap of peat, she went a few steps and suddenly noticed us. She quickly returned and hid. The children had also disappeared.

They had been watching us, it seemed. But then women and children came out of the shelter again. More and more of them appeared. And there were a few men's bearded faces. The entrance holes showed up black against the densely settled peat hills overgrown with grass. Probably a whole village was hiding in these burrows.

"You gave us such a fright, lads, we were really worried!" several women began to speak all at once as we approached. "Yesterday the Germans passed by, but they were over there, along that edge. They did not notice us. Here we thought that was it, that they were coming straight at us!"

"Did many go by?" the moustached commander asked.

"Yes, a lot! Perhaps three times as many as you are."

The partisans peeped into the shallow burrows in the peat; it was dark inside and under there feet blankets and bedding were scattered about, and by the entrances there were cast iron pots and buckets.

"Don't they cave in?"

"It comes down thick and fast at night. You get peat crumbs in your mouth and your ears. But it does keep the rain off."

"Are you hungry, lad?"

"Why, have you got something, girls?"

"It's obvious what! Baked potatoes. And nice sour sorrel. We use it instead of salt."

"This time we have got something to offer you. We borrowed it from the Germans," said the commander with the moustache. "Where's our quartermaster?"

But nobody turned down the baked potatoes either. The potatoes were soon ready here, and you could put as many of them on to bake in the red hot peat pit as you liked. A kind of funnel had formed in the ground, oblong, about five paces long, filled with whitish, smoking cinders. Everyone was curious to measure the depth of the hot peat, poking about in it with sticks and poles. The smoke was acrid and toxic, especially for my eyes. But I wanted to have a look as well. It appeared to be an ordinary fire, giving off heat, but there was something menacing and sinister about that fire that was devouring the very soil.

"Why did you light it so close to you, you won't be able to put it out now," we told our hosts, "watch out, or the fire will creep under you."

"God knows who set light to it! It just lies there and lies there and then bursts into flame," the women retorted, convinced. "It's all nice and dry like gunpowder! You won't find any water here. We go to the marshes for water. Then there's those mines, and the flares they keep releasing, what do you expect! Of course, everything's burning."

"You can't get near that forest. It's been burning since spring," the old man who was the stoker at the pit interrupted. "Yesterday the children saw a wild boar. Our people ran after it and drove it towards the fire, but they could not get near it. The ground would not hold them. There has been rainfall, but it's still smouldering there, and a crust has formed on top. One minute the boar was there, the next it had gone. All there was a shower of sparks. Perhaps it was a metre away and perhaps three. There was roast pork for you, and you could not get it."

"Girls, perhaps the fire is already under us, perhaps it's crept this far. You'll wake up one morning and you'll already be baked!"

The women laughed. There is a limit to man's sufferings beyond which the tears dry up and a person can no longer complain....

It is precisely over there that we had to go, where that ominous blue smoke was spreading above the horizon dissected by the peal hills. Somewhere we had to skirt round that ground fire.

The moustached commander remained with his detachment and his wounded. He could not bring himself to go any further, to leave the marshes. Kasach and he talked or argued about something for a long time. When we were already on the move, I heard him say to Kostya Chief of Staff, "It's enough that I listened to them there, in Perekhody."

Even now it is difficult to say who was right, the moustached commander or our own. But, as always happens in such alarming and uncertain situations, the slightest hesitation at the top soon multiplies into the anxiety of many, turning into real, serious disquiet. The main tiling was that we had almost two dozen wounded on our hands.

The next round of fighting began in confusion and was therefore ill-omened....

We had already gone some four kilometres but could not find any way round the burning strip of peat on the horizon. We got close to it several times. Kasach himself went to take a look. Those who went returned, excited and somewhat perplexed.

"Well, chaps, it is as quiet as a volcano!"

"The ground feels warm for half a kilometre away from it."

Finally we spotted some forest in the distance ahead. Owing to the smoky haze we could not tell whether it was a whole forest or just a patch of woodland, but all the same it was forest and not these wearisome green and rust-coloured "dunes" and the stunted little pines scattered about on all sides. People kept having terrible fits of coughing and their throats were dreadfully sore. Their eyes were so irritated, they were always rubbing their eyes. But for my eyes which had had soil in them the peaty, smoke-laden breeze was really harmful. Everything around me was swimming, coloured with a hot rainbow. I had an intense feeling of nausea. But the forest lay ahead, a real live forest and soon this revolting, black, dirty, friable, soft, smoking pillow would come to an end, and we would step on real ground. We had the sensation that in general we would return from somewhere to earth.

The wounded were at the back. The surviving members of the punitive squad were going with us, with the fighting group, still protected by our stunning, binding hatred for them.

The patrols had already approached the forest, when mines started to go bang in front of us, at the sides and behind us....

We all lay down, waiting for these first, most uncertain moments of such unexpected fighting to pass. The ground shuddered gently as if it were alive, and the black imprints of the explosions immediately began to smoulder dryly and to smoke.

It was strange that they were not firing at us from machine-guns or submachine-guns. Only mines were groping for us. From where were they bombarding us?

There were still no orders and that made everyone nervous. So long as no one jumped up and ran away! Then somebody leapt up and fled.

And another two or three. There could be nothing worse than that. They were keeping to the right, running towards the heaps of peat which, when you were lying down, looked like the backs of antediluvian creatures, hiding and warm. The air above them was quivering, spurting upwards....

Suddenly shots rang out, a round of machine-gun fire. One fell, three fled even more quickly, bending down and zigzagging. It was the prisoners who were running away, the members of the punitive squads!

It seemed that the first of those fleeing had stepped on a mine. A column of sparks rose over the spot where he had just been. Immediately another one, the last of those fleeing had vanished. They were disappearing into the hot peat, into the red-hot ground which had absorbed the heat!...

The one in the middle froze on the spot, then spun round, and we heard him not only screaming, but howling in inhuman terror....

"The 1st Company remains here, 1st Company!" shouted Kostya Chief of Staff, running ahead of us. And then the loud voice of Kasach was heard interrupted by the explosions.

"2nd Company! 2nd Company follow me!"

He ran towards the bushes, waving his submachine-gun.

That was the moment when everything that has been, is and will be looks you in the eyes, asking "Are you ready?" You must not miss it or give way to it!...

I leapt up and ran after Kasach, after Perekhod, after those who were in front of me. People were rising up from beneath the explosions and running towards an invisible enemy. The soft, springy ground was assisting us in our dash as if it were alive, somehow tilting us forward. We raced into the little hollow, going round the willow bushes. On the left was the horizon floating in the smoke, in the bluish fumes, broken by the peat mounds, on the right the green willow bushes growing densely like a wall. Ahead of us, somewhere beyond the willow bushes there was that still invisible enemy that was hurling mortar shells at us. Many of the faces, flushed as they were or turning grey with exhaustion, of the people running alongside me bore an expression of distrustful and alarmed curiosity as to what we were doing. We were running, not lying low, not waiting to see when the Germans would show themselves, when they would appear; we did not even try to find out where they were and how many of them there were, and from whence they were firing on us. Instead of that we were running in the direction where an ambush or a trap perhaps awaited us. But since we were doing that, even to our own amazement, and since our dash forward was so vicious and unrelenting, everything, from our faces, our heavy breathing, the noiseless flashing of our feet, to our tensed up shoulders and necks, and our elbows held away from our bodies, betrayed the growing conviction that right now we would fall upon our enemies and crush them for they would not be expecting us to race forward so blindly, taking such a risk.

Perekhod the elder was padding along in front unwieldily and heavily. His shapeless back, stone-grey in the tarpaulin, his head with its bull neck and those hurried gasps for breath indicated only one thing, that he must run where he was going, get there at last, become free of himself, so intolerably malicious and powerless in the face of his petrified fury.

We were skirting the endless willow bushes which seemed to go on and on forever, and still we did not come across those that we were trying to reach.

And then we saw them, two mortar barrels standing by the bushes and pointing in our direction. A round of submachine-gun fire spurted forth—that was Kasach. Those eyes of mine, blurred with pain, also caught sight of something flashing tip ahead. Without taking aim, I fired in that direction. Shots sounded, rending the air from behind and from the sides, Perekhod alone kept running without raising his submachine-gun and without firing.

The bushes straightened up to form a wall, and we saw men, five or six of them fleeing. They headed so helplessly and hurriedly for the distant edge of the willow bushes, especially one of them, who was lagging behind with his short legs in German soldier's trousers with their baggy seats, that all of a sudden everything took on the appearance of some kind of cruel merriment. And the most absurd thing was that from the acrid fumes and from all the running both we and they were coughing. As we kept on running, hurried shots sounded and the dead had just started to fall, but neither they nor we could refrain from that simple hacking cough that hindered us.

For some reason they did not fling themselves into the bushes but kept on fleeing before us, probably only seeing the edge of the willow bushes that would provide them with cover from us and from our shots. The closer they got to the edge of the bushes the more abrupt and hurried the firing became. Like something disintegrating, they fell one at a time, to the right, at the back, to the left. Two did manage to leap behind the willow bushes anyway. The very last of those in fight, the assiduous, clumsy little fat chap, still found time to look round with the eyes and twisted mouth of a person who saw his own death coming to him....

After firing a few shots into him, Kasach also looked round as if warning us not to linger round the dead. Perekhod kept on running without noticing those who had fallen, those he needed were ahead of him and he needed them alive, not dead....

There they were again, the two remaining ones. At first, we heard them, their hacking cough like a faint echo in re-sponse to the dozen of bouts of coughing on our side. The willow hushes straightened out again, and there they were in front of us again, out in the open and doomed. They looked round.

One of them immediately dropped his rifle and finally plunged into the bushes, breaking them down as he fell. The other one kept on running straight forward, although it was obvious that he himself felt and was aware that these were his last steps.

Perekhod wiped him out with a short, fastidious round and ran on, even without looking at the dead man. No, wounded man. Looking as if he had been run over by a tank, the latter stirred, and without lifting his head, crawled towards us. His hands, his blood-stained fingers, at which he seemed to be staring, greatly resembled goose feet....

He crawled along and stopped three paces from me, agreeing that he was dead!...

We were running after Perekhod and Kasach, drenched with sweat, and we could not get rid of that awkward coughing. We ran on as if we knew that these men were not the main ones, and that the main thing was up ahead.

"Vlasov's men, swine!" someone shouted belatedly about the dead men. I looked round and saw that a partisan had paused for a moment, turned over the body of the fat man and pulled out of his belt a long grenade. True, their rifles were not German ones! And their uniforms looked more yellow....

We skirted the willow bushes once more, keeping to our left the path beaten out by someone else. It veered away from under our feet into the smoke-laden distances of the burning peat.

At this moment we saw people in green, German uniform running out of the willow bushes in front of us. In helmets and with submachine-guns!... At that moment the Vlasov man who had plunged into the willow grove not long ago, emerged from the bushes and ran towards the Germans. Both he and we were racing along as if down a slope and over sharp stones. You realise, as happens in dreams, that you must stop before it's too late, but you cannot and are even afraid to; while you are running everything continues, but as soon as you stop, you will be dragged along, roll over the sharp stones, spattering them with blood....

Submachine-gun fire rounds screeched, ours, not ours, another, then another. Ten Germans, not more, ran out from behind the bushes, and we were out in the open, all one hundred of us, if not one hundred and fifty. And there was something inevitable about us racing straight towards them (we ourselves felt that, were aware of it as if seeing ourselves), because the Germans, instead of lying down and firing point-blank, rushed back and forth and suddenly, turning their hastening backs to our shots, they retreated.

Involuntarily I looked round at us, at our strength, which had had such an effect and had crushed the Germans like that. I was both glad and fearful. Rout them, rout them! These were short, fading minutes (you realised that) because the instant was approaching when both this chase across the springy peaty ground and that feeling would end. But we would still be drawn forward like a body rolling down a steep slope over sharp stones!...

Perekhod was still racing ahead. I could only feel the rest next to me and behind me, but I could see him. My eyes, watering, and stinging painfully, were fixed on him as if he was the most important and last part of what remained of me in the world, I reenacted his movements without thinking (perhaps not in actual fact, but only in my thoughts, deep down in my own muscles), increasingly becoming part of that huge, heavy person, fettered in that formless, stone-coloured tarpaulin.

Ever so slowly (as if pondering upon it), Perekhod lifted lus submachine-gun up with both hands like a heavy hammer, above the helmet of a dumpy German who was running right in front of him. But someone's bullet knocked the German out from under Perekhod's submachine-gun, and hurled him to one side. Without looking in that direction, Perekhod was already flying at the next one. It seems that he was (that you were) not capable of stopping while you were alive, while you were still going and that you would run round the forest like that as long as there was someone in front of you.

The Germans whom we were following and shooting on the run kept trying to skirt the willow bushes, to hide themselves in them, and we did not know who was up ahead, who could be lying in wait for us with machine-guns....

My eyes were completely swimming in a hot rainbow of dark blue, orange and red. Everything was unclear and floating apart, and I clung to that dark figure of Perekhod, keeping my eyes fixed on him as if he were the most real thing.

I do not know how long we were running, how long the spring was pressed down under our sudden impact. But I recall the wild, irrational relief (like that of someone who has stopped running, but is getting faster and faster down a stone slope and finally rolls to the bottom!) which slashed our souls with acute cold when we ran out into the open space and immediately saw in front of us the motionless German line, lying in wait beyond the peat hummocks. Helmets, helmets and more helmets....

But Perekhod did not stop or fall down, and that kept me on my feet, although everything in me immediately became heavy like stone.

"Lie down!" shouted Kasach, but did not fall down either. Perekhod prevented him from doing that, too. Perekhod was running even faster, tearing himself away from us, from the partisans who were sinking down one after another. There was neither the sound of shots nor human voices, but a mute silence, disappearing and falling into an invisible (although it was next to us) precipice.

Already prostrate on the ground, I felt something fly over us like a train whisking away the air from us, tearing me away from the ground, compelling me to press myself to it. The train kept racing forwards, endless, low, wide, right above my head, above my shoulders, just about to catch hold of you, drag you along, cutting us up carelessly. Machine-guns and submachine-guns were simply howling! When I tore my head away from the peat which reeked of burning, and looked through the swimming rainbow, Perekhod was still there, although it seemed as if a whole eternity had flown by. But he was no longer running but standing and slowly turning towards us as if being swung round by the machine-gun firing point-blank (I seemed to see both the flame bursting forth and even the hands of the German). Perekhod was facing us; his face was implausibly serene and attentive. He had not yet fallen, but light low clouds were scurrying over him, and it seemed that he was falling there, like the top of a felled shuddering tree which was still stationary down below....

From the moment when he fell and my eyes lost sight of him, it seemed that precisely from that moment everything changed.

The soft peat hummocks flared up before my very eyes, they emitted smoke and spluttered, not protecting but pointing the way to your head. When there is such a rumbling and roaring it seems a senseless occupation to fire. Yet you have to shoot as soon as you can so that you feel that even for a moment you can muffle everything.

Kasach was alive. I could see him in front of me. He was firing his submachine-gun and kept turning round, looking for something. I thought he was demandingly and impatiently trying to attract my attention. I raised my head although it was so hard to tear it away from the ground, from the triable tussock. Kasach's lips were saying something, shouting something angrily, and I could not make it out amidst the thunder and din of death. Finally, across the short silence, "Make your way round... To the chief of staff..."

He waved his hand, making a circular movement as if embracing the willow grove.

There is nothing more repulsive, but cheering as well, than retreating under fire, when you are not running away, nor are they routing you, but you yourself have to leave on a mission, on orders. The bullets flying close have con-strained something in you to a point, but have not captivated your whole body which has, on the contrary, become perfidiously huge, clumsy, and visible from everywhere. Every person whom you crawl past represents a pale overcome and left by you, on which there is someone's life and death, but not yet yours. Startled, inquiring eyes look you straight in the face or follow you ("... What? Are we retreating? Is it that bad?"), and so do angry or exactingly scornful looks ("Are you crawling away? So you want me to be here while you...") There is no time to reply or to explain, you have to show by your look that you are not fleeing or behaving in a cowardly manner, that you have been sent on a mission and commanded to crawl back.

I was still far from the safe fringe of the willow grove. Eyes, strange eyes kept seizing upon me, asking and demanding, and you had to look cheerful and at ease for it to be immediately understood why you were crawling. You do not flee with a face like that! My sight was bad and therefore I smiled at everyone just in case, the dead ones, too. Several limes I felt a tug at my sleeve, as if a dog was pulling at my elbow. I would freeze, expecting that this was the end of it all. And I was overcome by a desire, which it was hard to suppress, to jump up and run, to escape to the edge of the forest and beyond it. The wounded crawled away thither, and that was where they were dragged to. The wounded had a childish, dumbfounded look in their eyes as if a person was cast far, far away from the kind of life that he was living a moment ago. There were many wounded behind the willow bushes. Voices and groans could be heard, and the fighting sounded different from there. It was no longer a constant threatening din and a roar, but individual shots and rounds of machine-gun and submachine-gun fire. They seemed to be either getting their teeth into each other or rolling about one to one, and suddenly they went quiet for a while. Fighting like that would go on for a long time, for as long as there was ammunition. If only we had enough cartridges. On the faces and hands, under the tattered clothing of the people crawling somewhere, being carried away or tranquilly lying dead, there were seeping red patches. I was crawling, slipping past, farther, but my eyes kept seeing all that. I kept repeating, perhaps not even aloud, but to myself, "The commander ordered me to. I'm going to the first company. Kasach..."

Where we had recently pursued the Germans, I was already running upright up. There they were, the dead. There were no longer any weapons by the Germans and they were not lying as they had fallen. You can see straight away whether a dead man has been touched or not. I do not even know what it is about them, but you can tell. A last movement, a last attempt to save himself is always recorded in a dead man. And they always lie in different poses. All these were lying identically with their faces upwards. I raced over the immobile eyes of the dead and for some time I ran as if forgetting where and why.

No, I was making for the Chief of Staff, nothing has ended yet. We had to circumvent them, come up from the rear and rescue our people....

Up ahead Vlasov's men were lying in wait for me. They were further away from the firing, from the fighting, death had got at them earlier. Their bodies and poses had something more spread out and heavy about them. How long ago that all happened: we were running here, and they were in front of us, trying to escape our anger and death. And Perekhod was hot on their heels, running to his death. The fighting kept rumbling on, and no one knew how long it would last, or what would happen to me in fifteen minutes, in half an hour, and I was already remembering the fighting as something that took place long ago and far away.

I managed to race to my destination and caught sight of my own people. They were lying there, tense and poised for battle, and some were already standing around, smoking and waiting, just as they do in group photographs. There were no wounded or stretchers to be seen, they had been dragged away somewhere, perhaps hidden in the bushes, but there was no time to fathom everything out. I ran over to Kostya Chief of Stuff who was smoking, sitting on a kitbag. I called out Kasach's order to him.

"Around the willow bushes!... Go round them, at the double!... Otherwise, they'll smash our men, the commander gave orders!..."

Kostya looked at me just as before, without getting up, hut something had shifted abruptly and cruelly in his look and in his eyes. Finally, he shoved his cigarette under his boot and pressed on it hard as well, and then stood up: "Everyone who is not with the wounded, over here! Follow me, at the double!"

Now the willow bushes were on our left. We were running, skirting them and hearing the fighting on the opposite side of the forest. This forest, this patch of willow bushes was quite small and round. Only in some places did bushes which had broken away, branch out and grow into the peat bog, the brown and black heaps, and in one place there was an overgrown ditch which we were now passing. The old irrigation canal packed with willow bushes had long dried up and crept away to those same peat dunes.

"Back you go!" Kostya Chief of Staff halted and stopped one partisan. "You go back and tell them to bring the wounded to this ditch. Do you understand? Let them bring them and they can lie here. Lead them here."

The partisan ran back, and we headed round the willow bushes once again. But it seemed to us that the fighting was shifting away from us and moving increasingly to the left. As we ran I tried to tell Kostya Chief of Staff how we had chased the Vlasov men and the Germans, how there turned out to be a line of Germans with machine-guns in front of us, how Kasach had shouted to me and indicated that we should go round and strike at them from the rear. Kostya listened to both me and the fighting intently. The latter was indeed getting further away. It was withdrawing along the same circle. Surely they had not got the upper hand of Kasach and were ousting him out?

On the right, behind the garishly blue cover of transparent peat smoke we spotted trees in the distance (probably an orchard) and several roofs. And a road could be seen running to and from there. Had the Germans come along that road? There were even footprints here, apparently they had ridden on horseback. We would soon see them now, and they would see us! The peat bogs were smouldering, a bluish smoke consuming the distance and the roofs and trees melting in it and floating. The wind was blowing from there and once again we were choked by fits of coughing, hindering us and stopping us from running.

Ales Adamovich

We saw them near the saddled and loaded horses and immediately rushed at them. Rounds of submachine-gun fire intermingled, and rifle shots rang out sharply. People in green jumped to their feet and began to fire back. The wounded and dead horses sank very quietly to the ground, first kneeling and then lying down. They would stand as if waiting and suddenly, like a ripple on water, they would shiver from croup to neck and fall onto their hind quarters and then onto their fore legs....

We drove the Germans from the carts in the direction of the main fighting and in its wake. They defended themselves by shooting furiously and over and over again we had to go down, get up, crawl and fire.

Now the willow bushes, these woods, were, as it were, encircled by the firing. But this ring of fighting battle in a circle gradually rotated. The Germans had pressed Kasach and were continuing to do so, and we were bearing in on them. Kostya Chief of Staff sent a messenger once again, to tell those who remained in the ditch to take our wounded away, and follow us with them in a circle.

(What happened and how it turned out like that—just as in the diagram: the ring, the battle in a circle—is readily visible from here, from a distance, from the coach, from memory. At that time there was only a sensation of something unforeseen, of the strangeness of what was happening and even the impossibility of it. I would probably never have believed it, had it not actually happened to us.)

Here, it seemed, is the spot where we encountered the line of Germans with machine-guns. The peaty soil was smouldering, strewn with empty cartridge cases and dotted with rusty patches of blood that had seeped away, red and white dressings and shreds of clothing. But there were no dead to be seen. Kasach had removed ours. The Germans had cleared theirs away as well. The corpses of Vlasov's men remained lying on the spot, but they had been troubled again for they all had their belts and cartridge pouches missing and one was even bootless.

We needed to come to a halt and wait for our wounded (from that ditch); we needed to run faster to overtake the main Germans who were closing in on Kasach. But we did not have the time to wait, nor did we have the strength left to run. Now we would burst into a trot, now walk, being suffocated by the toxic fumes and coughing. The sun was like a round red hole in the sky that was astir with smoke and clouds.

The ring of fighting was rotating round the woods, with no possibility of breaking out: neither we nor the Germans could make up our minds to branch out sideways where the peat bogs were burning, or to leave along the road where you were unprotected from the machine-guns. The rounds of submachine-gun fire where Kasach and the Germans were, were becoming less frequent. There was no longer a battle but a sort of warning growl. That was on the opposite side of the round woods. Who was pursuing who now, who was chasing and who was withdrawing, who was behind and who was in front?

And the sun was large and red in the ever changing smoky sky like a red-hot muzzle aimed point-blank....

There was that ditch where we had left the wounded. Kostya Chief of Staff ordered that we should call a halt and wait a while. We lay down just in case. We were waiting for our own men, but who would appear in actual fact? I felt dizzy from the fumes and the nausea, my eyes were terribly irritated by the smoke, and coughing made my eyes water as well. Those whose sight was better could already see our men, and they were already conversing and laughing softly. It is always amusing to observe from the sidelines how people who know each other go cautiously, with circumspection, "on tiptoe". All I saw was my own tears, something like a rainbow, burning with pain. Then something dark appeared and began to move. The patrols had gone ahead, followed by threes and fours carrying stretchers. We had many wounded; the lads were absolutely exhausted, had turned grey, and were drenched with sweat; they lowered the stretchers, put them on the ground and lashed out at us:

"You keep running, you devils! From whom, from us?"

The wounded kept a heavy silence, listening alarmably to the firing. Only those who were unconscious kept muttering something. They were asking for water. All of us had an unbearable thirst. And their hoarse, fervent whispering made it even worse....

But the looks and eyes of some of the wounded were implausibly calm and concentrated. Those were the ones who were dying. They would die irrespective of how that improbable battle ended. When death is ready to take a person and does not leave him, he remains all alone, no matter how many people and who is with him. I once saw an elderly partisan dying in the forest. His two sons, also partisans, and his old woman stood by him. All those of us who were close by went up to the cart on which he was lying. No longer aware of his wounds, all white with dressings and bandages, the man looked at us completely sensibly, but just as if we were not there and he alone was there together with something else we could not see. The old woman rocked quietly over him, holding on to the cart with both hands and when the look on the dying man's face became even more distant from us, she began to talk and keen in a singsong voice: "Tikhon, I'm weeping, you can see, and the children are weeping. Tikhon, and your comrades are here. Tikhon, you can hear us crying..."

The woman was trying so naively and yet so understandably to break through the terrible solitude of death, the loneliness of man's last moments. Someone once told me that the last inevitable little tear of a dead man—Kasach also spoke about the last tear, the frozen one—was the little tear of loneliness, the terrifying sensation each person has of being abandoned in the face of death.

Kasach was to appear now with his men. That is, if everything was just as we had figured out, if they were really going round in a circle and directly in our wake. Kostya had decided to wait for them, and we, who were prepared for battle just in case, watched to see who would appear next.

We had four dead with us. We laid them on one side, but on stretchers as well. We had reshuffled, and now I was already with the stretchers, it was my turn to carry. I tried to position myself so that I would not have to carry a dead man. To walk round this blind circle, and with a dead man on your hands as well! It is easier to carry a live person. That was tried and tested, they did not gravitate towards the ground so much....

"Look at the way they are walking! You can see straight away, it's Kasach's men!"

"And there's Kasach himself, he's wounded. You can see, his shoulder's bandaged."

"That's not Kasach. No, it doesn't look like it."

"They've stopped, they've noticed. We should show ourselves, call to them, or they will start a fight as well. Comrade chief of staff!"

"Aha, are you afraid of Kasach's men!"

"You can rely upon them!"

Some of our men got up and climbed out of the ditch, waving their arms and signaling, moving their rifles up and down.

Three of the patrol men halted, gave the pass sign with their rifles and headed towards us in a more cheerful frame of mind. The whole chain of Kasach's men was coming out of the bushes in a long line, the front ones carrying rifles and submachine-guns. The people following them in groups of fours and sixes, had what was to us a familiar look, awkwardly and tiredly carrying the wounded and the dead. We counted them under our breath and aloud. Yes, the one with his right shoulder bandaged was Kasach. He was just in his soldier's blouse, not wearing a jacket or the cap he usually had on. His submachine-gun was under his left arm.

Kostya went to meet him, then stood still and waited.

We all left together, all the dead and wounded with us.

"The going is more even here, commander, they've already trodden a path," I heard Kostya Chief of Staff telling Kasach.

The latter replied, beginning to laugh briefly, "So, Kostya, you're overjoyed to see human footprints!" He gave the command, "Fire some shots, Chief of Staff, respond. Can't you hear, they're asking for it? (The Germans on the other side of the woods were firing shots from time to time.) We've squandered our cartridge drums, you know. And tell them to share their cartridges with us."

"Cartridges?" Kostya grinned mistrustfully. "Cartridges, you say!"

"Never mind, order them."

Kostya aimed his submachine-gun at the bushes, fired a round and then a second. The Germans responded immediately, with a whole volley of rounds. Were they pleased that we were there? Or that we were not close, far away?

Once again, like a marker on the track, dead horses. Two horses were peacefully wandering around near the peat hills. Shaking their heads, they moved from place to place, bothered by the smoke and fumes.

"They'll fall into the fire," said an elderly bearded partisan with a broken leg whom we were carrying in a blanket. He craned his neck to look out of his uncomfortable hammock.

"Just wait for me to run along and turn them back," Vedmed replied angrily, clutching the blanket, his heavy burden, with fingers turned white. Sweat was running into his eyes and down the lenses of his spectacles. Of short height it was especially hard for Vedmed because he had to keep lifting the corner of his blanket, pulling it upwards.

"I would make for it along that road that the Germans used to get here. How long are we supposed to go on walking round like this?" Vedmed complained.

Four of us were carrying our wounded man. You had to hold the corners of the blanket with both hands, but you could not sling your rifle on your back. You had to have it to hand. Your rifle got in the way, it kept banging your knees.

Each one thought that his neighbour was not holding it the right way, was not walking properly and was not saying the right thing in the necessary way.

"I suppose you have found out what is lying in wait for you on this road?"

"We'll find out all right."

"Hold it properly, will you! If we go back it would be better to walk towards the marshes through which we came. Crafty old whiskers is sitting back there now, baking potatoes. And we're wandering round and round like a blind horse."

"He is staying there and taking it easy," the tow-haired lad envied him phlegmatically.

"Keep in step," the fat man Pukhov who kept on putting us right, ordered angrily. "Why are you heading for the bush? He (this was to Vedmed again) wants to take the road. I'll get you with a machine-gun there! The Germans are just waiting for us to walk away from this accursed woodland. Don't pull the blanket, lift it up higher. If they go for you when you're out in the open, where will you take refuge? In the hot pits?"

"It's a pity about the horses, they'll fall through the hot crust," the wounded man was talking again. He could not hear us, he had been deafened by a mine. The bearded elderly fellow with his thin neck tried to stretch upwards out of his deep hammock like a bird.

"Sorry, lads, I'm heavy," the wounded man said."Never mind, old chap," said the tow-haired phlegmatic person. "It takes six of us to carry Perekhod. But why take a dead man?"

Vedmed was surprised all of a sudden, "True, the war is such that you are even afraid for a dead man. How could you possibly leave a wounded person to the enemy."

We were still going away from the Germans, taking with us our wounded and dead as if we even understood why we were going and why they were going, why they were not stopping, not laying down and forcing us to fight them (they had the cartridges for it, for some reason they always had the cartridges for it). We were expecting to walk into an ambush at any moment. As we went away from them, we were following in their wake, lending an ear to the menacing (perhaps warning) sound of firing.

Still, the first sensation that we experienced when we swooped down upon them, when we drove them off, overrunning them, probably continued to have its effect on us. The Germans themselves probably did not know definitely whether they were pursuing us or going away from us. They possibly feared that we lay in ambush as they withdrew. Perhaps they were thinking at that very moment how they could break out of that accursed circle, out of that endless orbit, without walking under our lire or falling into pits.

Perekhod, both Perekhods, the younger wounded one and the older dead one, were behind us. Up ahead they were carrying commissar Shardyko who, they said, was already dead. From time to time we changed places with those preceding the detachment and those following it up. Either you would carry the dead or you would wait for them to strike at you from ambush when you are in front. But we were so tired, that everyone was more eager to head the column. Sweat, pungent and acrid from the smoke, was running all over our bodies, and we simply drank it from our faces as it trickled down, wetting our lips. Now I was carrying the older Perekhod. Four of us were bearing him, using his tarpaulin raincoat instead of a stretcher. He was so heavy that it made your nails hurt since the dead body weighted down towards the ground. I myself wanted to collapse and to stay motionless, to immerse myself utterly and completely in my tiredness and enjoy the sensation of stillness. My eyes were swimming in the rainbow, a mass of different colours but a black strip was increasingly cast across it like a shadow. Suddenly everything that had accumulated within me in those days came to the surface and merged into a single dull feeling of the ultimate exhaustion after which you become quite indifferent, even to your own death.

The Germans were still firing beyond the woods, but we already remained silent. Our silence worried them, frightened them, and the firing became more and more intensive. How much had gone by since the moment when the first mine exploded and we rushed at the Vlasov men? There they lay, turned over, their eyes towards the heavens; for them a whole eternity had passed. Even a single second of death is an eternity like a million years. The live sun still moves above us, having completed the greater part of its semi-circle while we have been turning millstones. How many times they turned before we came along, too. We would skirt the forest many times more before the sun would slip down behind those smoky hills. And then what? You did not know what would happen then, but you just dreamt that it would hurry up and topple from the hot, smoky sky and stop melting and setting fire to us. I leaned towards my elbow to wipe my eyes and saw Perekhod's face close up. Somehow I was reluctantly surprised that there were no beads of sweat on it. What was I thinking about, whither had my attention slipped away?...

There was apparently nothing we could care for any longer, but one kept noticing even the minutest details. There was something fascinating about that wild walking in your own and someone else's footsteps. We and the Germans had already beaten out a path across the peat. How long had we been wandering in circles? And how much further had we still to go? No, we were not walking any longer. Our legs were sweetly stretched out, humming like a propeller, and when you closed your eyes, it was just as if you were being lifted, and your aching body with every muscle trembling, was swaying above the ground. The swaying made you feel increasingly sick, and you hastened to open your eyes. We were lying in that same ditch overgrown with willow bushes. They had left us there. Kostya Chief of Staff had suggested to Kasach that he hide a few men to watch which way the Germans were going, how many of them there were, what they had with them and what was to be expected of them. The Chief of Staff himself stayed with us. There were four of us in the ditch. We could still see Kasach's men and watched them leaving. The stretchers were numerous, far too many. People could hardly put one foot in front of the other, were reeling from exhaustion, from the heat and from the fumes. The living were being suffocated, overcome by fits of coughing. When you were lying quietly, the coughing did not bother you so much, but even then we were troubled with it, especially the corpulent Pukhov. From time to time Kostya would ask, "Well, not fed up yet?"

The man would try to muffle his outbursts of coughing with his hand or his cap, burying his face in the ground, looking up guiltily with watery red eyes. He would seek to justify himself by saying, "If only I had some water."

"The Germans will bring some in a minute," Kostya Chief of Staff would say, "Crawl along the ditch, old chap, further along there."

But then Zuyonak started coughing, followed by the Chief of Staff himself.

"Creep along there all the same. We've got enough wheezers here without you."

The stout partisan crawled along, still choking with coughing, and we indicated to him that it was still audible and that he would have to go even further away.

You could at least rub your eyes when you were lying down. When I could not, when my hands were busy with something else, it seemed that if only I could give my eyes a good rub, it could stop the irritating watering and soothe them. I did not, of course, have a handkerchief, and everything else was so caked with mud and soot that you could not touch your eyes with it. I pulled out my undershirt. It was yellowed and salty, but it was the cleanest thing I had and I rubbed my eyes with it. The sun was drifting in the billowing smoke; it, too, was inflamed, having some kind of ominous bluish tint. The sun was burning, ablaze, but I felt shivery. It seemed as if these shivers were spreading in the hot smoke-filled air, and the spines of the beast-like peat hills were quivering faintly, constantly.

There they were, the Germans, up ahead, the patrol! It is always a special feeling, the way you watch the enemy appear before you from ambush.

You have never seen each other, you do not know that the other is on earth, yet somewhere something has taken shape in such a way and not differently and now there are no people so tightly connected among themselves as you are. One life for the two, one death for the two, share them between you.

But it was not we who were an ambush: we ourselves were caught in a trap. We had to remain there. If the Germans suddenly decided to examine the ditch, we would give ourselves away by our coughing which suddenly began to become uncontrollable in Zuyonak, Kostya and me. They would kill us right there in the ditch. Our faces expressed fright and guilt in turn. We would throw ourselves down, burying our faces in the ground, covering our mouths with our hands, so that we were no longer coughing, but rumbling quietly and groaning.

The Germans were marching along in green uniforms and speckled cloaks, wearing helmets, individually and in groups. And they were all looking at the willow grove, guarded and standing back from the bushes. Were they waiting for us to appear from there? That was it. The Germans believed they had driven us into the willow bushes (we had not been answering their fire for a long time) and that we were sitting tight in the forest. They were walking along, expecting us to run out into the open. Then one German stopped and released a round of submachine-gun fire into the depths of the forest. Immediately a second and a third fired their rifles. They were shooting into the bushes. They did not look in our direction. A multitude of them, more than a hundred, tumbled out from behind the fringes of the willow bushes, and more and more kept appearing and were heading towards our ditch. Those in the middle of the column were not looking at the bushes. They were carrying the wounded and the dead, using raincoats and blankets as stretchers just as we were doing. Fours and sixes were carrying the burdens, stumbling, getting in each other's way, unsteady on their feet. Faint voices could be heard. The Germans were coming closer and closer, and we could hear their loud coughing which was our salvation. Our own coughs we were furiously holding back within ourselves, one using the palm of his hand, another—his sleeve. The last Germans had now emerged from behind the bushes, they huddled together in a tight little group, not eyeing the bushes but glancing round, expecting us to come from behind. Everything about them showed that it was not they who were pursuing us, but we who were pursuing them. Those in front were convinced that they had driven us into the bushes and were pursuing us, while to those at the back it seemed that the partisans were pressing them and driving them on. One of them would turn about, fire a round from his submachine-gun and catch up with the others, pulling out a fresh "horn" of cartridges from his boot or pouch as he walked along.

At first we fully expected that they would discover us.

But now they were right next to us, coughing, talking and firing shots, some fifty metres away. Our ditch ran right up to the willow bushes, and the Germans would have to clamber down into the ditch to cross it. They came closer and closer until it seemed as if they would step on our heads every minute. At the same time, everything seemed to recede into the distance as if you were not one of those who were lying there, or if you were, you were a different person from the one there at the moment, and all that had happened to you at one time and was now a thing of the past, something that had passed and was only recalled as terrifyingly real....

The Germans departed with their dead and wounded, leaving in the wake of our own people, and we began to wait for the partisans, for Kasach to appear again. Now it was our own men we were seeing from the sidelines and, although it was with different eyes, in a different way, with a feeling of gladness at your return to yourself, but again for an instant it seemed as if that was only a memory, too, of something that had happened to you long, long ago. Pukhov crawled up and joined us as well. He was still coughing, but now without holding it back, greeting us, life, safety with his joyful, no longer shy or restrained cough. Kostya Chief of Staff thumped Pukhov on his fat back with his fist, but then Kostya himself started coughing and burst out laughing.

We headed towards our own men, waved our weapons at them and were now walking towards them. We entered the column, were absorbed into it and its movement. Now we could give cheerful accounts of how close the Germans had been to us, how we had watched them and what they were like.

Once again we were walking round those woods, carrying away our dead and our wounded overtaking our enemies, yet moving away from them, and we could not believe that there had ever been anything except that endless walking under the huge, pitiless sun and that there might possibly be anything else. You gradually became more and more indifferent, distanced from yourself. We the living were becoming fewer as it were while those we were carrying, the dead and the wounded, were literally increasing. There were no longer any replacements for stretcher-bearers, and it was difficult for even six of us to drag along the burden of a dead or wounded man. The sun had almost completed its semicircle, leaving us on our own. The heat had subsided, but we felt even more tired than before, although at that time it had seemed that it was impossible to be more exhausted. The smoke from the peat became thicker and more toxic, choking everyone, the wounded included. Only the dead lay there tranquilly in their sagging blanket hammocks in which we carried them.

As the red sun with its smoky rim of deepening blue sank down below the darkening edge of the earth, beyond the peat hills, and the occasional stars managed to rise in the heavens, its own internal evil light came to rise from the dark earth and could be distinguished as it started to flicker and quiver. The peat smoke had also imparted a dark blue hue to it that inflamed light of the ground on fire. It was everywhere already, locking in an ever widening circle both us and the woods we were circumventing and the invisible Germans firing shots somewhere. You no longer knew where those paths were by which you and the Germans had come here, by which we could make our escape backwards or forwards. The fire was everywhere and it was advancing. Shining reflections of it were dancing on the willow bushes, on our faces and those of the dead. With every circle the Vlasov men that we and the Germans had left dead on the ground, changed in some way, lying in wait for us in a different way. The corpses scattered about were turning white; they were either closer together (or so it began to seem) or had crawled further apart, while we and the Germans were doing the next circle. Then you noticed that they were in exactly the same place as before. You noted that with the senseless, accidental interest of a person who was dead tired. We began to call a halt more and more often, putting the wounded on the ground and collapsing next to them as if we were dead. Then they would wake us up with their voices and hands on a general command. Someone there up front, Kasach, Kostya Chief of Staff, someone was giving the orders, but through the wounded now. They were the ones who were the freshest, the most lively, the least tormented. They would wake us, giving us a shove. And we would carry them again and take the dead, inertly and with difficulty. At that time, our enemies, who were probably just as exhausted as we were, were doing exactly what we were doing: they were withdrawing from us and catching us up. And both we and they were too worn out and fatigued that we could not stop and give battle.

Somewhere there is the road along which we had come and another one by which our enemies had come. We could try to flee the circle of burning ground which was closing in, along one of these roads. But immediately you lay yourself open to the other's machine-gun, the other will immediately take advantage as the pursuer. The fire from the ground kept blazing up under the darkening sky. It was enveloping us so closely that we could no longer believe that any roads or paths had survived. Where were they? But they must be there because the peat could not burn absolutely everywhere around in one day. We just had to find that road, but before that to ensure our safety from the pursuers.

We made a halt and tried to hear where the Germans were and where they were firing. You could collapse and just lie there... Again the wounded would wake us and shout, "Up you get, lads! Up you get! Wake that one over there!"

You had to get up. But for a moment more you could be in the state of sweet oblivion while they were not all up yet. Then they would poke you, and you had to get up....

Now we were on the spot where we had killed the horses. Nearby was the road along which the Germans had come. That meant that we would leave along it for we needed to break through in that direction. That meant that we would withdraw....

The drowsiness immediately disappeared and we even had supposedly forgotten about tiredness.

"Remove the wounded, the 2nd Company is to remove the wounded," a young partisan mumbled from a stretcher. His forehead had a dressing swollen with blood on it and a crust of dried blood had formed on his face which shone black.

"The 1st Company will engage the Germans," a wounded man, having listened intently, repeated the command in the usual way, looking sternly at us from the ground as if we were asleep or were not capable of catching it. Me, I was going to be with the First Company, we would face the Germans and in that time our people would take the wounded away as far as possible. And that is how that was finally to end — we would turn round and move towards the enemy, and everything that had happened in those days, that had accumulated during those endless circles would be less tense. Perhaps it would end in death, but the tension will be gone. My eyes were watering, but it was as if I was already accustomed to the tears, to the fact that everything I could see was spreading and melting away tinted by pain and the rainbow....

The partisans made a collection of cartridges and handed them over to those who would attack the Germans. I had a Herman rifle so I needed German cartridges. Aha, we were already on the march, leaving; what a good thing that was! We looked round at our own people while we could still see them. They were carrying away the wounded and the dead, awkwardly, tiredly and furiously clutching at the blanket or the tarpaulin or simply holding them by the arms and legs, and this alarming and hurried procession was departing in the direction of the smoky glow from the fires. No, we could no longer return to that road. We already knew that, we were tormented by the anguish that knowledge brought us, and we stepped up our pace to smother and suppress this knowledge within ourselves. The leaves of the willow bushes glistened all mottled, the vicious ground fire was casting its light on people's faces, and the shadows from the hummocks, ruts and bushes looked like black pits. We were already running, from somewhere we had found the energy to run, we were expending our emergency rations, the last reserves which we had previously saved without knowing it. Now there was no longer anything to save them for. Before we had covered a semi-circle we would find them, encounter those whom we were fleeing and pursuing. We had Kostya Chief of Staff with us. When he looked round at the double, it seemed to me that he had an unnaturally cheerful expression on his face, in his eyes.

But I had poor eyesight so perhaps I imagined many things.

We were already tired of running, there was no fresh air to breathe, so we went over to walking at a hasty pace. Our line had become very straggly, and the flank farther away from the forest was lagging behind. Like water trickling into a hollow, they were all being carried towards the forest, where there were not so many ruts and the circle was smaller.

On our right, there was a wall of willow bushes bathed in uneven light, on our left, the horizon with its dissected peat hills, devoured by the red, yellow, dark blue, and even black fire. Even the blackness seemed to be all ablaze and floating.

We crossed the ditch, then crossed another one and saw people lying there. These were dead Vlasov men who had been in the ambush. The white corpses formed familiar patches on the ground. There was something vengeful and gloating in their serenity....

Kostya Chief of Staff kept looking round at us as if weighing up how long those thirty or forty men could hold out. We had covered a sufficient distance from our own people, we had lost sight of them a long time before, and still there were no Germans. And we could not hear them firing shots any more.

But what if they had decided at the same time as we did to turn round and march in our direction? They would then be moving away from us again and they would soon bump into our wounded. Kostya was obviously worried by this. It was as if the Germans had disappeared. They were not firing shots any more, and until then we had heard them all the time.

"Look, there they are," someone shouted, their spirits raised and relieved. A kilometre or more from the willow bushes there were signs of life lit up by the smoky glow of the fires. Yes, they were withdrawing along the road that had brought us here.

There they would be met by the moustached commander and his detachment.

In the other direction, other Germans, those in the outer ring of the blockade were lying in wait for us.

We were completing our last circle to convince ourselves that the Germans had really departed, that all of them had left.

We had to catch our own people up. But why was it I could see Boris Boky in Kasach, and vice versa, Kasach in Boky? I did not really understand, you know, what Kasach was really like so as to compare them. I had never seen Boky, I had only heard his voice in arguments. Boky was wholly a product of books, of the library, of the radio and the newspapers, and all that Kasach knew, he had learned from the war. I probably could not have formulated precisely what that was. Was it hard, joyless, at times embittered ideas about people, about man? What one of them had derived in all its richness from his own life, the other possessed from the experience of others taken very personally. At times, (in Kasach) this would turn out as some kind of thought that had come to a halt (like his smile), swamped in action, swallowed up by it; in others, like Boky, reflection was a constant, agonizing process and it was action. Boky reminded one of a person who did not believe in an illness ending in a cure precisely because of an excruciating and passionate desire for things to turn out well. His thoughts like spasms were intercepted in flight by impatience, bitterness, and pain. (You could sense the same sort of spasm in Kasach well, but being or already transformed into bitterness. This had become particularly apparent in him after what happened at Perekhody and in those marshes.) Sometimes I imagined Boky to be Kasach who had suddenly warmed to his theme....

...But it must be said that today there is no calm understanding. If a person is calm, it means the person has not understood the entire threat. Before Boky I pretend to display a balanced understanding, but he obviously does not believe me, seeing in this a teasing polemic trick as well as the reflex of a blind person accustomed to avoiding abrupt movements. As my constant opponent he makes nothing but such movements! At times, he fumbles for and divines my own doubts, my pain so accurately that I could take him for my own opposing "I" without which there is no "stereoscopic", three-dimensional view of events, of the world and of oneself.

"Look, Flariyan Pyatrovich, what a patriotic festival they have made out of the trial of the My Lai murderers! They send thousands of letters to. Lieutenant William Calley who took upon himself the national burden of killing. And he parades and flaunts himself: 'If the majority tells me (yesterday they said, 'If the Führer says') to kill a whole country, I will kill it! I shall always put America's will above my conscience!' Note the difference: Claude Eatherly who was involved in the massacre of Hiroshima, asked to be tried and sent to prison himself until they hid the 'national hero' away in a lunatic asylum. There the war was against fascism for all that. But this chap just acts surprised: 'Murder? It's ridiculous! You sent me, I did my duty! What the hell!' —don't make Calley laugh. Today's Eatherlies would laugh at the trial of conscience, or any other trial for that matter. Although, unlike Claude Eatherly, they will know what the cargo is in the holds of their aircraft or in their missiles. That is what this speeding up and concentration means, and don't try to persuade me. Just as before, you are presuming on my divine patience, aren't you? All the markers have been set out and indicated. Choose, mankind, where you want to go! There are quite enough signs; Buchenwald, Khatyn and Hiroshima.... There is the last one somewhere, too. If you go there, there won't be any coming-back. Earlier nature went to pains for man. Now he has to take trouble for himself. Nature can no longer tackle his bombs and fascism. You yourself must deal with it, Homo sapiens!"

But that is not the whole story, my dear Boky! Once Hegel put forward the bitter idea that history only teaches that it has not taught anyone anything. It would seem that even today's man does have something to make him wallow in despair: those Khatyns and Adolfs are occurring again.... Once again simpletons are being found who are ready to believe anything and forget everything, people who do not look into the future, cruel people. They are like dry brushwood for the fire to creep across. And once again short-lived narcotic ideas and drugs instead of ideas are here.

The pointer has moved, quivered and almost returned to where it once was....

So, people have not learned anything from it? But, to be sure, we do not know, do we, Boky, where the world would be now with its bombs, if it had not been for the bitter experience of the Thirties and Forties!

And if it had not been for those fifteen minutes....

The Nuremberg judges, newsmen, guards and the public (as well as the accused) were shown film sequences which documented Nazi atrocities in Europe (in Byelorussia, outside Moscow, in the Ukraine, Poland and Yugoslavia), among them concentration camps like Oswiecim and obliterated communities like Khatyn. And when the lights went on, all those present stood up, faced the principal killers and stared at them for five, ten, fifteen minutes.... They were looking in silence at people, humans like themselves who had perpetrated all those inhuman things.

People have been staring point-blank at those people already for a quarter of a century rather than just fifteen minutes. In some places fascism has already come out of the dock, is flexing its benumbed muscles and has changed its humbly surprised and ingratiating look for an impudent grin. The lusty Bavarian roar can be heard already: "Germany is strong enough now. We have the right to demand that all the things past be forgotten!"

Yet new führers, wherever they emerge, are jittery all the same.

The stare is still there....

My Lai. Brings to mind Lidice, Oradour, Khatyn and suchlike....

Scenes of thugs belting people for reading books evoke memories of books burned on Berlin and Munich squares!

Strauss, Adolf von Thadden, Goldwater, Almirante—the names immediately conjure up a vision of snotty moustache.

People know all there is to know about new führers.

They also remember things about themselves... even though they would like so much to forget it all! They would like to forget how they sat captive and people in Nuremberg, Minsk, Kiev, Warsaw and Belgrade were scrutinising them, and victims were staring at them point-blank from the screen. The decade of despotism over the lives and destinies of millions vanished into thin air. They remember how they, Gorings and Kochs, curled their lips into ingratiating smiles in front of their victor, soldier guard. They remember how abjectly they, recent duces, looked, so unlike their former selves, under the guerrilla guns. ("I know they won't hurt me.") How those Kaltenbrunners squealed, unwilling to put their heads in the noose and how those Rosenbergs swooned like ladies, though I lie deaths of others, millions of other deaths they had planned bored them as routine. And how they, so-called Hitlers, mumbled and ran their trembling fingers over a poison vial.

No matter how impudent they are today behind the back of new authorities, they remember that at one time they had power over half the world but then, waking up, found themselves face to face with witness-judges whom they thought they had long wiped off....

Yes, the signs have been put up, lit up, right before the very eyes and memory of everybody!...

No deception can last for very long, it is impossible to deceive people forever. This is just as true today as it was in times past. But it is not such a consolation as it was formerly. Even a short-term deception of many people is too dangerous. This is because the Bomb exists, which takes very short time to explode. You stop the chain reaction with yourself! Do it in time, Homo sapiens, and tear out the wires connected to the Bomb!...

I remember how the man in the next bed in the army hospital, a sapper who had had his eyes burnt out, told me how he nearly drowned once, but they saved him and resuscitated him at the shore of a lake. According to him, he could hear the voices of those who had rescued him all the time, but at a certain moment he began to understand what they were saying. Suddenly he heard quite clearly, "Enough! What are we going to go on tormenting him for? It's forty minutes now and not a sign of life. It's hopeless!"

The man had wanted to cry out that he was alive, at least to groan, to move his lips, but he could not. He remembered how he had waited terrified that the others might consent, too, that it was hopeless.

Never cease your efforts, even when it seems that all possibilities have been exhausted and the battle is finally lost; that has always been the rule of military commanders. But then it was only the fate of someone's authority, or even a state that was at stake. Today, it is the destiny of man on the planet for eternity. In a direct and not philosophical sense, it is a question of "To be or not to be?" Too much is at stake and, no matter what the situation, man does not have the right to say. "Enough! It's hopeless!"

"The turn to Khatyn," they said in the bus. We were rocked and thrown into a list, and the humming in the bus became the close sounds of the forest.

"One... two... three...," Syarozha was counting aloud, probably reading the figures on the kilometre markers.

There was an open space again (the sound receded). We pulled up and made a sharp turn.

"We're there, Dad."

It was a very sunny, warm day.

When leaving a building or getting out of a car it is my habit to first seek out the tickling caress of the sun with my face, my skin and my eyelids. That is my general pointer in space, one might say.

The many voices all around were muffled. I could hear foreigners speaking. Now you would often hear them on the streets of our provincial town. Since I went blind, and especially in the last few years more and more of them have appeared as they have come closer to us.

There was the shuffling of feet on cement, the rustling of wheels and the noise of the engines of vehicles drawing up. A sharp metallic sound under my feet struck me. Here my cane sounded unusually and unpleasantly loud. I held it up, and put it under my elbow. I waited for Glasha's hand to find me. But a metallic sound, like an echo, reverberated in the space, making its way through to us from afar, through the voices and the shuffling of soles. Were those the bells of Khatyn? They say that the bells hang on tall stove chimneys where the cottages once stood. We were moving towards the sound, a faint sound as if disrupted. We stopped next to some people's voices repeating figures: "Two million two hundred and thirty thousand. Every fourth inhabitant of Byelorussia perished..."

"Dad, there's some steps," Syarozha warned me.

Glasha showed me where they were by squeezing my elbow, three paces and again—here were more steps. The path was rough and hard underfoot.

"Are those grave stones?" Syarozha asked quietly.

"No, this is simply a path."

Glasha's hand was prompting me and showing me where to walk, where to put my feet, her hand feeling different than it usually did at home or in the town street. Today her hand was like it was at that time in the forest when the mute firing (it was for me because I had gone deaf) thundered and Glasha, clutching my hand and hanging onto my arm, had shown me how close or how far away they were shooting....

The sound was already sharper and closer. Shuddering as it came into being, it died away like pain, suppressed and then immediately broke in two. Two bells, then three bells rang out, cymbal-like and disjointed, and also broke off as if someone had put the palm of their hand on them. But over and over again that disjointed cymbal-like sound rang out; you already expected it, and with it there emerged a distance which faded away and spread. In you yourself something spreads and expands. The sound seeks you out over and over again, groping along the bottom, summoning the echo.

Three paces, then a step. The slabs of stone are probably black. To Syarozha they looked like gravestones. Then more paces and we were slightly lower, one step lower.

"Mum, and no one managed to stay alive here?"

"Shush, Syarozha, don't talk, listen to what she is telling you."

The voice of a young woman was explaining what had occurred here more than a quarter of a century ago, how the punitive squads had swooped down, how they had driven everyone into a shed and set fire to it, and people ran out into the machine-gun fire....

The cymbal-like sounds of the bells, being carried away into the distance, recounting the dead stove pipes, kept ringing out in the background, beyond the voice of the young woman as if telling a truth that it was impossible to convey, but which was, nevertheless, the truth.

"Children eat more bread than adults," that was like a thorn in the side of a maniac at one end of Europe, so a few years later they came here, to the other end of the continent, to kill children. Those who "consume and eat more..."

The old man in stone holding a dead child has had his palm and his fingers exposed to fire. I do not know whether the sighted can see that. I saw it many times after the war. Almost all those who were put before a firing squad together with children but by chance managed to stay alive, had their hand deformed, the one with which they had covered the child's head and pressed it to the ground. A person would fall down with a dead man, while he and the child were still alive. They would be filled with terror and covered with the blood of the dead. They must not move or stir, no matter what happened!... But the child wanted to get up, it wanted to cry and to scream. But the hand of his father or mother held it down and buried its face in the ground, begging and pleading the child not to summon death.... Death had already come close to them, it was looking point-blank, and aiming. It fired at the head of the child and at the hand that sought to protect and hide that head so round and warm like the ground in summer.

The sounds kept breaking up into twos and threes and fading away, they kept counting and counting.... In the midst of the village that no longer exists I heard voices reading from the lists I could not see the names and surnames of the people burnt to death and the villages exterminated. I heard the names of towns and the whispered figures for the thousands of people tortured to death in concentration camps: eighty thousand... one hundred and eighty thousand... two hundred and fifty....

The sun tickles my eyelids, and tries to open them, although they are already open.

At one time I used to like to look at the sun with my eyes closed, through the live, melting redness of my eyelids. I liked to sit down, or to stand like that or to stroll slowly towards the sun and look at it coloured by my own live blood and just as if it were warmed by my blood.

Now my eyelids were black; only jabs of pain rushed through the black, ever hot sky....

The sound of the Khatyn bells counting the stove pipes was already behind us. We were going away, and it remained, but caught us up again, got its way and asked: "How did you carry it out, carry it out, carry it out? Do you understand, understand?..."

Three paces and there is a step. Three paces, and we have moved a step away. I lowered my cane, and it made a strangely loud tinkling on the slabs of stone. One needs time to get used to that sound. All it was the tapping of a metal cane on stone. I was going somewhere and nothing more....

But is there anything in the world now about which you can say, "and nothing more"?

The sound behind us becomes fainter, and my cane, our footsteps, the voices of those walking along, seem to sound louder and more casual.

"Well, are you ready to go now?" the voice of our young driver inquired.

1965, 1968-1971